SWEET TASTE OF REVENGE

SWEET TASTE OF REVENGE

Mary Ellis

This first world edition published 2018
in Great Britain and 2019 in the USA by
SEVERN HOUSE PUBLISHERS LTD of
Eardley House, 4 Uxbridge Street, London W8 7SY.
Trade paperback edition first published
in Great Britain and the USA 2019 by
SEVERN HOUSE PUBLISHERS LTD.

British Library Cataloguing in Publication Data
A CIP catalogue record for this title is available from the British Library.

ISBN-13: 978-0-7278-8834-1 (cased)
ISBN-13: 978-1-84751-959-7 (trade paper)
ISBN-13: 978-1-4483-0169-0 (e-book)

All Severn House titles are printed on acid-free paper.

Severn House Publishers support the Forest Stewardship Council™ [FSC™],
the leading international forest certification organisation.
All our titles that are printed on FSC certified paper carry the FSC logo.

MIX
Paper from
responsible sources
FSC® C013056

Typeset by Palimpsest Book Production Ltd.,
Falkirk, Stirlingshire, Scotland.
Printed and bound in Great Britain by
TJ International, Padstow, Cornwall.

ONE

Kate Weller leaned back against the headrest and tried not to think about a very tall, dark, and handsome man who cooked the best Italian food she'd ever tasted. An ambitious man, who almost single-handedly built the family's trattoria into one of Charleston's most sought-after restaurants. A man who respected the elderly, was kind to animals, and knew how to make a woman feel like a queen. She was leaving behind a trophy fish, pulled from the sea of eligible bachelors. As Kate forced away painful memories of Eric Manfredi, she tried to imagine what she would find when she visited her brother for the first time in years.

What had sixteen years in prison done to Liam? Would he be coarse and foul-mouthed, muscle-bound and covered in tats to indicate his prison-yard allegiances? Or would her brother still be the same shaggy-haired dreamer who'd wanted to make a better life for them after their parents died? Shame and guilt over never visiting after his arrest washed over Kate. So she forced thoughts of Liam into the same corner of her mind that Eric inhabited.

'Yoo-hoo, Kate. Did you see that sign?' Beth Kirby took her hand off the wheel long enough to deliver a jab with her elbow. 'Welcome to Florida. Getting homesick yet?'

Kate straightened. 'The Florida–Georgia line is still a long way from Pensacola. It'll be another four hours before things start looking familiar.' She slouched back down in the seat.

'Will you look for a place to live near your brother's prison?'

'No, that would be too depressing. I want to find a cheap hotel near the beach in Pensacola. I really enjoyed being close to water in Charleston.'

Her best friend rolled her eyes. 'First of all, there is no such thing as a *cheap hotel* near the beach unless it's slated for demolition. Secondly, you need something more long-term than a hotel. Let's look for an apartment that leases by the month.'

'I'm not staying that long.' Kate rubbed a knot in her left shoulder. 'I plan to find out why Liam wants to see me, and why after all these years someone is stirring up the past.'

Beth's face scrunched into a frown. 'Are you crazy? Someone has been threatening you. And that someone blew up your boyfriend's car. It was only by the grace of God that Eric wasn't inside at the time. That's a far cry from posting embarrassing photos from your high school days.'

'I realize that, but it doesn't change the fact I need to work. Last time I looked at my bank account, I wasn't independently wealthy. And since I'm the roving PI, I have to go wherever the boss finds the next case. In the meantime, I just hope Nate doesn't fire me. Oh, and for the record, Eric is no longer my boyfriend. I broke it off.'

'Nate isn't going to fire you. He's really nice guy. Why do you think he insisted I come with you to Pensacola?'

Kate's mouth dropped open. 'You're staying only until I find a place to live. Then you're going back to your fiancé in Savannah. Don't you have a wedding to plan?'

'Everything is already organized. Mom has the situation well under control. I just need to show up. Oh, and fit into my dress.' Beth tossed the rest of her donut out the window.

'Stop littering.' Kate sipped her cold coffee. 'I know you mean well, but I don't need a bodyguard. I have my permit to carry a firearm and plenty of ammunition. Can't you have some faith in your protégée?'

Beth glanced into the rearview mirror before changing lanes. 'I've got lots of faith, but two Annie Oakleys are better than one.' She patted the Beretta concealed beneath her cardigan. Beth Kirby was the only woman who packed heat while wearing a girly dress, high heels, and a big hat.

Kate's own handgun was tucked in her purse at her feet. Hopefully, she'd have time to dig it out if they ran into trouble. 'Three days and that's it,' she said. 'Even if your wedding is set, I'm sure Michael needs help on the case you two are working.'

'Nope, he's just finishing the paperwork on our last one before he joins us.'

Kate pivoted on the seat. 'He's picking you up and taking you home, right?'

'Wrong. You're going to have *two* bodyguards. Nate doesn't want his newest agent to end up like your boyfriend's SUV.'

'I can't believe this is happening.' Kate remembered Eric's Expedition exploding in a cloud of smoke and twisted metal with a sour taste in her mouth.

'Believe it, girlfriend. I'm treating this trip like my final vacation as a single woman. I can bunk with you, while Michael sleeps on the couch.'

'Beth, I don't have a couch. I own a few boxes of books and photo albums, a plastic crate of work stuff, one suitcase of clothes, and my laptop. Did you hear the word *couch* anywhere in that list?'

'We'll find you a furnished place just like you had in Charleston. Every furnished apartment has at least one couch.'

Without warning, Kate's eyes filled with tears. 'But it won't be *just like* Charleston, will it?' Despite her best intentions, tears streamed down her face as the image of Eric Manfredi in his white chef's coat danced through her mind – all six foot three inches of him.

'No, adorable landlords like Eric are hard to find. But now that he's your boyfriend, the landlord can look like Quasimodo.'

'You're not listening. Right before I left town, we broke up.'

'Oh, I heard you just fine. But I also know he still loves you.' Beth switched the air conditioning to high.

Kate squeezed her eyes shut, willing herself to stop crying. 'Someone connected to my jailbird brother sent me a very clear message, all because I failed to listen at the last two places I lived. Now the nicest man in the world almost died in the crossfire. I can't, I *won't* let that happen again.'

'Eric Manfredi is built like a prizefighter. Don't you think he can take care of himself?'

'But he's *not* a prizefighter! He's a chef who takes his grandmother to church on Sundays and cooks exquisite *pappardelle Bolognese*. So no, I don't think Eric can deal with sociopaths who plant car bombs in the parking lot of Office Max.'

When Beth opened her mouth to argue, Kate held up her

hand. 'Please, let's not talk about him. Nothing can be done about the situation so the less said the better.'

'Okay, I won't bring up Eric, but just remember that Michael and I go wherever the boss sends us. Nate wants Michael to use his techy superpowers to find out who's sending those warnings and I'm supposed to dog you like a bloodhound. Anybody who gets too close will be shot.' Beth patted her weapon lovingly.

'If you get arrested I won't testify at the trial that you were temporarily insane. Because we both know in your case it's permanent. Wake me when we get close to Pensacola.'

Kate leaned her seat back and closed her eyes. She knew she wouldn't sleep, but she needed time to strategize. Everything had happened so fast. Just as her last case was wrapping up in Charleston, someone with an axe to grind had found her, despite her every effort to cover her tracks. And she only had a vague idea who they were.

After her brother went to jail, his old cronies would occasionally follow her around Pensacola. Sometimes they parked outside her apartment, always in a different car with mud obscuring the license plate. Since Liam had been the only member of their pack of thieves to go to jail, she knew their intimidation was meant to keep her quiet, which is exactly what she had done.

Not that she had much choice. Whatever Kate had witnessed the night Liam graduated to big-league crime, she had buried so deep in her child's mind that she couldn't make trouble if she wanted to. Her sole intentions were to finish college and forget she even had a big brother. Then, after several years of no drive-bys, someone started leaving vile obscenities and thinly veiled threats on her answering machine. Kate considered going to the police, but feared retaliation against her brother in prison. Inmates killed fellow inmates all the time – crimes not considered newsworthy enough to make the newspaper. Even though she wanted no contact with Liam, she didn't want him to end up dead because of some foul-mouthed punks.

So instead she had packed her bags, changed her name, and left town in the dead of night. William Faulkner would have been proud, except that she hadn't bought a bus ticket. Her rusty old car made it to Tallahassee where she lived on savings until she found a job.

For a few years Kate maintained a low profile, telling only one person the truth about her identity: her boss and mentor at the Florida Bureau of Worker's Compensation. Life had been good. Then the threats started up again, this time not so thinly veiled. Her boss transferred her to a different division, in Georgia, where she was sent to work as a fraud investigator. Meeting Beth and Michael in Savannah had been a dream come true, since they wanted to hire a PI willing to travel. During her training, Kate and Beth had clicked immediately. When she was sent to Charleston – the first case she worked solo – Kate had met the love of her life. But a woman on the run can't afford to fall in love. Getting involved with her had almost cost Eric his life.

Kate was done with romance. But she was also done with running and hiding. She went back to her real name and was on her way home to Pensacola. If someone was out to get her, they might as well get it over with. That is, once Beth and Michael were safely back in Savannah.

'Wake up, sleepy head.' Beth nudged her shoulder. 'We're almost to Pensacola. What do you want me to do?'

Unfortunately, Kate had fallen asleep without formulating a strategy. 'Exit I-10 at I-110. Stay on that until it dead-ends at the Gulf of Mexico. I'll watch for signs to Main Street. Pensacola's historic district isn't quite as grand as Savannah's or Charleston's, but it's close to the water. That's where I hope to find a place to live.'

'I guess I woke you in the nick of time.' Beth cut across three lanes of traffic to reach the exit lane. 'As soon as you see water, keep your eyes peeled for signs that say, "Condemned" or "Sheriff's Auction."' A corner of Beth's mouth twitched as she fought back a grin.

'Very funny. I'll Google places on Main Street in the down-town area. There's got to be something I can afford within walking distance of the bay, even if I have to jog half a mile.' Kate pulled out her phone.

'What, you don't want to rent a villa on the beach?'

'Those would be over on Santa Rosa Island and out of my price range. Besides, I want to stay on this side of Pensacola Bay so I won't have to fight the traffic every day.'

'Like this?' Beth braked hard as cars slowed to a crawl.

She glanced up from her Google search. 'Exactly.'

While Beth fumed over the traffic, Kate checked out the long-term rental hotels, those reasonably priced and part of a national chain. But Pensacola was no Daytona or Miami Beach. She quickly narrowed the limited possibilities down to one.

'When you see a sign for Scenic Highway 90, take it to the east,' she said impulsively. 'I want to show you one of my favorite places from my youth.'

'Was this the local Lovers' Lane? Somewhere little Katie kissed a boy for the first time?'

She snorted. 'Nope, I had lots of friends in high school but no boyfriends. Even in college, the guy I hung with was more of a pal than anything else. The month we graduated, Larry got engaged to my best friend.'

'Did you want to kill him?' Beth lowered her voice to a whisper.

'Nope. I was overjoyed for them.'

'And yet . . . you're so willing to give up on Eric Manfredi – your first real boyfriend?'

Sweat ran down Kate's neck. 'What part of "knowing me could be dangerous to his health" don't you understand?' She enunciated each word carefully.

'I understand just fine, but I never pegged you for a quitter or a scaredy-cat.'

'Well, now you know the truth. And what happened to our agreement of not talking about him?'

Beth ducked her head. 'Sorry. Michael will attest to me having the memory of a mayfly.'

'Write it on the back of your hand in ink. Don't make me hurt you.'

'Here's the exit for Highway 90. What are we looking for?' Beth slowed as she headed down the ramp.

'Bay Bluffs Park. My mother brought Liam and me here for picnics. This is where Liam taught me to swim. My mentor at the Florida Bureau heard they had fixed up the area.

Supposedly they have a nice boardwalk down to the beach through a protected habitat.'

While watching for the park, Beth switched off the AC and rolled down the windows of Kate's car. 'There's the sign,' Beth hooted.

'Turn down the next road and park anywhere. I can't wait to get out of this car and stretch my legs.' The moment the Toyota stopped, Kate jumped out and started to run.

It didn't take Beth long to catch up to her. 'What's the big hurry? Is there an ice-cream stand at the end of the boardwalk?'

'I'm just happy to be here after all these years.' She didn't slow down until totally breathless.

'Which mother brought you here – the lady who adopted you and Liam or one of the foster moms?' Beth leaned back against the rail, not breathing anywhere near as hard as Kate.

'Both. My adoptive mom was first to show us this place. Then I talked a few *nice* foster mothers into coming here whenever I'd earned some kind of reward.'

Beth peered up with narrowed eyes. 'You say *nice* as though some of them weren't.'

'I don't mean abusive, or anything close. None of my foster parents were mean to me, but some had bitten off more than they could chew with the number of kids they took in. They didn't have the time or energy to give more than the minimum.' Kate didn't like where the conversation had veered. 'But I got along just fine. Plenty of natural parents wouldn't win any parenting awards either.'

'That's for sure. I'd say you turned out pretty well.' Beth wrapped an arm around her shoulder and squeezed.

'Thanks,' Kate murmured, returning the hug. 'Check out that view.'

Beth turned to see crystal blue water and sand so white the reflected glare hurt their eyes. 'Wow. This is better than any old ice-cream stand.' For several minutes they watched speed-boats and sailboats out on Escambia Bay, mesmerized. Then Beth asked, 'Do you remember the last time you came here with your brother?'

Kate shook her head. 'Liam didn't thrive well in the foster care system. Like I told you, we were never placed in the same home after our adoptive parents died. I was only seven, but Liam was already fifteen. He thought he didn't need any more supervision and wanted to be on his own.'

'He left his little sister behind?'

'No,' said Kate, much too defensively. 'Liam wanted to get a job so he could save money. Then he planned to petition the court for my custody as soon as he turned eighteen. But by then he'd fallen into a rough crowd and landed in trouble. Juvenile hall did nothing to improve his ethical sense of right and wrong. It became harder and harder for us to keep in touch.' She felt a drop of rain, the first harbinger of a storm on the horizon. 'Enough past history. Let's get out of here before we get soaked.'

Like teenagers, they raced back to the car, arriving almost at the same time. 'I beat you by a foot,' Kate crowed.

'Only because I let you win.' Beth unlocked the doors with a press of a button. 'And that's enough sightseeing. We'd better search for a place to stay.'

'I've already made up my mind. Set your GPS for the Vacation Inn and Suites on West Main Street. They have a free breakfast bar, free WiFi and free parking. No doubt there'll be a couch in the room. All the reviews say it's very clean, with an outdoor pool if you want to soak your head before heading home to Savannah.'

'Shouldn't we check out more than one place?'

'Why bother? This one I can afford if I don't stay too long. Plus Main Street turns into Bay Front Parkway, so I'll be within jogging distance of water.'

Beth headed back to the highway. 'Fine, but with your impulsive mindset you'll probably marry the next man you meet.'

Kate turned her face to the window as unbidden thoughts of Eric surfaced. Eric had been her first boyfriend – the first man she ever cared about. Now marriage to him was out of the question. 'I intend to grow old with dogs, cats, and maybe a pet lizard. Let's just get to the Vacation Inn so I can check in and unpack. Tomorrow is Saturday, visiting day at Santa Rosa Prison, and I still want to get in a swim tonight.'

As Beth stepped on the gas, Kate leaned back and tried to picture Liam as a hardened inmate. But no matter how hard she tried, an image of a lanky, sandy-haired boy with freckles simply refused to budge.

Kate awoke to the sound of Beth snoring in the other queen-size bed. She thought about burying her head beneath the pillow, but the first rays of dawn were already streaking the sky. Kate decided to let Beth sleep while she started the coffee and went for a run. Nothing like running along the bay in the cool morning air to clear away cobwebs. Last night she and Beth had splashed around in the pool, eaten greasy pizza, and fallen asleep listening to country music on her iPod. Actually, she liked having Beth's company for a few days, especially since Beth kept a small Beretta and large Glock with her at all times. But when she faced Liam Weller for the first time since his incarceration, she would be alone.

'There you are.' Beth shoved a cup of coffee into her hand the moment she walked through the door. 'Drink this, then jump in the shower. We'd better get a move on.'

Kate added a fake creamer, since no one stopped to buy milk. 'What's the big hurry? I told you Milton is less than an hour from here.'

'Yeah, but visiting hours end at two and no one will be processed after one o'clock.'

'Where are you getting all this information?' Kate gingerly sipped before gulping a mouthful.

'From a page on their website – Frequently Asked Visitation Questions.' Beth tapped the screen on her phone. 'Did you fill out and mail the visitation application?'

'Yeah, right before I left Savannah.'

Beth's eyes bugged out. 'That's only a little over a week ago. You're sunk! It takes thirty days for approval.'

'Will you please relax? I called my friend at the Florida Industrial Commission. She has friends in high places and promised to ask the warden for special permission for me.'

'Just you? I don't get to meet your brother?'

'Not until you're both in your forties.'

'Fine, but you'd better get moving. If they still need to call the warden, it will take extra time.' Beth pushed her toward the bathroom. 'You can drink your second cup along the way.'

'What about the free breakfast?' Kate called through the door.

'We'll fill our pockets and eat on the road. If I didn't know better, I'd say you were purposely dragging your feet.'

Kate turned on the water and stared into the mirror. *You might just be right.*

'And remember,' Beth hollered. 'No shorts, tank tops, Spandex, tight clothing, or fishnet stockings. And nothing either desert tan or jungle green camouflage and nothing see-through.'

The image of someone wearing all those clothes simultaneously made Kate smile. 'I'll wear nothing but long, black and baggy.'

After wolfing down scrambled eggs with hash browns and filling their to-go mugs, they set out for Milton in a somber mood.

Beth was first to break the silence. 'You know Liam will have changed a lot since you last saw him.'

'I'm prepared for that.' Kate glanced in the mirror to make sure no one was following them.

'The website said you have to lock your firearm in the trunk and take in only a small coin purse with less than fifty dollars.'

'I know, Beth. I read the rules, all except the dress code. What I don't know is how to approach this. Hey, Liam, I was just curious: Who have you been talking to that resulted in my boyfriend's car blowing up and threats against my life?'

'Maybe he's talking in order to save his life inside.'

'Then I need to know that. And his attorney needs to know, if Liam even has a lawyer.'

'Sounds like you might be softening a little toward your old swimming instructor.'

A lump of emotion rose up and lodged in her throat. 'I might be, but all that could change the moment I see him. Liam could be nothing but a trash-talking, hate-filled criminal who isn't the least bit interested in a relationship with me.'

'How can I help?' Beth asked.

'I might have an answer for you on the way home, but right now I need to mull this over in my head.'

Her friend remained silent for the rest of the drive. But once the razor-wire fence and imposing guard tower loomed into view, Kate's gut twisted into a knot. Everything she knew about prisons was from the movies and TV shows with dubious accuracy. She remembered watching a program about a Civil War prisoner camp from which some Pennsylvania coal miners tunneled their way to freedom. Nothing that would prepare her for Santa Rosa.

Once on the grounds, Kate followed the signs to visitor parking and chose a spot between two pickup trucks. After locking her purse and gun in the trunk, she hugged Beth as though she might never be released.

Beth took hold of her shoulders. 'Be brave. Remember, deep inside this is the same boy who taught you to swim.'

'I'll be fine. You make sure you don't attract the attention of the guard tower. They have even more firepower than you.'

Without a backward glance, Kate marched through the door and joined the other females in line at registration. She tried to look tough and savvy, but pulled off only aloof and bored.

'What's your old man in here for?' asked a voice over her shoulder.

Kate half turned to a buxom redhead wearing enough makeup for three women. 'My old man is dead. I'm here to see my brother.' Turning back around, Kate realized the redhead was asking about a spouse, not her father. *No matter . . . I don't have either one.* Advancing one position, she concentrated on not making eye contact. When it was finally her turn, Kate repeated the explanation she'd rehearsed a dozen times.

The guard stared, then frowned, and then pointed at the wall. 'Wait over there while I call the warden. Next.'

Just as she concluded this visitation wasn't going to happen, another guard materialized on her left. 'Come with me. Your brother is waiting in the visitation park.'

As she followed him down the hall, Kate visualized a *park* with swing sets, sandboxes, and colorful umbrella tables, where loved ones caught up on family news while birds chirped in branches overhead. What she found when the guard opened the door was a dozen picnic tables arranged in a grid in a fenced-in dirt courtyard. No colorful umbrellas, no sandboxes, no swing sets, and certainly no trees for Tarzan-like escapes. But there were families, young and old, black and white, all reconnecting with sons, brothers, husbands, and boyfriends. Inmate dads rocked babies in their arms or held toddlers in laps. The sound of their laughter was better than noisy birds anyway.

The guard pointed in the general direction, and Kate threaded her way between tables to where one man sat alone. With his back to her, the man was so still he might have been sleeping.

Inhaling a deep breath, she stepped around the table. 'Liam?'

A ruddy-faced, clean-shaven man with short hair the color of wet sand half rose to his feet. 'Yep, it's your big brother.' Gone were the long, tousled locks and closely clipped beard. Liam had gained at least forty pounds, but there wasn't an ounce of fat on his muscular frame. 'Good to see you, Katie.'

'What happened to your freckles?' She sat on the opposite bench.

'Haven't a clue. Sixteen years, and *that's* your first question?' A smile deepened the crow's feet around his piercing green eyes. Those were the only things that had remained the same.

'Sorry,' she sputtered. 'I'm a fish out of water at this.'

Liam sat down and reached across to clasp her hand. 'It's okay. I'm so happy to see you, nothing you say could be wrong.'

With a pang of guilt, she broke eye contact. 'Sorry I didn't visit sooner.'

'You were angry, and you had every right to be.' Liam squeezed her fingers. 'I promised to bust you out of the foster system, but instead I started breaking into cars and hanging around with creeps. I was on a downhill slide with no inclination to stop. I'm the one who's sorry.'

'Well, I'm not mad anymore.' Kate managed a small smile. She was practically giddy that he still had all his teeth and his speech wasn't peppered with expletives.

'You think *I've* changed? The last time I saw you, Katie-girl, you had knobby knees, hair down to your waist, and braces on your teeth. Look at you now.' Liam whistled through his teeth. 'What are you – twenty-five? Get hitched yet?' He glanced at her ring finger.

'No-oo.' She dragged the word into two syllables. 'Nothing has even come close to marriage and I'm twenty-six.'

'Any kids?'

'Of course not. That's not how we were raised.' Kate regretted her harsh tone the moment the words left her mouth.

'Begging your pardon, Miss Priss,' he drawled. 'I forgot your foster homes worked out better than mine. You turned out to be a respectable woman.'

'S'pose so. Hey, I bought food at the canteen. The website said you could take this back with you. Are you hungry?' She pulled the bag of snacks up to the table, spread out a napkin, and dumped out the bag. 'Save the bag. I wrote down my cell number should you need it.'

'I'm always hungry.' Liam picked up an apple and took a bite. 'Since you're not a housewife changing diapers all day, tell me what you've done for the last sixteen years.'

Kate pondered for a moment. 'Let's see. I was ten when you went away so I was in fourth grade. After that came middle and high school.' She ticked off details on her fingers. 'In my senior year, my foster mom helped me apply for scholarships. When the University of Florida offered me a full, four-year ride, I studied criminal justice. Go Gators,' she added as an afterthought.

Liam grinned. 'I'm proud of you.'

'I had planned to go to law school, but I soon disabused myself of that notion. I can never remember trivial facts, and law school involves tons of memorization.'

'I've never heard anyone use "disabuse" in a sentence before.' Liam laughed from his belly. 'But I know what you mean about law books. I'm doing research in our library and have fallen asleep more than once.'

'I'm glad they have a library and law books available here,' she said, even though she couldn't remember ever seeing Liam with a book.

'Wha'cha do after college?'

'I came back to Pensacola and found a job in a law office. Then this lady – the sister of someone I met at church – helped me get a job at the Florida Industrial Commission in Tallahassee.' Kate jumped ahead in the story. No need to mention why she had to leave Pensacola in a hurry. 'Government jobs pay well and have great benefits.'

Liam finished the apple and tucked the core into his shirt pocket. 'Are you still working there, building up a fat retirement for old age?'

She shook her head. 'No, I quit and became a private investigator. The pay isn't so great and no fat pension after forty years, but it's a lot more exciting.'

Liam studied her, as though contemplating how much of what she said was the truth. 'Makes sense. Anyone who can hold their breath under water as long as you and run a six-minute mile shouldn't sit behind a desk all day.'

'That six minutes might take seven or eight now, but I'm working on it.' Kate opened the bag of chips, not because she was hungry but for a distraction. 'What about you? Are they treating you okay in here?' As she shifted her focus to the imposing gray building with armed guards posted everywhere, she realized the stupidity of her question.

Liam merely shrugged. 'We don't get milk and cookies at bedtime. They read my mail and listen in on phone calls, but I'm okay. Last month I fired my worthless lawyer and requested a new public defender. But at least I'm staying in shape.' He flexed an impressive bicep. 'I got a few friends. The gangs usually leave me alone. And I just got transferred to the kitchen. They're training me to work in a restaurant when I get out.'

Kate thought about mentioning Eric's restaurant, but what was the point? She and Eric had broken up, and Liam wasn't getting released soon. It was time to get to the point of her visit. Visiting hours would end while she was dancing around the subject.

'Come to think of it, I did have one serious boyfriend. We just broke up.'

'The guy's probably kicking himself for letting you get away. What went wrong? Did he try to tame the wild-child too soon?'

'Actually, he's probably grateful he didn't end up dead. Knowing me could be hazardous to a person's health.' As she locked gazes with him, his expression sobered.

'Better give me the details, sister. You're freakin' me out.'

Kate cleared her throat. 'I left out some past history.' Kate cleared her throat. 'After your trial and conviction, every once in a while someone would call the house and ask for me. When I came to the phone, the guy would just breathe heavily and hang up. My foster mom thought it was some lovesick boy.'

'But you didn't. You thought it had something to do with me?'

'Not at first, but after I started driving it seemed like I was being followed.'

'You get the guy's license plate?'

'That's what made me suspicious. Even though it was always a different car, mud was always spattered on the front plate. Then, right before I left for college, I picked up the phone and someone said, "You remember anything yet, sweetheart? I strongly advise against it."'

Liam's ruddy complexion paled. 'You think he was referring to the robbery.' He issued a statement, didn't ask a question.

'What else could it be? Then I went away to college and heard nothing until my junior year when the hang-ups started again. Right before graduation, I got another warning about not regaining my memory.'

'Why didn't you go to the police?' Liam demanded.

'Because I was afraid it would come back on you. I've seen prison movies – men getting stabbed with plastic forks sharpened into blades.'

Liam neither agreed nor denied, but his eyes darkened. 'Tell me the rest.'

'When I came back to Pensacola, the threats got nastier. I was living alone in a tiny apartment then.'

'Did you at least tape-record some of them?'

'No, what was the point if I wasn't going to the police? But I changed my name before I moved to Tallahassee to work for the Florida IC and for a long time I was left alone.'

'Then the guy tracked you down in Tallahassee, so

you high-tailed it again.' Liam's expression registered
disappointment.

'Yeah, but this time I bought a gun, learned to shoot, and
took self-defense classes. Plus, now my co-workers are a bunch
of pistol-packing PIs instead of secretaries and clerks.'

This made her brother smile. 'Little Katie-girl . . . who
would have thought? I still don't understand what this has to
do with your *ex-boyfriend.*'

'I'm getting there. Sixteen years is a long time. My new
boss at the detective agency sent me to Charleston for a missing
person case. That's where I met Eric, because I rented a room
above his family's restaurant. I thought he could be *the one,*
until my mysterious enemy resurfaced and blew up his car. I
can't take a chance on Eric getting caught in the crossfire.'

Liam's jaw tightened while his fists clenched. 'Someone
blew up his car and you're sure it's the same man?'

'Yep, it was the same voice. And the guy called me Kathryn
and Kaitlyn and Jill – that was my most recent name change.
In Charleston, I'd been using a car titled to someone else, my
phone was registered to the company, and I'd cut my hair
short. Yet the guy still found me.' Kate let a few moments
pass. 'And his final threat was more specific. He said my
boyfriend shouldn't turn the key in his black Expedition
parked outside Office Max. And *if my brother* didn't keep his
mouth shut, there wouldn't be any advance warning next time.
I called Eric in the nick of time.'

'A bomb . . .' he asked, 'hooked to the ignition?'

'Yes. Eric didn't believe the threat was real, so I pressed
the remote start button and his car exploded.'

Liam lifted his eyebrows. 'So you blew up his car? How
did that go over?'

'At first not well. So, to make a long story a tad shorter . . .
Eric and I broke up. I left Charleston in a hurry and came
home to deal with this mess once and for all.' She waited
until her brother met her eye. 'Now I want the truth, Liam:
Who have you been talking to?'

TWO

'What do you mean Liam doesn't have a clue?' Beth asked for the third time once they reached the interstate.

'Exactly that.' Kate took her eyes off the road long enough to scowl at her best friend. 'Liam insists he hasn't been talking to anyone. He's the only member of the gang who went to jail, and he hasn't had any phone calls or visits from the ones still free as birds.'

'What makes you so sure?' Beth dug two bottles of water from her soft cooler and handed Kate one.

'Because he's my brother and I would know if he's lying.'

'You haven't seen him in sixteen years.'

'He has no reason to lie. Besides, the prison keeps records of every visitor, and inmate telephone calls are logged in and monitored.' She took a long sip of water.

That shut Beth up for a full two minutes. Then she began with less passion. 'What could that guy have meant? You know, right before he blew up Eric's car?'

'No need to get sarcastic, missy.' Kate clenched down on her back teeth. 'I remember the creep's words and actions all too well.'

'Sorry, it's just that you're so sweet and innocent. Prison can turn people into master manipulators. I can see how an older brother could maneuver you.'

She blew out a whoosh of exasperation. 'I might be a sucker for kitten videos and stray dogs, but my brother was telling the truth. I saw his face when I described the threats turning violent. You didn't.'

'You're right. I apologize. But try to remember everything your brother said. *Someone* must be keeping an eye on Liam and got spooked by something.'

For several minutes, Kate kept her focus on Route 10 while her mind scanned every word Liam said. 'He told me he'd started using the prison's law library. This is something new.'

'After sixteen years of incarceration, now your brother is researching the law?'

Kate smacked her forehead. 'And he also fired his lawyer and requested a new public defender.'

'Okay, now we're getting somewhere.' Beth clapped her hands.

Kate tried to put it all together and got zip. 'I doubt it. Whoever got worried about Liam firing his lawyer must work here, and I'm certain none of his partners-in-crime became prison guards after their lucky break.'

'As far as we know,' said Beth, always playing the devil's advocate. 'I would love to know their names.'

'So would the district attorney. There's no statute of limitations since someone died during the commission of a robbery.'

'My money says one of the former gang members has an inside informant.' Beth crunched her water bottle with one hand.

'And maybe you watch too many crime shows on TV.' Kate slowed down for the I-110 exit. 'You just make sure that goes into the recycle bin.'

'Will do, partner.'

'Beth, I appreciate everything you've done for me, but we can't *partner* on this. I'm on a leave of absence from work, but you need to get back to your case in Savannah. Plus, I'm sure Michael can't live another day without you.'

Beth dismissed the logic with a wave of her hand. 'I'm treating this like my bachelorette getaway before I fall under my new husband's thumb.'

Kate burst out laughing. 'First of all, Michael will *never* hold you down under his thumb. And secondly, women on bachelorette getaways don't visit prisons.'

'If some of their pals are inmates, they might. Take this exit,' Beth ordered. 'I saw a sign for Chick-Fil-A and I'm starving. And tonight we're pulling out the stops – extra time in the pool, a deluxe pizza whenever we get hungry, and then a chick-flick on TV.'

Kate shook her head. Arguing with her former mentor would be pointless.

Later that afternoon, Beth floated in the pool for several

hours, then called for pizza delivery. Kate stayed in their room and researched the newspaper online archives, trying to find an update on Liam's infamous crime from years ago. But she found nothing. The case was closed, period.

Nobody cared that Liam Weller hadn't pulled off an armoured car robbery alone.

When Kate finally wandered down to Beth's patio table, her friend was talking mushy-stuff to her fiancé. So she wolfed down two slices of cold, greasy pepperoni pizza. Just as she was ready to head upstairs for an antacid, her phone rang. According to caller-ID, it was their boss at the agency.

'Hello, Nate. What's up? Beth is sitting next to me, in case this involves both of us.'

'It involves mainly you, Kate, but Beth will be happy to hear I found you a case in Pensacola.'

Kate was dumbfounded for several moments. 'But I thought I was on a family leave of absence.'

'Family leaves are unpaid. Beth had indicated the situation with your brother might take a while. She also mentioned you don't have a lot of savings.'

Kate shot a dagger-look across the table. Beth swiveled around in her chair but kept talking to Michael.

'That's true, Mr Price. But I'm not sure I can devote the time your case might need.' The formal moniker was a sure sign her feathers had been ruffled.

'Beth and Michael have complete faith in you, *Miss . . . Weller*.' Nate struggled to remember her real last name, considering all the pseudonyms she used. 'And after your Charleston performance, I do too. This new case shouldn't command your attention twenty-four/seven. Or would you prefer that I fire you?'

'No, sir, I don't. I appreciate you beating the bushes for local work.'

'It wasn't too hard, since I have a friend for life in Mobile. This case involves a wealthy woman who was found dead on her yacht. Apparently she was alone at the time, but her daughter got it in her head she'll be suspected of murder.'

'Was it murder?' Kate asked.

'Who knows? So far it looks like suicide, and I told the

daughter that. But she insists she needs a detective to look into Mom's death. She doesn't trust the police and has hired our firm based on Mrs Baer's recommendation. That's my friend from Mobile.'

Kate rubbed her temples with her fingertips. 'What do you want me to do, boss?'

'Beth agreed to stay another day or two, so I want you *both* to visit the daughter tomorrow. Her name is Lainey Westin, and her mother's name was Agnes. Beth has great instincts with these things. She'll be able to tell if Miss Westin needs our help or is simply paranoid.'

'I see,' Kate said coolly.

Nate picked up on her tone. 'After that you can send Beth back to Savannah. This is your case, Kate, if there is a case at all.'

'Sorry, boss, it's been a long day.'

'Days sort of get that way around Beth. Bless her heart. Poor Michael, eh? Talk to Lainey tomorrow and then discuss it with Beth. One of you should call me tomorrow night so I'll know if I should extend your family leave of absence or put you on Miss Westin's expense retainer.'

Kate's eyes filled with moisture. 'Will do, Nate, and thanks. You've gone out of your way for me and I won't forget this.'

'Don't go all emotional with me. I'm already dealing with a pregnant wife, remember?'

'I do. Tell Isabelle I said hey, and we'll talk tomorrow.' Kate hung up with Nate Price just as Beth clicked off with Michael. 'I don't know whether I should beat the tar out of you or hug you.'

'You better pick the latter, because we both know you couldn't beat the tar out of a four-year-old. And who ate the rest of my pizza?'

'I did. You need to fit into your wedding dress. I ordered the maid-of-honor dress one size too big.'

'You sly fox!'

'Tomorrow we interview Miss Lainey Westin so we'd better get a good night's sleep. Nate will email us with the particulars.' Kate picked up the empty pizza box. 'Thanks, Beth. I know you're the reason Nate looked for PI work in Pensacola. Once again, I'm in your debt.'

Beth's pretty face bloomed with a smile. 'That's what I like – gratitude. Maybe you might not wake me up tonight when I snore.'

Kate awoke to sunlight streaming through the open blinds and the sound of a blender going haywire. She padded into the kitchen/living room where she found Beth jamming ice cubes into the appliance. 'What are you doing?'

'Crushing ice. I'm making orange juice slushies for the road. Did you sleep well?'

'Yes, until that machine woke me up.' Kate frowned at the blender, then headed for the coffeemaker.

'It was time to get up anyway. I woke up early so I printed the information Nate sent us. Then I called Michael so he can start background checks on Lainey and Agnes Westin. And I called Ms Westin and asked what time would be convenient for us to make a social call.' Beth rolled her eyes. 'Lainey can squeeze us in between beach yoga and brunch with her future in-laws. Our window of opportunity is from 10.00 to 10.45. *La-Dee-Dah*,' she drawled.

Kate glanced at her watch. 'Give me ten minutes to get ready, then we need to hustle. Who knows how long it'll take to find Miss Westin's address on Santa Rosa Island?'

'She lives in Gulf Breeze. I did a Google search and plotted our course.' Beth filled two water bottles with juice and ice.

'On second thought, maybe I'll just hang out in the pool today. It doesn't sound like you need me.'

'Nope, this is your case. But after your emotional day yesterday, I thought I'd let you sleep in.'

As Kate headed to the bathroom with her coffee, memories of her brother in yellow prison garb flooded back, along with the fact she was no closer to knowing who was threatening her than before. But today she needed to earn a living, since employers like Nate Price were hard to find and co-workers like Beth and Michael were even harder.

Considering it was still early on a Sunday, the traffic was light. Thanks to Beth's diligence, they easily found the client's residence. Lainey Westin lived on the top floor of a high-rise condo which faced the crystal blue Santa Rosa Sound.

With the exceptionally nice weather, the Sound was filled with sailboats. When they entered the building, a doorman verified their identities and allowed access to the elevator. Then a uniformed maid opened the door to the Westin suite and showed them into a starkly under-furnished living room. Or maybe it only looked under-furnished because the room was so huge. The furniture was either ultra-modern or retro Art Deco, while framed landscapes of mountains adorned the walls.

As though on cue, a tall ash-blonde, dressed to the nines, turned from her sentinel position at the windows. 'Miss Kirby? What a pleasure to meet you. I'm Lainey Westin.' The woman extended her hand to Kate.

'No, ma'am, I'm Kate Weller. That's Beth Kirby.' Kate indicated her partner. 'Beth made the initial contact, but I'll be the one handling your case.'

'Miss Kirby.' Westin shook with Beth as well. 'You both came well recommended by Mr Price. He came well recommended by an old friend of the Westin family.'

'I hope we're not keeping you from beach yoga,' Beth murmured.

Westin frowned. 'I decided to forgo my class today. Shall we get started?' She gestured to a white silk sofa and then lowered herself to a matching brocade chaise lounge. *Apparently the woman had no pets.*

'Absolutely.' Kate sat down and pulled out her notepad. 'First of all, Beth and I would like to extend our deepest sympathy at the loss of your mother.'

Westin glanced up from an inspection of her cuticles. 'Thank you, Miss Weller. I haven't heard that as much as one would think. The medical examiner hasn't released Mom's body yet, so I'm unable to plan an appropriate funeral. My mother was well known in the community and well loved by everyone who didn't know her.'

'That sounds contradictory,' said Beth. 'Could you clarify that for us?'

'It's simple. My mother loved the arts, animals, and mankind – in that order. She was legendary at raising great sums of money for museum acquisitions, a new exhibit at the zoo, or for an orphanage in Zaire. But individual people irritated her no end. The closer you got to Agnes, the better your chances for tongue-lashings at regular intervals.'

'I take it you were the primary recipient of her wrath?' asked Kate.

'Precisely. You're very astute, Miss Weller.'

'Kate, please,' she said, glancing up from taking notes. 'If we can go over the particulars, since Mr Price didn't provide much background. Are you an only child? Did your mother live here with you? By the way, your condo is stunning.'

'Yes, no, and thank you.' Westin grinned at her cleverness. 'I wish I did have siblings. That way Agnes's wrath could have been spread out among us. My mother had a condo along the beach, four miles to the east. If she had lived here, her untimely death would have happened that much sooner.' The corners of Lainey's mouth turned up.

'That sounds like a confession,' said Beth. 'Did you kill your mother? We need to know this right now.'

Westin's nose wrinkled, as though she smelled something particularly foul. 'No, Miss Kirby, I didn't. I hired your agency to find out who did. I'm guilty only of making an inappropriate joke.'

Kate shot a pointed look at Beth. 'With that out of the way, may I assume you were your mother's principal heir?'

'Correct: principal and sole, except for a few minor bequests to charity. But there were none over one hundred k.' Westin leaned back while the maid delivered a tray with a carafe and several mugs to the low table.

Kate heard Beth clear her throat but chose to ignore her. 'Is there anything in particular that makes you think you'll be suspected of her murder, other than you were her heir and your relationship was less than perfect? That is, if the police declare this a homicide. I believe all mothers and daughters argue from time to time, Miss Westin.'

'These weren't disagreements over the correct way to fold linens. These were shouting matches that could be heard in Alabama. Would you like coffee?' Lainey directed her question at Kate.

'Yes, please. Just cream for me, but Beth likes cream and sugar.'

'Oh, they'll declare it a homicide all right. Agnes wasn't

lunching alone on the *Arrivederci Sorrento*, but I don't know who she was with.' Westin handed Kate her cup but set Beth's on the edge of the table. 'And please, call me "Lainey."'

Kate took a sip. 'I gather the *Arrivederci Sorrento* is the name of your mother's boat?'

'What you called a boat is a 110-foot sailing yacht, the largest in our club's marina.'

'If the vessel is that large, wouldn't it have a captain and crew? Certainly your mother couldn't sail it alone.'

Westin laughed. 'Of course not, she might break a nail. Yes, we have a captain and full crew. But other than their small monthly retainer, they are only paid when someone takes the *Arrivederci* out. Other times, they are free to offer their services on other yachts when my mother will be *entertaining* dockside.' She imbued the word with innuendo.

Beth couldn't sit quietly on the sidelines any longer. 'Sounds to me like everything you're *not* telling us could fill up the *Queen Mary*. Why don't we just let the police do the job they're paid for? Right now we don't even know if there's been a murder, let alone that you're a suspect.' She picked up her coffee and finished the cup in several gulps.

With great dignity, Lainey rose to her feet and glared down her nose at Beth, her four-inch heels offering an imperious position. 'This isn't your decision, Miss Kirby. Mr Price already hired me, and Miss Weller will be handling my case. Perhaps you could walk the beach while Kate and I finish up?'

Kate jumped up too, her sneakers adding nothing to her five foot four. 'Instead of taking a walk, would you please check to see if the police have released the *Arrivederci Sorrento*? I would love to view the crime scene.'

Beth set her cup in the saucer with a clatter. 'Be happy to.' She marched toward the door, pulling out her phone along the way.

'Please excuse her, Lainey. Beth is about to get married and I think she's more nervous than she lets on.'

Westin nodded. 'Say no more. But in the future, any assistance from Miss Kirby must be behind the scenes.'

'Agreed.' Kate sat down. 'Now that it's just the two of us, and I assure you of my complete discretion, tell me who would point the police in your direction, if indeed your mom was murdered.'

'Just about everyone . . . let's see.' Lainey held up her index finger. 'Mom's housekeeper warned me about eternal damnation because of the way I talked to her. The ship's captain was witness to a few of our legendary fights.' She held up a third finger. 'Then we have Martha Collier, my mom's best friend. Agnes was always telling the woman she planned to disinherit me and give everything to the Audubon Society. Of course it was just talk. My mother didn't even like birds and she hated seagulls.' Lainey glanced at her watch, while Kate jotted down Martha Collier's name.

'I know you have another appointment, but may I have the names of the marina, the ship's captain, and your mother's housekeeper?'

'That would be the Santa Rosa Yacht Club, Captain Roger Holcomb, and Luisa Gonzalez.' While she spoke, Lainey led Kate down the hallway to the front door. 'Please call me with updates. Here's my card with my business number and cell phone.'

'I certainly will. Oh, one more thing. I'm assuming your mom was single. Was she divorced or was your father never in the picture?'

Lainey's blue eyes grew round with indignation. 'Yes, they were married! Once upon a time, my dad and I were very close, but they divorced at least fifteen years ago.'

'I beg your pardon.' Kate ducked her head to hide her embarrassment. 'May I have his name?'

'Robert Westin.'

'Westin – your mom continued to use her married name?'

'Yes, she's rather old-fashioned. Plus she never liked her maiden name. Now, if you'll excuse me . . .'

Dutifully, Kate walked out the door. 'Again, my sympathies on your loss.'

On the elevator ride down to the lobby, Kate arrived at three conclusions: Agnes Westin didn't sound the least bit old-fashioned.

Lainey Westin was as likeable as a millipede.

And Beth had definitely dodged a bullet on this case.

*   *   *

Eric Manfredi picked up his phone on the first ring. 'Beth? Where are you? Is Jill – er, I mean Kate with you? Is everything okay?'

'Would you please relax?' Beth leaned her backside against the car's fender. 'Kate, formerly known as Jill, is upstairs interviewing her new client. Thank goodness I'll be heading home soon. I'd bet my next month's salary this woman killed her mother and thinks we'll cover it up. Women that arrogant think they can commit murder and get away with it.'

As appreciative as he was of Beth, Eric didn't have time for one of her tirades now. 'Could you save this story for another day? I've got plenty to do before you get back to the Vacation Inn and Suites. That's where Kate rented a room, right? On West Main Street in downtown?'

'Yes, she's staying on the fourth floor with a lovely view of the parking lot. But I hope you have your ducks in a row, Manfredi. If Kate suspects you came to Pensacola to keep an eye on her, she'll blow a gasket. She got mad when I insisted on driving here with her. Wait until Michael shows up in a few days.'

Eric grunted. 'Michael should stay in Savannah and you should join him. I'm capable of watching Kate's back, whether she wants me here or not.'

'I understand, Prince Charming, but Nate wants us to investigate Liam Weller's robbery/homicide from sixteen years ago. The only reason someone is threatening Kate is because the truth never came out at trial. The boss says Kate will never be safe until her brother's accomplices land in the slammer.' Suddenly, Beth abruptly changed her tone of voice. 'Thanks so much for letting us know,' she drawled. 'And we'll check back tomorrow for another update.' Then the line went dead.

Eric surmised that Kate had finished interviewing her new client. Slipping his phone in his pocket, he hurried toward the hotel office. He didn't care what he paid for a night, a week, a month at the Village Inn and Suites. If they had no vacancy, he would bribe someone to check out. What good was money in the bank or a portfolio of investments if he lost the woman he loved? He hadn't handled things well when his car blew up. With his pride kicking in, he'd reacted with anger that some cretin had gotten too close. Next time Kate would be his target. So Eric had to make sure he took care of the cretin first.

Eric marched up to the registration desk and produced his friendliest smile for the clerk. Soon he had the keys to a large suite on the fourth floor. Although his suite faced in the opposite direction as Kate's, the view wasn't much better than the parking lot. But he hadn't come for the view, and his unit was only two down from hers. No fat bribe had been necessary. With two bedrooms, two baths, and a queen-size pullout couch, he had far more space than he needed. But that too wasn't important.

Climbing into his new SUV, a replacement vehicle from the insurance company, Eric Googled the nearest grocery store and headed in that direction. As sweet as Kate was, he wanted to make his lame excuse sound as plausible as possible. So he needed plenty of groceries, along with the simple necessities of a chef's life. An hour later, Eric was hefting his last load of cooking utensils from his vehicle along with three bags of groceries when a female voice screeched his name.

'Eric Manfredi, what on earth are you doing here?'

Shifting his armload of boxes, he saw two women with bare legs and knotted bathrobes blocking his path. 'Kate! Beth! Are you two staying *here*? Of all the places I could have picked in town.' His smile was even more magnanimous than the one offered to the desk clerk.

Kate's face scrunched into a scowl. 'Bah-lon-nee! How naïve do you think I am? No way could this be a coincidence.' She turned on her heel to glare at Beth, who was frantically searching for something in her purse.

Eric moved closer. 'Since you're from Pensacola, I assumed you would stay with relatives, like an aunt or uncle, or maybe a godmother.'

'I don't have a godmother.' Kate crossed her arms. 'I told you I had little family. So I'll ask you once more . . . why are you here? Did you forget that we broke up?'

Eric didn't have to feign a hurt expression. His feelings were as raw as they had been in Charleston. But before he could open his mouth, Beth turned on Kate like a feral raccoon.

'Look, missy. If you're gonna be mean to one of your few *friends*, I'm heading to the pool.' Beth stomped past Eric to the elevator. 'Maybe you should come too, and soak that rock-head of yours,' she called over her shoulder.

Kate modified her tone. 'She's right. I'm sorry, Eric. What's goin' on with you?'

He shifted the load of boxes. 'Would you like to step into my suite? These are heavy.'

'No, thank you. I'm comfortable right here.' Despite a softened tone, she remained rigid and guarded.

Eric lowered his burdens to the carpeted hallway. 'When you left, I felt . . . conflicted. I was sad, of course, that you and I couldn't work things out. But it was more than that.' He leaned one shoulder against the wall. 'I was also a little envious.'

Kate's chin snapped up. 'Have you lost your mind? You were jealous because a bomb-making madman was stalking me?'

'Of course not. But the moment you realized the situation was getting worse, you packed up your car and left town. Just like that, with very little baggage, literally or figuratively.'

'I didn't have much choice.'

'I understand that, Kate, but it got me thinking. I'm not even thirty, yet it seems I have a life sentence at Bella Trattoria. I can't even remember the last time I went on vacation.'

'But you love to cook. It's more than your job; it's your passion.'

He smiled at that. 'The passion of my life is garlic, olive oil, and veal cutlets? I'm even more pathetic than I thought.'

'You know what I mean.'

'I do, but I'm too young to settle down like my parents, and owning a restaurant traps a person. I might enjoy cooking, but I'm not sure I want to stay in Charleston forever. So I asked my parents if they'd ever considered a second location for Bella Trattoria, maybe somewhere in Florida. I expected them to laugh me out of the kitchen, but they were open to the idea. Mom said she'd been thinking about a place to go for vacations, maybe two or three months at a time. She has always loved the ocean. Dad said if Mom wanted to stay away that long, he'd need another restaurant to dabble in.'

Kate put her hands on her hips. 'You're saying it was your parents who suggested Pensacola?' Skepticism dripped from her words like candle wax.

'Not exactly.' Eric looked her in the eye. 'They were thinking about Amelia Island outside of Jacksonville. But when I told them you were moving here, they asked if the area could support another high-end restaurant. My dad really liked you, Kate, and you sort of grew on Irena.' He held up his hands. 'Now, before you blow your stack, they know we've broken up. But having friends in the area is like money in the bank.'

She considered this. 'If you opened a restaurant here, who would run Bella in Charleston? Your father's talking at least semi-retirement.'

'My sister can run that place with her eyes closed. And she would have my aunt and grandmother's help.'

'So you're not here to replace Beth as my bodyguard?' Her crooked smile almost broke his heart.

'Nope. I'm here to give Bernadette a trial run to see how she does without me. And to look at commercial real estate close to the water. I'd love to find an out-of-business restaurant.'

'Wouldn't the fact they're out of business tell you something?'

'Not necessarily, unless the place served northern Italian cuisine.'

She shrugged. 'It would be nice to have a friend in town when Beth leaves.'

'If you need my help, call me. Otherwise, I'll stay out of your way.' Eric picked up the boxes and unlocked the door into his suite. 'Right now, I need to put these groceries away, so go enjoy your swim.' He walked in and shut the door on her, something he thought would have been hard to do.

But after his half-truths and white lies, it proved very easy. Despite all the groceries he'd bought, he wouldn't invite Kate and Beth over for dinner. Maybe someday they could give their relationship another chance. He needed to play by Kate's rules. And he'd do anything short of first-degree murder to keep that woman safe.

THREE

Last night Kate had swum laps until every muscle in her body screamed for mercy and her lungs burned from holding her breath. Then she had floated on her back and watched cloud formations form and dissolve in the sky, half hoping and half fearing Eric would show up with a pizza and six-pack of soda.

But he hadn't.

Kate knew his tale of 'scouting the area for a second location' was pure fiction. Or, at least, partial fiction. When this mess with her brother was over – if she hadn't been fired yet – Nate would send her on a case in another town. Wasn't that exactly what she wanted – no strings attached?

At least it was what she used to want.

Now the idea of Eric close by comforted her. Despite everything that happened at Bella Trattoria, she'd loved waking up to the sound of Eric in the kitchen below. Unfortunately, that's what almost got him killed.

Better for him to think she didn't love him.

On that bright and sunny Monday morning, Kate had drunk two cups of coffee and finished her run along the bay before Beth dragged herself out of bed. 'Good morning, sunshine,' she cooed when her roommate appeared in the doorway.

'What happened last night?' Beth held her stomach with one hand, while her other tried to work out a nasty knot in her hair.

'Looks like you tangled with an octopus. *Mommy* warned you to apply conditioner and comb out the snarls, but you didn't listen.' Kate handed her a cup of coffee.

'That explains my coiffure, but what about my bellyache?'

'I also said it was a bad idea to have pizza two nights in a row.'

Beth slumped over the kitchen counter. 'Nobody ever listens to the voice of reason until it's too late.'

'Take these.' Kate placed two antacids in a saucer. 'Aspirin are in my makeup bag. I'll be back in a few hours.'

Beth straightened immediately. 'Where are you off to this early?'

'It's almost ten. I want to check out where the Westins keep the *Arrivederci Sorrento*. Even if the police haven't released the crime scene, plenty can be learned from talking to people in the marina.'

'I want to go too,' Beth whined like an eight-year-old.

'No, I'm tired of sitting around here. You take a hot shower and feel better. Tonight we'll stop at a grocery store for salad fixings. I don't want to see greasy pizza for six months.'

'If I take the fastest shower on record and I promise to be good, can I come? *Pul-leaze?*' Beth pressed her fingers together as though praying. 'You can check the internet for info on the Westins while I get dressed.'

Kate rolled her eyes. 'Michael already sent me more than I'll ever need. The late Mrs Agnes Westin left a huge footprint in this area. She had her well-manicured fingers into everything.' She opened the file she'd printed that morning in the hotel's business center. 'And look how beautiful she was. The way Lainey talked, I was expecting a look-alike for Madame Defarge.'

'Who's Madame Defarge?'

'Didn't you ever read *A Tale of Two Cities*?'

'Very little of it. I kept nodding off.' Beth studied the printed photo. 'She's certainly attractive, but that surprised look on her face is a dead giveaway for a facelift.'

Kate took another look at the smiling, sixtyish blonde. 'You and I won't look surprised. We'll look like topography maps of Colorado.' She slipped the picture into her file folder. 'Okay, I'll study Michael's notes for fifteen minutes. If you can get ready that fast, you can come. And it's only because I don't want you chumming around with Eric while I'm gone. He's here with a purpose and it has nothing to do with me.'

Beth nodded, picked up her coffee, and headed to the bathroom.

The fact she'd said *nothing* about Eric last night at the pool

spoke volumes. Neither one of them liked to lie, but Beth
thought omission of the truth wasn't lying.

Kate shook off Beth's ethical code and concentrated on the
life of Agnes Westin. To say the woman had lived well would
be an understatement. She owned beautiful homes here and
in Nice, France, plus a condo in Manhattan's theater district.
After her graduation from the University of Florida with a
Master's in Art History, she'd studied in Paris for a year.
Although Lainey was her only child, plenty of orphans on
three continents had benefited from her big heart and deep
pockets. She married only once, to her college sweetheart,
Robert Westin, who worked for a while in the family business.
The serious money came from her family, not his. Mrs Westin
was daughter of John and Delia Cook, founders of the largest
yacht manufacturer on the Gulf of Mexico. Although John had
died several years ago, Delia Cook was still on the company's
board of directors, although she wasn't the chairwoman. When
John Cook died, his wife inherited his voting shares of stock,
while his daughter, Agnes, received a huge portfolio of investments
which, according to Michael, were generating large dividends.
The woman had money to burn, lived well, and donated plenty
to charity. So even if she wasn't mother-of-the-year, at least she
was generous.

Kate paused for a moment, trying to imagine what Lainey's
young life had been like. All that money everywhere she looked,
and yet the woman had grown up to be downright mean-spirited
and hostile. *Poor little Lainey – didn't Mommy have enough
time for you?* Kate thought about fellow kids in the foster care
system who had endured miserable lives before finally being
removed from an abusive parent. Any compassion she might
have mustered for the poor little rich girl drained away.

'Did I beat the deadline?' A fresh-scrubbed Beth bounded
into the room. Her damp red hair was in a long plait down
her back to match Kate's braid.

'You did, but I didn't think we were going as the Bobbsey
Twins. Have you ever read a book in your life?' asked Kate,
in response to Beth's look of confusion. She grabbed her bag
on her way out the door.

'Do you mean all the way to the end?' Beth pressed the button for the elevator.

'Of course, I mean to the end.'

'I'm sure I have, let me think for a minute.'

When after five minutes, Beth still came up empty, Kate filled her in on the Westin details for the remainder of the drive.

At the gate for the Santa Rosa Yacht Club, Kate handed her PI license to the uniformed guard in the booth. 'I work for Lainey Westin,' she said. 'Could you point me in the direction of the *Arrivederci Sorrento*?'

The guard studied her license. 'Sure, Miss Weller, but I'll need to photocopy this first.' When he handed back her license, he also wrote down the Westin dock and slip numbers. 'Good luck finding a place to park. The police and crime lab techs are still crawling all over that boat.'

'How come the guard is allowed to call it a boat, when we were told not to?' Beth asked as they left the booth.

'Don't worry about that.' Kate pulled out her notepad. 'You just remember this is *my* case. You're here to take notes while I do the talking. Got that?'

'Yes, ma'am.' With a salute Beth took the tablet and opened to a clean page.

As they drove through the marina, the yachts become larger and fancier the further they went from the gate. Soon Kate saw the commotion the guard referred to – several police cars and a forensic van were parked haphazardly at the end of dock 7.

'Good grief.' Beth raised a finger to point. 'Have you ever seen a sailboat that huge?'

Kate had seen a picture of the *Arrivederci Sorrento* in the file Michael sent, but a photo couldn't compare to up-close and personal. 'I've seen a few regattas out on the Gulf, but boats must look a lot smaller on the water.' Kate stopped the car to stare. 'Three masts, two decks, all that brass. The thought of sailing across the Atlantic grows more romantic by the minute.'

'Especially if the new bride has a gourmet chef for a bridegroom.' Beth pinched her arm.

'You need to stop reading romance novels,' Kate muttered, shaking off the mental picture of Eric. 'It's bad for your practical nature.' Parking in a spot marked 'Reserved for the *Dancing Fool*,' she jumped out of the car.

'What happens if that boat's owner shows up?' asked Beth, following her down the gangway.

'We'll just say we're helping the police. And it won't be a lie. Uh-oh.' Kate spotted the double band of yellow *Do Not Cross* tape, preventing them from joining the cops and lab techs that covered the main deck like ants.

'What's the plan, boss?' Beth leaned one shoulder against a dock post.

'We'll wait here until someone in authority leaves the ship. Then I'll place my irresistible self into his or her path. I won't let them get past me until my questions are answered.'

'While you carry out that foolproof plan, I'll check out the rest of the marina. I need to stretch my legs.'

'Don't fall in or wander too far away,' Kate warned. 'I might send you an SOS text.'

Beth saluted again and hiked up the gangway.

From her fine vantage point, Kate watched the comings and goings on the *Arrivederci*. Once most of the techs closed up their kits and disembarked, the only people left were cops. And it wasn't hard to tell which one of them was in charge. A tall man with close-cropped black hair and a trimmed goatee was wearing a sport coat and tan Dockers with a sharp crease, while the others wore uniforms with Santa Rosa County Sheriff's Department insignias.

Kate locked eyes with him once while he talked on the phone, then resumed studying the boats entering and leaving the marina. When the man finished his conversation, he slipped the phone into his pocket and walked to the narrow plank connecting the dock to the *Arrivederci*.

'Can I help you with something, miss?' He stopped on his side of the police tape. 'I would be a terrible detective if I didn't notice you watching every move made on this sailboat.' Instead of a drawl, he spoke with a lilting British accent with a hint of the islands, perhaps Bahamian or Jamaican.

Kate approached the plank with a friendly yet professional

expression. 'Good afternoon, sir. Forgive me for disturbing you. I'm Kate Weller of Price Investigations. I've been hired by Lainey Westin to assist with the investigation.' She pulled out both her PI license and a photocopy of the contract and passed them across the yellow barrier.

He inspected both carefully and even held the contract up to the light, as though waiting for the ink to disappear. When satisfied, he offered Kate his hand. 'I'm Lieutenant Julian Buckley of the Sheriff's Department. You haven't disturbed me, but it'll be at least another day or two before we release the *Arrivederci Sorrento* to Miss Westin or her representative. This is an ongoing homicide investigation, Miss Weller.'

'Yes, sir, I understand, and I wouldn't dream of crossing your tape.' *But I could listen to your charming accent all day*, she thought, hiking her leather tote up her shoulder. 'From your terminology, may I assume natural causes have been ruled out in Mrs Westin's death?'

A slow smile revealed sparkling white teeth. 'You may not. Until the medical examiner finishes his autopsy and all evidence has been processed, nothing has been ruled out. But we do prefer to err on the side of caution.'

'Very wise.' She nodded energetically. 'May I ask who made the initial 911 call?'

He frowned. 'Why would I tell you that, Miss Weller?'

'Knowing who made the call would go a long way in easing the daughter's mind, because whoever made the call most likely discovered Mrs Westin's body. And Miss Lainey Westin is hoping her mother hadn't over-imbibed and fallen overboard.' Looking appropriately mortified, Kate dropped her voice to a whisper. 'The daughter hopes that Mom hadn't been spotted by a fisherman floating face down in the inlet. The poor woman would have been at the mercy of carnivorous fish or worse . . . sharks.' Kate clutched her throat with the mental picture.

'Stop surmising, PI. First of all, sharks don't usually come into Santa Rosa Sound, so I caution you against starting baseless rumors. And secondly, although the tox screen will reveal whether or not she had over-imbibed, I assure you Mrs Westin was never in the water.' Buckley pushed his sunglasses up his nose. 'There, you wormed something out of me. So if you can return to your post, I'd like to finish up here.'

'Thank you, Lieutenant, for sharing that with me. I came all the way down from Natchez, Mississippi to work this case.' Kate pumped his hand like a well handle.

He discreetly extracted his hand. 'So I noticed on your license.'

Just then they both heard sounds of a scuffle, along with irate male and female voices. Buckley most likely recognized the male voice, while Kate knew exactly who the female voice belonged to.

A portly uniformed officer dragged Beth Kirby around the ship's main cabin. 'I found this woman sneaking onto the crime scene, Lieutenant. She crawled under the tape and was heading down the crew staircase.'

'I tried to explain to your officer that this is all a misunderstanding.' Beth shook off the cop's hold. 'I was cutting across the *Arrivederci* from the *Dancing Fool* on my way to the dock. I know the Westins wouldn't mind me stepping over their yellow party ribbon.'

'Oh, yeah? Then why were you headed down the crew staircase?' The officer didn't loosen his grip on Beth's arm.

'I got scared when I saw all the cops. So I tried to hide below deck.'

Beth might have gotten away with her bizarre explanation if not for growling sounds coming from Kate's throat. And the fact that when the lieutenant demanded Beth's ID, a Mississippi driver's license was one coincidence too many.

'I take it you know this woman, Miss Weller?' asked Buckley.

'Yes, sir, unfortunately I do. Miss Kirby is a brand-new investigator who's still learning the ropes. I hope you won't formally charge her.' To Beth, Kate muttered, 'What did you think "Crime Scene – Do Not Cross" meant, Kirby?'

Beth played along with the juxtaposition of roles. 'Sorry, Miss Weller, I thought it didn't apply to me because I'm an investigator. Please don't tell the boss. He'll fire me for sure this time.'

Buckley handed back Beth's driver's license. 'If I see you

anywhere near my crime scene again, I'll get the real owners of the *Dancing Fool* to press trespassing charges at the very minimum. Now get out of my sight.' He pointed at the plank leading to the dock.

'See you back at the car, Miss Weller,' Beth said meekly.

After a final scowl, Kate turned back to the police. 'Thank you, Lieutenant. I'm grateful you didn't throw her in jail.'

'I've already got a mountain of paperwork with this case.' Buckley studied Kate for a long moment, and then handed her his business card. 'The ship's captain along with two crew members found Mrs Westin slumped in a chair. The captain called in the 911. No one else was on the ship.'

Kate nodded. 'Thank you, sir. Now if I might return the professional courtesy. Miss Westin said her mother often entertained here without staff – both for business and with personal friends. But if the captain and crew showed up, she must have planned an evening sail. Mrs Westin was a stickler for privacy. Although if she allowed other boats to raft off the *Arrivederci*, I don't know how much privacy she had.'

'The *Dancing Fool* was tied up snuggly in its own slip when I arrived.' Buckley peered down his nose at Kate. 'My guess is your protégée took it upon herself to untie the ropes and raft the *Dancing Fool* off the *Arrivederci* – something owners of expensive ships would never do.'

Kate's expression revealed utter shock. 'Oh, no, I'll take care of that right now.'

Buckley waved off her suggestion. 'No. Since I have sailing experience, I'll return the *Dancing Fool* to her slip. You just keep the new PI away from me.'

'You have my word.'

Buckley studied her face for a second time. 'Why don't you call me in a few days? I might have some information I can share. In the meantime, let me give you some advice: Tell your boss about Kirby's stunt. If he fires her now, it'll save you plenty of stress down the road.' Buckley turned on his heel and walked away.

Kate had no idea why the police detective was being so nice, but she smiled all the way to her car.

Santa Rosa Correctional Institution

At the appointed hour, all the doors in the cellblock slid back, allowing Liam and his fellow inmates to proceed in orderly fashion to the dining hall. No pushing, shoving, or talking in line. It was very much like elementary school except that, instead of a young pretty teacher who could make you spend recess on the bench, guards armed with batons made the rules. And, since every single movement made inside prison walls was caught on video, other guards armed with highly lethal weapons could materialize at a moment's notice. That succinct fact had been made clear to Liam and every inmate upon arrival. Liam had no desire to tunnel beneath concrete walls sunk well below ground level, or to make his grand escape in the back of a garbage truck. He planned to learn a trade and serve his time, so when released he would never end up back here.

He had never fallen victim to the addictive allure of alcohol or drugs. Money and the power it conveyed had been his personal Achilles' heel. But his plan to share in great wealth had earned him twenty years, stripped of privacy and without the ability to change the tiniest variable in his life. Thus, Liam queued silently with the others to receive a tray of nutritious but barely palatable food and take his assigned place in the dining hall. Although talking was permitted, most men had little to say to those they had nothing in common with, except for current circumstances. Familiarity breeds contempt, never more so than among incarcerated prisoners.

Liam peered at the roast beef in dark gravy over mashed potatoes and began to eat, starting with the canned green beans first. Nothing tasted particularly different than usual in the two-week rotation of meal menus. But as he sopped up gravy with his sole slice of bread, Liam felt an uncomfortable rumble deep in his gut. He set his fork on the tray, took a drink of water, and swallowed. After a moment, the uncomfortable rumbles morphed into wrenching spasms that made it difficult to breathe. Liam pushed away the tray and glanced around the table. None of the other men seemed to be struggling with the bland potatoes and overcooked beef.

'What's the matter with you, man?' asked a burly man named Carlos.

But Liam couldn't speak. Gripping the edge of the table, he waited for the spasms to pass.

'Try drinking some water,' suggested the helpful Carlos. 'This horsemeat won't go down without it.'

But water wouldn't help in this situation. Soon the spasms turned into a pain so intense, Liam expected to see blood staining his shirt. Struggling to his feet, he prayed he would reach the men's room in time. But as he tried to step over the bench, he tripped and sprawled helplessly into the aisle. Falling, he tasted both blood and the bile that had risen up his throat. Although Liam couldn't be sure, he thought he heard Carlos say, 'Man, that guy's been poisoned,' right before his head hit the hard concrete floor.

When Liam awoke, he was lying on a narrow hospital bed and staring at a dingy white ceiling. A thin beige blanket had been pulled up to his throat and, surprisingly, his wrists weren't tied to the bed frame.

'Where am I?' he croaked, his throat painfully dry.

'In the infirmary.' A wrinkled, weathered face appeared above him. 'You passed out in the dining hall. I'm Doc Murphy. Try to sit up and drink this. You're no doubt dehydrated, considering you threw up all over yourself. The man who has to mop that up ain't gonna be happy with you, Weller.'

'What happened?' Liam struggled to a sitting position and sipped from a plastic cup. His insides churned as the water hit his stomach, but at least the searing pain had stopped.

'Who knows? Something sure didn't agree with you.'

'Did anybody else get sick?' he rasped.

'Nope.' The doctor refilled his cup from the pitcher.

'Doesn't that strike you as strange?' Liam supported himself with his elbows.

'Nope, funny thing about food in this place. Some men can tolerate it just fine, others don't handle it well. I notified the warden, but he said if nobody else gets sick, I'm to write this up as stomach flu in my report.'

'Yeah, maybe that's it.' Liam studied the aging medical practitioner, but Murphy returned the gaze with benign interest.

Nothing about his behavior indicated he was part of a conspiracy to poison certain inmates.

Just then the phone on the wall rang. Doc Murphy took his time answering it. 'Infirmary,' he finally barked into the mouthpiece.

'*Right now?*' he asked.

'But I've got a patient in here . . .'

'Fine, no need to get hot under the collar.'

Doc Murphy hung up the phone and turned back to Liam. 'Sorry, but I gotta step out for a little while and protocol says I must lock you down. Nothing personal.' Adroitly, he snapped a handcuff on Liam's wrist and attached the other end to the metal frame. A second pair secured his other arm in the same fashion. 'I'll be back soon. In the meantime, try to get some sleep. The Donnatal I gave you for the cramping should make you drowsy. If this is the flu, sleep is the best cure I can offer.' Murphy punched a code into the keypad on the wall, and when the door unlocked he stepped into the hallway. A cool draft blew in behind him.

With not much else to do, Liam closed his eyes and felt his muscles relax one by one. But his fitful slumber didn't last long. Without warning, someone jerked him by the shoulder, upright enough to slip a black hood over his head. Instinctively, Liam fought to free his arms from the wrist restraints. The cloth smelled foul, but he was no match for cold steel, even if he hadn't been sedated.

'Relax, Weller,' a voice whispered next to his ear. 'I ain't here to kill you, not this time anyway.' The hand on his chest pushed him down on the bed.

'What do you want?' Liam asked, fighting back a wave of nausea.

'Just to give a smart boy like you a bit of advice.' The hand exerted pressure on Liam's ribs. 'How did ya like that special seasoning on your meat? Kinda put an extra kick into dinner, no?'

Straining against his restraints, Liam let loose with a string of expletives. But with each name, the pressure on his chest increased until he gasped for breath.

'I'd shut that mouth of yours, Weller, and just listen. Or I'll accidentally wring your neck like a chicken.'

As the rough, nasty cloth tightened against his face, Liam let his body go limp.

'As I was saying . . . this is only a warning. Stop whatever it is you're doing in the law library. And, if I were you, I wouldn't tell that new lawyer of yours to start digging up the past. You might get a stronger dose of seasoning that kills with just one bite. So, unless you plan the longest hunger strike in prison history, let the sleeping dogs lie.'

Suddenly the pressure on his chest lifted. For a moment, Liam thought his tormentor had gone. Then the man whispered in his other ear. 'And that sister of yours? What a pretty thing little Katie turned into, or so I'm told. Why did she come back to town, Weller?'

'Who knows?' Liam rasped. 'Whatever her reason, it's got nothing to do with me.'

'Then how come she came to visit you with that red-haired PI from Savannah?'

Liam had never felt so helpless in his entire life. 'I didn't see no redheads, and I don't know no PIs, from Savannah or anywhere else. My sister wanted to see what I looked like these days. She probably won't be back for another sixteen years. We're not exactly close.'

'You'd better hope that's the case, or little Katie will find something very bad in her morning yogurt.'

This creep knew what his sister ate for breakfast? Lunging against his restraints, Liam launched another volley of expletives. But it was doubtful his tormentor heard them, because the man's hands closed around Liam's throat and squeezed until Liam saw thousands of flashing lights before his eyes. Then his world went dark and he was aware of nothing at all.

'Weller,' called a voice from far away.

'Weller, wake up! What happened in here?'

Liam finally roused to consciousness as Doc Murphy removed the left handcuff. 'You tell me. I woke up to someone pulling a hood over my head. Then someone tried to choke me.'

Murphy turned Liam's face to the side to examine his neck. 'Good golly. Who did that?'

Struggling to sit up, Liam knocked away the doctor's hand.

'How would I know? You left me drugged and tied to the table.'

Murphy uncuffed his other wrist. 'Man, somebody's really got it out for you.'

'And you're helping them.' Liam coughed up blood into his palm.

'I swear I'm not. I got called to the loading dock for an order of pharmaceuticals that just arrived. I'm the only one allowed to sign for them. But deliveries never come this late in the day.'

'Let me guess: Nothing was waiting when you got there, right?'

Murphy just stared at him.

'If you're not with them, you just played right into their hands.'

'Not on purpose. I do my best for the inmates. I'm not out to do anyone harm.' Indignation resonated in Murphy's voice.

'If that's true, you need to get a message to my sister.'

The doctor lifted a bushy white eyebrow. 'I also don't get involved in inmate squabbles.'

'Whoever sneaked in here and tried to kill me also plans to kill her. Warn her to stay away from Santa Rosa Prison and *anything* that has to do with me.'

'Is that it?'

When Liam nodded, Murphy produced a pen and paper. 'Write down her name and number. When I'm far away from this place, I'll give her a call, but only this once. So don't ask again.'

Liam wrote down the number he'd committed to memory during Kate's visit. Then he took a long look at his physician. Murphy had to be at least seventy, and the broken capillaries in his nose indicated a lifetime of alcohol abuse. The man walked with a limp, while his general demeanor could best be described as dazed and confused. Hopefully, he could rally his faculties long enough to see that no harm came to his sister.

Because this old man was the best hope Liam had.

FOUR

L ost in her thoughts, Kate almost didn't hear her cell
phone ring.

'Good morning, sunshine,' said Michael Preston.
'Did I wake you?'

'Of course not. You're talking to me, not to your fiancée.
I'm out for my morning run in beautiful downtown Pensacola.
What's up?'

'Is my intended bride with you?' he asked with a laugh.

'Let me repeat – *of course not.* It's early. Did you want to
talk to Beth?'

'No, it's you I need.'

'Did Beth tell you about her shenanigans yesterday at my
crime scene?'

'She did.' All frivolity vanished from Michael's voice. 'Beth
felt terrible about jamming you up with that detective. Living
in upstate Mississippi, she's not had much boating experience,
and none on sailboats that size. She didn't realize the potential
consequences of untying that yacht.'

'Beth was lucky the bumpers were out on the *Dancing Fool*
when it drifted up against the *Arrivederci Sorrento.*'

'You're not kidding, or she and I would be paying off
damages for years.'

Kate checked her watch. 'Is that why you called? Because
she and I have resolved our differences: Beth is hereby banned
from my crime scene, plus she buys me lunch for a year.'

'Well done, Weller, but no. I called because I have information. I did some checking on Agnes Westin. Should I wait
until you're back at the hotel to tell you?'

'No way, let's hear it now.' Kate plopped down on a retaining
wall.

'Not that long ago, police were summoned to the yacht club
marina by an anonymous caller, specifically to the *Arrivederci
Sorrento.* According to the report, Agnes Westin and her

ex-husband, Robert, were in the midst of a heated argument when police arrived. A dining table and several wine glasses had been smashed, and one of the deckchairs was in the water, floating away with the current.'

'My, my, those two had been divorced for years. What could they still be squabbling about?'

'If I may venture a guess as an about-to-be married man . . . money. The term "over my dead body," uttered by Mrs Westin, had been noted in the police report.'

'Had there ever been any physical violence?' she asked.

'Apparently not. Both seemed to prefer smashing objects instead of each other. But due to the level of hostility, a thorough search was made of the boat. And guess what the police found?'

Kate decided to let Michael's misuse of nautical terms slide. 'I'm holding my breath with anticipation.'

'A thirty-eight-caliber handgun, registered to Robert Westin, hidden behind a loose panel in the galley. A galley is a kitchen.'

'I know that, Mr Natchez. I was born in Florida,' Kate teased. 'What am I missing here? There was no mention of a gunshot wound in the preliminary report.'

'I know,' Michael agreed. 'But now we know a gun had been on the boat. Mrs Westin was so shocked when the gun was discovered that she started throwing more stuff at Robert until physically restrained by a woman cop.'

Kate pondered this. 'What did Mr Westin say about the weapon?'

'Not much. He said he hid the gun there years earlier before a trip to the Bahamas. He wanted protection from pirates in the Caribbean, no pun intended. Then, after their divorce, he'd forgotten about it.'

'That could be true. I read about well-armed thieves robbing pleasure boats of all sizes.'

'Yeah, except, according to the registration, the brand-new Smith and Wesson had been purchased long *after* their divorce.'

Kate felt a spike of anger. 'Doesn't anyone tell the truth to the police anymore? I thought rich folks had too much class to outright lie.'

'I have no answer to that, but I scanned the report and sent it to your email. So what are you two ladies doing today?'

'We're not *ladies*; we're professional private investigators. And don't you forget it.'

'Yes, ma'am. Tell sweet Beth I'll talk to her tonight. And whatever you're doing, be safe.'

'Wait, Michael, there's something else.' Kate sucked in a breath. 'I know you tapped my new work phone so don't bother to deny it. I need to know who called me last night around eleven o'clock.'

'Hey, it was the boss who told me to record your incoming calls. He's worried about you and wants to know immediately about any threats against you. I haven't checked the machine yet, so tell me about this phone call while I do that now.'

'Some man said I should stay away from Santa Rosa Correctional and stop digging into my brother's business. Otherwise, Liam wasn't safe and neither was I. I told him I wasn't digging into anything, but the guy hung up. That's it. So I want to know who called.'

Michael was silent a moment. 'If he used a prepaid cell phone, all I'll be able to get is the closest cell tower it bounced off of. It'll take a little while. I'll call you back.'

Just like that, Michael hung up. And Kate fumed all the way back to the hotel. When she walked into their suite, Beth was at the kitchen counter, sipping coffee.

'Michael called five minutes ago and woke me up. He told me about your late-night whacko and wants me with you today. No arguments.'

Kate toed off her sneakers. 'Did he find out who the mystery caller was?'

'Yep. His name is Elias Murphy. He's a retired osteopathic physician from Mobile. Apparently, he didn't like retirement, because he now works for the Florida Department of Corrections.'

'At Santa Rosa Prison,' Kate said.

'Correct. Murphy used his personal cell phone from home – so much for being secretive. Michael checked and the doctor still works there.'

Kate felt lightheaded. She sat down hard at the table. 'Did something happen to Liam?'

'Nothing that Michael found so far, but he'll delve deeper

today. In the meantime, let's take the good doctor's advice and stay away from Liam.'

Kate ran a hand through her damp hair. As much as she wanted to drive to the prison with every piece of firepower Beth owned, she knew two people couldn't storm a prison. Breaking someone out of a maximum-security facility only worked in the movies. 'We have no other choice. Let's head to the home of Robert Westin. While I take a shower, you find out where the ex-husband lives. Oh, and print out Michael's emails. He sent a police report about a recent fight between Robert and Agnes on the *Arrivederci*. We'll talk more along the way.'

Beth met Kate's eye. The two women – formerly mentor and trainee – shared complete understanding with one look. 'You got it, boss. Then tonight we'll figure out a strategy for your brother.'

Kate showered and dressed as fast as she could, then called Robert Westin. Westin answered on the first ring and, after the briefest of explanations, said she could come over any time since he worked at home. His wife, however, was at Pilates, and then would be shopping for several hours.

During the short drive across the Pensacola Bay Bridge, Kate explained her desire to cultivate Robert Westin as an ally, not an enemy. Beth promised not to aggravate the guy under penalty of death.

The town of Gulf Breeze, home to the Westins, sat on a narrow band of land with Pensacola Bay on one side and the Santa Rosa Sound on the other. Further to the south was an even narrower ribbon of land called Santa Rosa Island, which contained Gulf Islands National Seashore, Pensacola Beach, Navarre Beach and, finally, to the east, Fort Walton Beach. South of this narrow ribbon was the Gulf of Mexico. Only when one viewed an overhead map could a person understand the vulnerability of barrier islands during a hurricane. But today was crystal clear, without a cloud in the sky. And from the moment Robert Westin opened his front door, Kate knew she'd have no trouble cultivating a new friend.

'Mr Westin? I'm Kate Weller and this is Beth Kirby. We both work for Price Investigations.'

'Come in, come in. What can I get you to drink? That sun is a scorcher today.'

'Nothing, sir. We're good.'

'The name's Robert. No *sirs* allowed in this house. Let's talk in the Florida room where we'll be more comfortable.' Westin led them through a well-appointed living room, past a gourmet kitchen larger than her last apartment, and into a casual area with furniture in small groupings, tall potted palms, and a ten-person Jacuzzi.

'Wow. I would spend my entire life in this room,' Beth murmured.

'Thanks, I pretty much do. I take no credit for anything. Kim did it all with her decorator friend. The best part is that the ceiling slides back so we can stargaze on cool nights.'

Both Kate and Beth turned their focuses skyward.

'And those wall panels open to the pool area for parties.'

'That was a good idea,' said Kate, stating the obvious.

'But you didn't come to admire my wife's handiwork. Please make yourself comfortable. Didn't you mention you're friends with my daughter?' Westin perched on the arm of the sofa.

'Not exactly. Your daughter hired me to investigate her mother's death.' Kate settled in a rattan chair.

Westin's smile never wavered. 'I'm ashamed to admit I still haven't called Lainey. How's she taking the death of her mother?'

'I'm not a good judge of emotional states, but for some reason your daughter doesn't think the police will conduct a thorough investigation.'

'I'm afraid Lainey had a few run-ins with authority when she was younger. How can I help, Kate?'

'Did you happen to be the one having lunch with Mrs Westin on the afternoon she died?'

He chuckled as though she'd cracked a joke. 'I'm afraid not. It's been years since Agnes entertained me in *that* fashion on the *Arrivederci.*'

'What does that mean?'

Westin flourished a hand through the air. 'Nothing, sorry. For all I know, Agnes might have invited a committee member to lunch. But if there was plenty of wine involved, then most likely her guest was male.'

Kate nodded. 'Several glasses were found on the table, along with at least one wine bottle. They were sent to the lab as evidence.'

'Evidence of what?' He blinked in disbelief. 'I heard she had a heart attack and went face down on the table.'

'We don't know the cause of death yet.' Kate stole a glance at Beth, who was studying Westin as though under a magnifying glass.

'Oh-hh.' He dragged out the word. 'That's why my daughter hired you. And that's why you're here,' Westin added, as though details had finally clicked in his head.

'I don't follow you,' Kate said.

Westin looked her dead in the eye. 'If the police suspect foul play, Lainey would sic the dogs on me, first and foremost.'

'Actually, Lainey said you'd been a good father while she was growing up. Only after the divorce did her relationship with you suffer. She didn't point us in your direction. We're trying to cover all bases.'

Westin jumped to his feet. 'Forgive me, Kate, Beth. I have a bad habit of jumping to conclusions. Please, won't you have something to drink?'

'Iced tea, if you got it,' said Beth. She glanced at Kate to make sure she hadn't overstepped their agreement.

'I do. My wife made a pitcher this morning.' Westin disappeared into the kitchen, returning with two glasses of tea and a tumbler of something amber.

At eleven o'clock in the morning? Kate thought. But the interruption gave her time to phrase her next question. 'Actually, I did want to ask about your relationship with your ex-wife.'

Westin took a long swallow of the amber liquid before replying. 'Would you like three words or less? I hated her.'

'And if I wished for a longer explanation?' Kate sipped her tea.

'In my life, after traveling extensively over four continents, I have never met a nastier, more controlling woman than Agnes Westin.'

'Thank you for your honesty, Robert.'

'You're welcome, Kate.' His smile turned ordinary features downright handsome. 'And to save you from asking . . . I didn't kill my ex-wife, if indeed it turns out she was murdered.' He looked from one PI to the other, waiting for a reaction. When both remained silent, he continued. 'I considered it many times when we were married and, at one point, I probably was very close to fulfilling my fantasy.' Westin sipped his drink. 'But I have no reason to kill her now. I have a beautiful house, a pretty wife, and work that I enjoy. Agnes – she has only her bitterness and lust for power.'

'Not anymore she doesn't,' Kate said, annoyed by his smugness.

Westin nodded. 'You're right. But I'm only sorry for my daughter's sake. Agnes did everything in her power to turn Lainey into a duplicate of herself. Her shenanigans in that regard still turn my stomach.' He started to pace the room.

'Let's not talk ill of the dead, darling.' A beautiful young woman with Asian features swept into the room. She was fine-boned with waist-length black hair, flawless skin, and a slim, athletic figure. To describe Robert's wife as merely pretty would be like describing a giraffe as *on the tall side*. She marched straight toward them and extended her hand first to Kate and then to Beth. 'How do you do? I'm Kim Westin.'

'Nice to meet you, Mrs Westin. I'm Kate Weller and that's Beth Kirby. We've been hired by Lainey Westin to investigate her mother's death.'

A smile lifted one corner of her mouth. 'Good luck with that. If she didn't choke on a chicken bone, the list of potential murderers will be longer than a political speech.' She poured herself tea from the pitcher and sat next to her husband on the couch.

'I'm glad you came straight home instead of going to the mall.' Robert buzzed Kim's cheek with a kiss.

'I'm sick of shopping in Pensacola. I'd rather save your money for our next trip to Europe.' Kim returned the kiss. 'Now, what do you need from us?' she asked Kate.

'You said the list of suspects would be long. Sounds like you hated Robert's first wife.' She was fishing with such a statement, but the bait and tackle paid off.

Kim laughed. 'You're joking, right?'

'No, Mrs Westin, I assure you I'm not.'

After an expression Kate couldn't decipher, Kim shrugged. 'Simply put, Robert received a substantial settlement in the divorce, his fair share considering how long he put up with that witch's abuse. Keep in mind Robert helped build that business into what it is today.'

'Kim, please. They didn't come to hear this.'

'Sorry, darling,' she murmured. 'But I believe these investigators deserve the truth.' She took a drink of tea. 'Agnes went to court and pleaded limited liquid assets. Her lawyer was so convincing that the judge dispersed Robert's settlement over a period of twenty years, like *alimony*.' Kim added a negative inflection. 'Her claims of cash-poor were false, but Robert has no choice but to put up with her nonsense.'

'And in the eventuality of Agnes's death?' Beth asked, while Kate silently thanked Michael for insisting Beth tag along. That question hadn't occurred to her.

Kim tossed back her silky hair and smiled. 'If the first Mrs Westin died, the balance of Robert's settlement will be paid in full from her estate. Then we can buy a place in Europe and go there when Florida gets too hot . . . like it is now.' She looked from Kate to Beth. 'I won't pretend that I'm sorry she's dead. Agnes couldn't even be civil to me. She called me horrible names, even though I didn't meet Robert until *a year* after their divorce. It was as though she hated the idea of Robert being happy when nothing on God's green earth would make Agnes content.' Kim's grip tightened on the glass until her husband pulled it from her fingers.

'Calm down, my dear. Agnes's death might not be accidental, as we assumed.'

'Is that right?' She shrugged. 'Then we owe *someone* a debt of gratitude. Why don't I make us more tea?' Kim smiled as she strode from the room with perfect composure.

Westin sighed wearily. 'Please don't tell my daughter about Kim's reaction. Lainey doesn't need any more reason to despise us.'

'You have my word,' said Kate. 'But I'm curious as to what happened between you and Lainey.'

Westin thought for a bit. 'So am I. When I was married to Agnes, I attended every ballet recital, art show, and junior sailing regatta. I loved my daughter; I still do. But after the divorce, Agnes poisoned Lainey against me. She told me the wrong dates or times for her events, and then denied doing it. She would do anything to keep Lainey home during my scheduled weekends. Once I met Kim, Agnes's lies became more vicious. She insisted we'd been carrying on an affair for years, but I'd never once been unfaithful during our marriage.' Robert's face turned red as a tomato. 'It's no wonder Kim has little sympathy with her death.'

An icy chill ran up Kate's spine. Her intuition said Westin was telling the truth. But that didn't mean he wasn't a killer. If his wife didn't beat him to it.

'We've taken up enough of your time, Robert.' Kate rose to her feet. 'Please thank your wife for her hospitality.'

Beth jumped up too. 'And pass along our compliments on her decorating. This house is gorgeous.'

Westin walked them to the door, then neither of them spoke until they reached the car.

'Wow, if Westin is the killer,' Beth was first to break the ice. 'No one could say he didn't have good reason.'

Kate nodded. 'Kim might be right about a long list of suspects, but, in my opinion, she and Robert just tied Lainey for first place.'

Kate felt out of sorts on the drive back from the Westins' and, thankfully, Beth didn't feel like chatting either. She stared out the car window until they reached their hotel. Once inside their suite, she went to the kitchen to reheat the breakfast coffee. Kate pulled out her laptop to do some paperwork. By the time Beth returned with two steaming mugs, Kate had come to a conclusion. 'I think what bothers me is the realization our victim wasn't very nice. Even a saint might be tempted to slap that woman silly.'

Sitting down, Beth propped her chin with her fists. 'Are you saying nasty people have it coming and we shouldn't look too hard for their killers?'

'Of course not. I intend to find who did this, even if it turns out to be our client.'

'Well, don't expect a big bonus from Lainey if you throw her under the bus.' Beth blew lightly on the surface of her mug. 'What do you want to do now – swim, rent mopeds, veg out in front of the TV? You're officially the boss while I'm in Pensacola.'

Kate smiled at her friend. 'Because two people have already declared you *persona non grata*, effectively banning you from their personal space, you can pursue any of the above. But, since the boss assigned me a case and I'm on Lainey's retainer for expenses, I need to update the case file and email it to Nate.'

'Fine, but you must have something for me to do.'

'You can ask your handsome fiancé to find out everything about the crime that sent Liam to jail sixteen years ago.'

Beth's forehead furrowed. 'But weren't you two close back then? A big brother's involvement in a robbery would be hard to forget.'

'One would think,' Kate murmured. 'Rumor has it I witnessed all or part of the heist, but I don't remember anything.'

'You had amnesia? Somebody conk you on the head?'

'I don't think so. My foster mother said I suppressed the memory because it was upsetting. She liked to think of herself as a kiddie-shrink without the degree, so she gave away free *expert* advice.'

'Do you agree with her diagnosis?'

'I guess so. I can remember everything else from my childhood and troubled youth. Just not the day Liam and his cronies crashed a stolen car into an armored truck, pulled ski masks over their faces, and leveled guns at the driver.'

'Yikes! What could possibly go wrong with that genius plan?' asked Beth wryly.

Kate shrugged. 'The plan worked fine for three of the accomplices. They got clean away, with the cash, no less.'

'How much money?'

'That I don't know. I also don't know the names of Liam's cronies or the identity of the two security guards.'

'I'm afraid to ask, but what happened to them?'

'One ended up shot to death during the robbery. The

other supposedly ran off, which in itself sounds awfully suspicious.'

'It does to me too. I'll ask Michael to dig up everything he can about the case.'

'Find out the name of the investigating officer and if the case is still open. If someone died during the commission of another felony, there's no statute of limitations.'

Beth quickly fit the pieces together. 'That's why someone is getting nervous about your memory coming back.'

'But nothing has changed. I still don't remember anything more than a week after it happened.'

Beth considered this. 'True, but you weren't a private investigator until recently, with professional PI pals.' She huffed on her knuckles and rubbed her shirt. 'Some thug doesn't want to go to jail.'

Kate snorted. 'That's where part two of my plan comes in. I'm going to find a hypnotist in Pensacola. I heard hypnosis works for people trying to lose weight or quit smoking. So why not for suppressed memories?'

'Michael gave me just the thing.' Beth disappeared into the bedroom, then returned with a silver locket on a long chain. Perching on the stool across from Kate, she uttered in a low, somber tone: 'Listen to the sound of my voice and let your eyes follow the undulating pendant. You are getting *very* sleepy. Soon you will fall into a deep slumber where I will have total control over you.'

Kate snatched the necklace from Beth's fingers. 'Stop that!' she demanded, trying not to laugh. 'I'm serious about this.'

'Relax. I would only make you cluck like a chicken.'

'And I thought you wanted to help.' Kate tapped on the Price Investigations shortcut on her laptop.

'I do. That's why I'm giving you some sisterly advice. The last thing you need is some fortune-teller in a turban conning you out of your hard-earned money.'

Despite herself, Kate laughed at the mental image. 'Will she have on red lipstick and bright purple eyeshadow?'

'You know it, Katie girl. She'll be living in a VW van with "Woodstock or bust" still on the bumper.' Beth patted her back. 'Legitimate psychiatrists who use hypnosis to coax repressed memories are few and far between. And they cost a bundle. What's the chance of you finding one in Pensacola?'

'Good point, but I need to try. So run along, *Sis,* and call your future husband. I've got work to do.'

Three hours later, Kate had finished her case update, caught up with email and, best of all, located a hypnotherapist in Gulf Breeze, a thirty-minute drive away. Unfortunately, she had no one to tell the good news. Her partner had marched out the door two hours ago and not returned. Just as Kate picked up her phone, Beth strolled in, whistling an unrecognizable tune.

'I've got both good news and bad – which do you want to hear first?'

Kate sighed. 'Give me the bad first.'

Beth slouched into a chair. 'Michael found information on your brother. As you know, he was the only perp arrested and convicted in the robbery homicide, mainly because Liam refused to name his accomplices. And he found the Escambia County detective who had caught the case, but his file is mighty slim.'

'Why on earth would that be?' Kate asked.

'Liam initially pleaded "not guilty," as advised by counsel – standard in capital cases. But then he changed his plea to "guilty" right before the trial started.' Beth let a few moments pass. 'And he admitted to shooting the security guard.'

'Liam was no killer!' Kate gasped. 'He wouldn't even kill a snake that slithered into our kitchen. He picked it up with a shovel and carried it to the woods.'

'I'm just giving you the facts in the file, sketchy as they might be.'

'No wonder he got life with no chance of parole for twenty years.' Kate dropped her face into her hands.

'At least they took the death penalty off the table.'

Would an entire life behind bars in a Florida maximum security be better? It was a thought Kate couldn't voice, not even to her best friend.

'I wrote down everything Michael said for you to read later. And he promised to keep digging.'

'Thanks,' she said, her face still against her arm.

'Ready for my good news?' Beth shook her like a ragdoll.

'I'm desperate for some.' She uncovered her eyes but didn't lift her head.

'I walked to the grocery store and bought a ton of healthy stuff to eat – fresh veggies, salad, hummus, grilled chicken breast, cut-up fruit, even wholegrain tortillas to make wraps.'

'Where is this cornucopia of goodness? You walked into the suite empty-handed.'

'Stashed in the fridge down by the pool. I already staked out an umbrella table with towels. I thought we'd go for a swim after you finished researching carnivals traveling through the area.'

'Very funny. For your information I found a hypnotherapist in Gulf Breeze, the same town where Kim and Robert live. She can see me tomorrow morning at seven before leaving on a business trip.'

'Is the sideshow moving their tents to Mobile?' Beth almost choked on her laughter. 'Or maybe she's trying to stay one step ahead of the fraud squad.'

'Would you please stop? She's a licensed professional with a great website.'

'Okay, how much will this *professional* cost?'

'Seventy-five bucks, unless our session runs over forty-five minutes.'

'Well then, she ain't no shrink. They won't even say "hello" for less than three hundred.'

'Are you speaking from experience?' Kate was happy to turn the tables. 'Besides, I don't need a shrink because I'm not crazy. I just want to remember one particular day in my life.'

'Can I tag along in case she makes you bark like a dog?'

Kate produced her best evil eye. 'I prefer to take my chances.'

Beth threw up her hands. 'Enough about tomorrow. Let's put on our swimsuits and hit the pool before the best part of the day slips away.'

'That's the best idea you've had.'

While changing clothes, Kate realized what she loved about Beth – she thought *any time* was the day's best. As annoying as Beth could be, she never pouted or held grudges.

Her positive attitude went far beyond being a good person. Beth was a downright optimist. And that went a long way in smoothing out her rough edges.

Down at their table, Kate noticed towels had been draped over three chairs. 'Expecting someone?' she asked.

'Nope. He's already here.' Beth inclined her head toward the pool, where a tall man with dark hair and amazing biceps was swimming laps.

'If we weren't surrounded by witnesses, I would throttle you,' Kate hissed under her breath.

'Why would you do that?' Beth feigned innocence. 'I bought way too much food at the store. But then I remembered your old pal from Charleston was staying here. So I thought: Why not knock on his door? Turned out Eric was dying for a swim.' Beth pulled off her cover-up, ran to the pool, and jumped in the water, thus ending their conversation.

Sinking into a chair, Kate watched Beth splash around like a duck. Then her attention locked on the sleek seal swimming just beneath the surface from one end of the pool to the other. In the sunlight, droplets of water glistened on his shoulders, and for several minutes Kate was mesmerized.

My old pal from Charleston? Eric Manfredi had advanced well past friendship during their brief acquaintance. For a few blissful days, she'd made up her mind to marry the guy. And got the feeling he felt the same. Now their relationship was past history. Only Beth never got the message.

Suddenly, Eric lifted his head from the water and caught her staring at him. 'Hey, Kate. How's it goin'?' He boosted himself from the pool and wrapped a towel around his waist, letting his hair drip.

'All good,' she called, making up her mind to be nice to him. Not encouraging, but nice. For all she knew, Eric truly was here to research locations for a second restaurant. She would take him at his word, at least for now. 'Find any commercial properties you liked?' Kate asked when he took the chair opposite hers.

'I looked at several establishments up for sale, but it was easy to see why they went belly-up. They were too far from the beach to attract tourists, and the neighborhoods couldn't support high-end cuisine. Restaurants can't support them-selves with only Friday and Saturday reservations. You need people willing to pay twenty-plus per entrée on Tuesdays and Wednesdays too.'

'I sure wouldn't pay that much on a Monday night.'

Eric released a deep baritone laugh – the one she'd come to love. 'Not even with me cooking?'

Kate pretended to ponder the question. 'Only if I had something to celebrate, like winning the lottery or the Publishers Clearing House.'

For several moments, their gazes locked, until Beth barged into the conversation. 'Did I hear we have some-thing to celebrate?' she asked. 'You found a spot for Bella Trattoria II?'

'Nothing even close to appropriate, at any price. I'll keep looking, but I'll also Google job openings at local restaurants. If someone needs a *sous chef*, I can find out plenty from the head chef about the area.'

'You're looking for a *job*?' Beth asked.

'Yes, I'll make it clear that it'll be temporary – a month or two. Restaurants have high turnover. I might just get lucky.' Although Beth had asked the question, Eric aimed his answer directly at Kate.

With her cheeks aflame for no apparent reason, Kate rose from the table. 'Time for me to get wet.'

'Good idea,' said Beth. 'I'll set out the grub while you swim.'

Without looking back, Kate walked to the deep end of the pool and dove in. The cool water felt wonderful on her over-heated skin. Hopefully, it would also wash away the stupid fantasies that refused to stay buried in the past.

The next morning Kate was out the door by six o'clock with her to-go cup filled to the brim. She wouldn't take any chances on heavy traffic causing her to miss the appointment, now that the proverbial ball was rolling. Her GPS guided her to a rambling Victorian house a block from the water, on the oppo-site of Gulf Breeze from the Westins. According to a cutesy sign, she had reached the Sweet Dreams Bed and Breakfast.

A small shingle hanging beneath the sign indicated Leslie Faraday, Licensed Hypnotherapist, resided within.

'Miss Faraday?' Kate asked when a fortyish woman in a cream-colored suit answered her knock.

'And you must be Kathryn Weller. Nice to meet you. Please come to my office so we can get started. I'm glad you're a tad early.'

'Please call me Kate. Do you also run a B&B?' She followed the woman down a hallway with pink flowery wallpaper.

'Mainly my husband runs it. This white elephant—' she flourished her hand at the ten-foot ceilings – 'was his retirement dream, but I'm glad he talked me into it. It's fun meeting people from all over the world.' They entered a spacious room with an antique desk, expensive leather furniture, and framed seascapes on the walls.

'You have a great office,' Kate said. 'My friend thought you would live in a tent and wear a silk turban.'

Faraday hesitated but then smiled. 'I do have big hoop earrings if they would make you more comfortable.'

'No, I'm fine with everything as it is.'

'Good. Then let's get started. Slip off your shoes, sit on the couch, relax, but don't lie down. I'm sure your friend will ask about my qualifications. I'm a psychiatric registered nurse by degree and formerly worked in a clinical setting for twenty stressful years. When I left there, I trained as a hypnotherapist at the Florida Institute. Keep in mind hypnosis can be highly enlightening or a major disappointment for the patient. In other words, I offer no guarantees you'll find what you're looking for. But I won't make up any *probable scenario* based on any intuitive assumptions. Do you still wish to proceed?'

'I would be skeptical if you operated any other way. I'm in.'

'Very well.' Faraday wheeled her chair within four feet of the couch. 'Before you arrived, I reviewed the information you provided on the phone. You wish to unblock memories from a particular day when you were ten years old and your brother was eighteen. Since you have no other "black holes" in your childhood, you are assuming you witnessed something traumatic.'

'That's correct.'

As Kate watched, Faraday closed the heavy drapes, dimmed the lights, and turned down the AC. 'We want no chilly drafts or street noise to distract you. If you are comfortable, I'd like you to close your eyes and imagine yourself standing alone on a beach.' Faraday paused about five seconds between commands. 'Feel the warm sun on your face and hear the gentle waves as they roll toward shore. You are completely safe, now and at all times. If errant thoughts come to mind, such as what you want for lunch or you'll do tomorrow, simply send them on their way.'

Faraday's voice was soft as a mother's kiss and Kate followed the instructions as best she could.

'Instead of attempting to reach one specific day immediately, let's go back in stages, so your subconscious mind feels perfectly safe and comfortable as you voice what your inner eye is seeing.'

Inner eye? She imagined Beth's opinion of such a thing, but gently sent the thought on its way.

'Kate, you are standing in front of a beautiful golden staircase. You feel completely relaxed as you walk slowly down the stairs. With each deep breath that you inhale, you go deeper into your past. Let's pause for a moment on the step you're on, Kate, because today is your high school prom,' said Faraday. 'You are surrounded by friends and classmates. Tell me what you see and hear and feel.'

'Loud music. People talking and laughing. I feel the wood floor vibrating from dancing. I smell popcorn and burnt sugar. Caramel corn.'

'Do you eat some caramel corn?'

'No, I don't like it.'

'What do you see, Kate?'

'Dresses – pink, blue, green. Like a rainbow.'

'Sounds beautiful. What color is your dress?'

'Don't know. I only see my friends.'

'You're right there, Kate, at the prom with your friends. Just look down at your clothes.'

'Soft yellow, like a buttercup. And my sandals are white with a high platform.'

'You're doing well, Kate. Now try to remember how you felt that day. Did anything make you sad at the prom?'

After a long pause, Kate's expression turned sorrowful. 'I was dancing slow with one of my friends. It was the last dance. When the music stopped, he tried to kiss me. Not on the cheek either. I said: "Don't be ridiculous, Carl. Try that again and I'll flatten you right here on the dance floor".' Her voice became agitated, while her fingers curled into a fist. 'I could have done it, too. Carl was real skinny.'

'How did Carl react?'

'He didn't laugh. He stomped off to find his friends. He didn't drive me home like he promised.' Kate sounded on the verge of tears.

'How did you get home?'

'My girlfriend and her date. Carl and me were friends since grade school. He wouldn't talk to me after that night. I felt so bad.'

'As painful as that was to lose Carl's friendship, you survived and have thrived ever since. Sometimes when we endure a painful experience, we pave the way for a better situation for everyone.'

After a brief pause, Faraday continued. 'Now, let's breathe deeply and move down a few steps on that golden staircase to the summer when you were ten years old. Remember, Kate. You're perfectly safe. Nothing in the past can hurt you.'

After a pause, Kate nodded.

'You loved your brother. Liam and you tried to stay close despite being in different foster homes. Tell me what was going on that summer with you two.'

Kate remained silent for a while. 'Liam got into trouble with his foster mother. Again. She was having him put back into the system. So I begged my foster parents to take him for six months until he turned eighteen. They said yes.'

'Then Liam would be on his own and on the streets?'

'Yes.'

'Did you like having Liam back with you?'

She nodded vigorously. 'I was so happy. We went swimming at the beach and fishing in the bay. Like the old days, but better because Liam had his driver's license and a car.'

'Did he get along with your foster parents?'

'Yes. He tried real hard to do what they said, but his pals wouldn't quit. They kept calling to do stuff.'

'What did you do, Kate?'

'I listened when Liam was on the phone. I heard them planning somethin' on Friday night. Dad was out of town and Mom had to work the late shift. Liam was told to watch me, but he was going out instead.'

'Did you tell anyone?'

She shrugged. 'No.'

'What happened on Friday?'

'He told me to stay in my room and be a good girl. So, when he was in the shower, I snuck into the back of his pickup under a smelly old tarp.'

'Didn't he check on you before he left?'

'I dunno. I put the TV on real loud in my room.'

'Where do you think Liam was going?'

'To town. We crossed the bumpy railroad tracks.'

'Go on, Kate. Remember, nothing can hurt you.'

'I'm not scared, but I couldn't stay under the tarp one more minute. I came up for air. Liam saw me in his mirror and blew his stack. He pulled to the side of the road so fast I almost flew out. He yelled at me and made me climb out. I started crying, but he wouldn't let me get back in the truck.'

'What happened next, Kate?'

'He drove away and left me standing on the sidewalk.'

'Weren't you scared then?'

'Maybe a little. I was afraid he would tell Mom. But then he'd get in trouble too.'

'Were you wondering how to get home?'

'No. I knew he'd come back once he cooled off.'

'Did you wait in that spot?'

'No. I saw his truck stuck behind a red light. So I ran after him and hid behind a telephone pole.'

'Very smart. Could you keep up with him when the light turned green?'

Kate nodded. 'Yes. I run fast. He only went three more blocks.'

'Tell me the rest of the story,' Faraday prodded. 'Did Liam see you behind the pole and blow his stack again?'

A negative head-shake. 'He parked by the curb and walked over to his pals. They were in the street, yelling at each other.'

'What are his friends' names?'

A shrug. 'Don't know. Liam never told me.'

'Look around, Kate. What do you see?'

'Bunch of dark buildings. No lights on.'

'Are these shops or houses that people live in?'

Another shrug. 'Just dark buildings.'

'What else do you see?'

'A shiny black van and a red car. A car accident. The black van has blinkers on and the front of the red car is smashed.' Kate's agitation escalated.

'Take a deep breath and calm down. You're perfectly safe with me. Can you hear what the loud voices are saying?'

'No.'

'Why are Liam's friends in the street?'

'They're looking at something on the ground.'

'What's on the ground?'

'I don't know. It's dark.'

'If there are sidewalks, there must be streetlights. Remember, nothing from the past can hurt you. Please look at what's lying in the street.'

'It's a man in a white shirt. He's not moving.'

'What did Liam do when he walked up to his friends in the middle of the street?'

'He started yelling too.'

'Then what happened?'

'I don't know.'

'Try to remember, Kate. What happened next?'

Her agitation reached a critical threshold. 'Don't know,' she cried. 'I ran away. I want to stop.'

'Listen to the sound of my voice, Kate, as I count backwards from *five*. We're coming up the steps two at a time. *Four.* You're feeling safe and warm. *Three.* As we approach the top of the stairs we waken from our slumber. *Two.* You feel the warm sun on your face from my office window. *One.* You are fully awake in my office at Sweet Dreams Bed and Breakfast.'

When Kate awoke she stumbled off the couch into the arms of Mrs Faraday. Tears were streaming down her face.

'Everything is fine, Kate. You're in my office in Gulf Breeze and the sun is shining. Let's go to the window so you can see for yourself.'

Kate sucked air into her aching lungs. 'Liam didn't shoot that man. That man was already lying in the street when Liam got there.' She pressed her fingertips to her eyes and then staggered to where she'd left her purse. 'Here's your check, Mrs Faraday. Thanks.' She thrust the check at the woman.

'We still have more time. Don't you wish to continue?'

'No. I want to get out of here.' Kate started for the door on shaky legs.

'Wait, here's an audio copy of our session. You can download to your computer and listen at your convenience.' Faraday had to chase Kate down the hallway to give her the audio. 'Call me if you need a second appointment.'

Kate grabbed the memory stick and bolted out the front door of the bed and breakfast, startling the tourists eating breakfast on the porch. Once inside her car, she pounded the steering wheel. *Liam didn't shoot anyone.* He wasn't even there when the guard was shot. So *why did he confess?* became her new, million-dollar question.

With visiting at the prison not until Saturday, Kate headed to the only other person in the world who could shed light on that day – her foster mother, hoping all the way there that she still lived at the same address.

FIVE

Kate had wanted to leave their hotel suite as quietly as possible, but her eagle-eyed roommate curtailed her well-laid plans.

Beth cornered Kate in the kitchen. 'Where are you off to so early two mornings in a row?'

'For normal people, nine o'clock isn't remotely early. And I'm on my way to see Detective Julian Buckley. He said he'd be in his office all morning. But after your little stunt on the *Dancing Fool*, he doesn't want to see you.'

'You weren't even going to tell me?'

'I thought I'd let you sleep in and text you later.' Kate pulled out the cereal and a bowl.

With hands on hips, Beth blocked her path to the refrigerator. 'What part of "you could be in danger" do you not understand?'

Kate began eating her cereal dry. 'I have my firearm, which I'll lock in my trunk when I get to the Sheriff's Department. Nobody will jump in my car between here and there.'

'You don't know that. Now sit down and eat like a civilized person.' Beth took the milk from the fridge. 'Before you leave I want to hear about the visit to your foster mother. Last night, you only talked about the hypnotist appointment before falling dead asleep. Frankly, I don't know why I couldn't come along. *Your mom* hasn't taken out a restraining order against me.'

Kate sat and poured milk over her cereal. 'Next time you can come. Since Dolores and I have been out of touch, I didn't know how she would react. Or if I'd even find her.'

'Why haven't you kept in contact? Not even Christmas or birthday cards?' Beth poured herself a bowl of cereal.

Kate pushed the milk across the counter. 'I'm not good with cards and letters. And Dolores has taken in so many foster kids over the years she can't stay in touch with all of them.'

'So, how did the visit go? Did she remember you?'

'She not only remembered, she gave me a big hug. They still live in the same house, but since I moved out, her husband added two more bedrooms and another bath. Now they can accommodate six kids. Plus, they hired a tutor for three afternoons per week.'

'Dolores must have tons of patience.'

'She does. I took her and two of her kids to lunch. Everyone seems happy.'

'Except that *you* don't sound happy.'

Beth . . . always picking up subtle nuances. 'As much as I enjoyed the walk down memory lane, Mom wasn't much help with the night Liam got into trouble. She never knew I sneaked out and hid in Liam's truck. I got back before she came home from work—'

'You walked all the way from downtown Pensacola?' Beth interrupted.

'Hitchhiked. I tried to wait up for Liam but I fell asleep. When I woke up, Mom was making breakfast and we found out later Liam had been arrested. Dolores never knew the name of his cronies, so she wasn't much help with my missing pieces.' Kate finished eating and drank the milk from the bowl. 'But it was really nice seeing her again. Okay, that's the story. I'm off to see that detective.'

'Hang on there, missy. I'm coming too, even if you make me sit in the car.'

Kate turned on her heel. 'That's ridiculous. Why don't you stay here and swim? Just think how much scheming you and Eric can do behind my back.'

'First of all, it's raining. Secondly, the boss isn't covering my expenses just so I can work on my tan. Nate is worried about you. We all are. Someone tried to kill your boyfriend in Charleston.'

Kate stared at her. *Nate was paying for Beth's expenses?* 'I want you to listen very carefully. Eric is not my boyfriend. And nobody tried to kill him. They were trying to send *me* a message. That's why you, Michael, Nate, and Eric should stay away from me.'

'Eric is busy looking at restaurants, while I'm supposed to be on my final fling as a single woman. So that means I'm

coming too.' The volume of Beth's voice increased dramatic-
ally as she strapped on her shoulder holster, covering it with
a lightweight sweater.

'Fine, but you're staying in the parking lot. Nothing will
happen inside the sheriff's department.'

Life with a personal bodyguard was downright complicated.
Now Kate knew how the British monarchy and TV reality
stars felt. At the station, she gave her name at the desk and
waited on a folding chair for ninety minutes for Detective
Buckley to finally appear.

'Good morning, Miss Weller. I hope this won't take long.
I need to be somewhere by eleven.'

'I'll be brief. Thanks for making time.' Kate followed him
to a small conference room.

'Please have a seat. You said you had information for me.'
Buckley straightened his tie.

'I do, but I'm hoping for *quid pro quo* regarding
information.'

Buckley's brows drew together over the bridge of his nose.
'That depends on what you have.'

'For starters, Mrs Westin and her daughter didn't get along.
Mrs Westin had threatened several times to write Lainey out
of her will.'

He huffed out a breath. 'Anyone who spends five minutes
with Lainey finds out there was no love lost between those
two. Hopefully you didn't drive all the way to Milton to tell
me that.'

Kate smiled. 'No, sir, that's just my opener. I also talked
with Robert and Kim Westin. Robert and Agnes's divorce was
especially hostile. Agnes hated the new Mrs Westin, even
though Kim had nothing to do with the divorce. Plus, Robert
hated Agnes for turning Lainey against him.'

Buckley sighed. 'Truly one big made-for-television mess.
What else?'

'Mrs Westin asked the judge to spread out the divorce
settlement over twenty years, even though she could afford to
pay Robert his share. And the judge agreed.'

'Some women know how to make a man miserable long
after a split.' He glanced at his watch.

'That particular clause in the divorce settlement bothered wife-number-two more than it did Robert. He insisted he doesn't need the money and is quite content with his life. Kim, however, dreams of a villa in France. And I saved the best part for last.' Kate paused to up the drama. 'Upon Mrs Westin's death, Robert's settlement must be paid in full from her estate.' Kate waited until the cop met her gaze, then wiggled her eyebrows.

'Well, well, Miss Weller. Not bad.' Buckley leaned forward in his chair. 'What would you like to know?'

'Tell me about the handgun found on the boat.'

'It hadn't been fired recently, so definitely not the murder weapon.'

'Had Agnes been shot with a different gun?'

'The medical examiner hasn't finished the autopsy yet, but I saw no gunshot wounds, no signs of blunt-force trauma, and no indication of strangulation. So what supposition would you make?'

Kate didn't answer immediately. 'I'm betting against drug overdose or suicide. So most likely Mrs Westin ingested something that proved fatal, either accidentally or by someone else's hand. As in murder,' she added needlessly.

'Look at you . . . drawing conclusions like the big dogs.' Buckley laughed.

'Thanks, I think.' Kate felt color flood into her cheeks. 'I wonder if Mrs Westin was allergic to anything.'

'No medic-alert medallion around her neck or wrist, so it looks like you have work to do.'

'What about fingerprints on the boat?'

'Tons of them, mostly the victim's, the captain's, and members of the crew.'

'Were any of them Robert Westin's?'

'Maybe, I'll know soon enough.' Buckley glanced at his watch a second time. 'I'll throw you one more bone, Miss PI. Three wine glasses were found at the scene with three different sets of prints. One set belonged to the victim, but the other two aren't in the system. Two of the wine glasses had lipstick, one glass did not.'

'So one of the unknown sets belongs to a female,' Kate mused.

'Your time is up, Miss Weller. I gotta go.' Buckley jumped up and headed for the door.

Kate followed close to his heels. 'If I bring you DNA samples of possible suspects, could you check them against the lipstick?'

The detective turned on a dime. 'What good would that do me? You're not a cop. Without a proper chain of evidence, anything we uncover wouldn't be admissible in court.'

'True, but it could point you in the right direction and save valuable time.'

Buckley kept walking, right out of the station house. 'If ordinary citizens wish to help the police,' he said over his shoulder, 'who am I to say no? Just don't interfere with my investigation.'

'You have my word.' Kate practically skipped to her car. She found Beth filing her nails in the passenger seat with the windows rolled down.

'Good news, I take it?' Beth asked.

'Not yet, but it will be as soon as we pay the lovely Kim Westin a second visit.'

'We can't now. I'm starving and buying lunch, remember? Then I need to get back to the hotel. Something has run off-track for our wedding.'

Kate lifted an eyebrow. 'What ran off-track?'

'Something with the caterer. Michael texted while you were inside. He said I should check my email and then call him.'

'Check from your phone on the way to Gulf Breeze.'

'No, he sent photos to my work email. Let's go see Kim tomorrow. She's probably out shopping anyway.'

Kate argued with Beth the entire time they sat in the drive-thru lane and halfway back to the hotel. But soon the true reason for Beth's excuses became clear. Eric Manfredi was waiting for them in the lobby, looking like a million bucks as usual.

Beth certainly had plenty of time for scheming behind her back.

'Good afternoon, ladies,' Eric drawled, exaggerating his low-country accent. 'You both look exceptionally pretty today.'

Beth grinned like a beauty pageant contestant. 'Thanks, Eric. You look downright presentable yourself.'

'What a *surprise* seeing you so soon, Mr Manfredi,' Kate said wryly. 'What can we do for you?'

'I was wondering if you two could look at properties with me in Gulf Breeze and out by the National Seashore. I've exhausted the possibilities in Pensacola in terms of restaurants for sale, and I don't want to build from the ground up. Lunch will be my treat.'

Kate answered for both of them. 'Sorry, but we just ate lunch. Beth got hungry early. And now I've got work to do.'

'Then let me buy dinner tonight, somewhere along the ocean. *Please?*' he begged, peering from one to the other. 'I could really use another perspective. Maybe I'm being too picky with the places I've rejected.'

'I would love to join you,' said Beth. 'But I've got wedding problems. Apparently the caterer is balking at gluten-free selections on the buffet, after several guests indicated "no gluten" on their RSVP cards. Gluten free – what nonsense!'

'It's not nonsense,' said Kate. 'Plenty of Americans have developed gluten sensitivity or full-blown celiac disease.'

Beth put her arm around Kate's shoulder. 'You're absolutely right. So while I explain this to my boorish caterer, you can go with Eric and provide some objectivity. I promise we'll call on Kim Westin tomorrow, early, before she runs off somewhere.' She hurried toward the elevator.

'Beth just played me like a hand of poker.' Kate peered up at him. 'Looks like I'm your voice of reason.'

Eric tried not to laugh. 'It's my good fortune, since you're far more reasonable than Beth. She'd talk me into a houseboat for a floating Italian trattoria. Do you need to get some work done first? I can wait.'

'No. If I go upstairs something bad might happen to Beth. And I don't need Michael after me too.'

Eric held the door as they walked out into the humid afternoon. 'Why don't I drive? You haven't seen my new set of wheels.' He pointed at a shiny Expedition in the back row of the parking lot, the sight of his old car exploding into a fireball of shattered glass and twisted metal a distant memory.

Kate stared where he pointed. 'I see you went with red this time. I love the high-metallic shine. Did you have any trouble with the police or your insurance agent?'

'Some trouble with the police. They couldn't believe I had no clue who rigged the bomb. But finally they took my word for it. The insurance adjuster declared the vehicle a total loss due to an explosion of undetermined origin. I had the replacement check within a week.'

She met his eye when he opened her door. 'Aren't you worried about me in your new car? I still don't know who's targeting me.'

'Not worried a bit.' He climbed in beside her. 'I'm happy you're willing to look at real estate.'

'Not worried, my foot. I noticed that you started the engine while still twenty feet away.' Kate buckled her seatbelt. 'Where are these for-sale restaurants?'

Eric pulled onto the side street. 'Two locations are in Gulf Breeze along the Parkway, but I don't have much hope for either. One is a sandwich/ice-cream shop that's bound to be too small with limited parking. The other, according to their defunct website, won't be much bigger. After we check out those, we'll take the toll bridge over to Pensacola Beach. I was surprised how many restaurants are along the coast. I was picturing the Gulf Islands National Seashore as a pristine wilderness for backpackers and birdwatchers.'

'The barrier islands might protect the rest of Florida, but tourists love to eat, as do the local folk. I've been to the beach lots of times but, by the end of this case, I should know Gulf Breeze like the back of my hand too.' Kate smiled.

It was the first one he'd seen in a long time. Eric sat back and relaxed, heading off the mainland in no particular hurry. The longer it took them to drive by every restaurant in the area, the happier he would be. In the meantime, he kept Kate talking about events that had transpired since their break-up in Charleston. Although he often had to prod her with specific questions, eventually he heard about her first visit to her brother in sixteen years, along with details on her current PI case.

'Why are you pulling into here?' she asked, interrupting her narrative about Liam. 'This place isn't for sale, and it would have way too small a kitchen even if it was.' Her expression turned skeptical. 'Didn't you print up a list of the places for sale?'

'I did. But I wanted to see every restaurant in Gulf Breeze and Pensacola Beach. You never know when an owner will stick a for-sale sign in the window, hoping to attract a local buyer instead of a corporate conglomerate.' In order to explain why he was dragging out the afternoon, Eric pulled that rationale off the top of his head.

Kate focused out the window at the passing scenery. 'I suppose that makes sense.'

'Why are you so jumpy?' he asked. 'I thought you had nothing going on with the case until tomorrow. Don't you trust me?'

She turned to face him. 'Why wouldn't I trust you? I'm the one who's unsafe to be around.'

'Let's *please* give that a rest. I feel perfectly safe. And just because you don't love me anymore, there's no reason we can't be friends. I'll need all the friends I can get if I open a restaurant down here.'

Kate's mouth dropped open. For a moment it seemed like she would offer an argument but changed her mind. 'Looks like there's a chowder house up ahead. Maybe this will be your lucky day, Manfredi.'

It was not his lucky day. Although the waterfront location, building dimensions, and amount of parking would be perfect, the place was not for sale. And since the lot overflowed with cars, most likely the owners wouldn't be selling soon. The next few establishments heading east on Route 399 also weren't for sale. So, unless he wanted to relocate in Fort Walton, which certainly wouldn't suit his true agenda, the afternoon with his former girlfriend was drawing to a close. Eric returned to the most upscale of the restaurants they saw and turned off the ignition.

'There's no sign out front or in any window. Do you know something I don't?'

'No. But according to the reviews, they have great food and I'm starving. I promised you and Beth dinner. Your roommate is on her own.'

Kate squirmed in her seat. 'I don't know if—'

'You don't know *what?* It's just dinner, Kate. No strings attached. Besides, the owner might know of properties about to go on the market.'

'All right, fine. But I need to get back early.' She climbed from the car and made a beeline for the front door, without waiting for him. By the time he reached the hostess stand, she'd already requested the first available table. The woman was definitely in a hurry.

'Have you already picked out what you want to eat?' he whispered next to her ear.

'Very funny,' she whispered on the way to the table, then held up the menu in front of her face.

Eric, however, took his time choosing his meal. When the waiter returned a second time, he ordered the broiled grouper with fried green tomatoes. 'How come Liam was the only foster sibling you stayed in touch with?' he asked without preamble.

She shook her head. 'Liam was my brother before we ever entered the foster system. We were adopted together, then our parents were killed. Even though we were eight years apart, he always looked out for me. When I was little, Liam read me stories, built me a treehouse, and taught me to play ball.'

'How old were you when your parents died?'

'I was seven, he was fifteen. At first the county placed us together in a foster home with four other kids, all boys.' Kate suddenly grew quiet as she picked at her salad.

'What happened?'

'Nothing, because Liam knew better than to leave me alone with those boys. Unfortunately, the foster mother complained that Liam caused *dissention* in the household.' Kate tightened her grip on the water glass. 'The county placed us separately after that. Liam had turned sixteen and started getting into trouble at school, too. For a year and a half he bounced around between homes but still tried to stay in touch. Finally, my foster family took Liam in for the last few months before he turned eighteen. You know how that turned out.'

'You had it rough, Kate.'

She shrugged. 'No, not me. Liam made sure nothing bad

happened in my first home, and then Dolores and Ken took me in until I left for college in the fall, well past my eighteenth birthday. They didn't have to let me stay. I'm grateful to them.'

'I wish we'd grown up in the same neighborhood. I would've forced Irena and Alfonzo to take you in.'

Kate chuckled – a sound that was like music to his ears. 'Could you see your mother raising me? But at least I would know how to cook.'

They were both quiet then, until the silence grew uncomfortable. 'Speaking of food, what do you think of the food here?' Eric pushed away his empty plate.

'It's great, but the place isn't for sale. Are you planning to hold the owner hostage until he agrees to part with it?' She popped another fried shrimp in her mouth.

'No, but I did apply online for a job here as under-chef.'

Kate glanced around the room. 'Let me get this straight. So you're a head chef going undercover because you want to be a line cook?' She pressed her fist to her mouth.

'Why not see firsthand what I'm walking into? I like the food. The protocol for the staff is consistent and professional. If the manager hires me, I think I'll enjoy my temporary gig.'

Leaning into the aisle, Kate waved to the waiter. 'Who am I to judge? But I can't eat another bite. I'll take this home for tomorrow.'

Eric didn't want the evening to end. 'Tell me about your visit to the hypnotherapist. Beth said you remembered details about the crime that put Liam in jail.'

Her eyes narrowed. 'I *knew* you and Beth were talking behind my back!'

'Why shouldn't we? We're all friends. And we're both worried about you. Beth doesn't want you going anywhere alone.'

While they waited for the check, Kate glared at him while he stared back with equal determination.

'I guess I should be grateful,' she said at long last.

'That would be nice.'

'I'm not used to all this . . . hovering.'

'That's what friends do.'

'Fine, I'll stop fighting my babysitters.' Kate picked up her takeout box. 'While you pay the check, I'm going to the ladies' room. But I won't walk outside until you're holding my hand.'

'Great idea, but what about your hypnosis? I want to hear the details.' Eric set his credit card inside the folder. Although he personally would lump hypnosis in the same category as Santa Claus and the Easter Bunny, if Kate found it helpful, he would keep his opinion to himself.

'I'll tell you in the car. I need to get back.'

Eric watched Kate leave the room. With his dinner churning in his gut, he realized his feelings for her had not diminished one bit. On the drive back to Pensacola, she relayed the therapy session, as much as she could remember from the recording. When finished, Kate turned her huge brown eyes in his direction, waiting for a reaction.

'Are you convinced your brother didn't shoot the armored car driver?'

'I am. But I don't know why Liam said he did.'

'What's your next step – back to the hypnotist for a second session?'

'No, I'm heading to Santa Rosa Correctional on Saturday to ask him face-to-face. I will know if he's lying or telling the truth.'

'Will Beth go with you?' Eric turned into the parking lot for the Vacation Inn and Suites.

'I guess so. I haven't thought that far ahead yet.'

'If you need my help, call me. Otherwise, I'll see you around the pool.'

Kate reached for her purse and opened the car door. Then she hesitated. 'Thanks for dinner, Eric. It was nice . . . talking to you again. I'd forgotten how well we get along.'

'Compared to you and Beth?' he asked with a laugh.

'Compared to me and . . . *anybody*.' Kate jumped out, slammed the door, and ran for the entrance.

Eric waited until she was in the elevator before turning off the ignition. *That's good, because I'm not just anybody. And the sooner you realize that, the better off we'll both be.*

SIX

On Friday morning, Kate awoke to the smell of coffee and something sweet. When she stumbled out to the kitchen, she found Beth already showered, dressed, and sitting at the table.

'You're up mighty early, missy. Feeling guilty about something perhaps?' Kate poured herself a cup of coffee. 'Your machinations to get Eric and me back together aren't fooling anyone.'

'I have no idea what you're talking about. Can't a person cook breakfast for her best friend and maid of honor?'

'You might have hoodwinked poor Michael, but I know you can't cook any better than me.' She grinned over the rim of her cup.

Beth leaned very close and whispered, 'That's why *one* of us should marry a gourmet chef, or we'll all starve.'

'You're the one getting married, not me.'

Just then two waffles sprang up in the toaster. Beth laid them on a plate, ladled on strawberry preserves, and topped the heap with whipped cream. '*Voilà*,' she said, and set the plate in front of her. 'Just like House of Pancakes down the road.'

'Thanks. Aren't you having any?' Kate spooned up some whipped cream.

'Second batch coming up.' Beth pushed two waffles into the toaster. 'While these heat, care to share highlights from last night?'

'There's nothing to share. I told Eric about my case and about the hypnosis appointment. And we looked at every food establishment in Gulf Breeze and Pensacola Beach, whether for sale or not.'

'Did he buy you dinner?'

'Yes, at the place where he applied for a job. Why he wants to work here is beyond me. If he can't find an appropriate location, he should go back to Charleston to his *perfectly fine* trattoria, with his *perfectly fine* family, and live in his *perfectly fine* condo down the street.'

Beth blinked several times. 'Whoa, that sounded a tad resentful. Eric can't help it if he has a cool life.'

Kate scrubbed her face with her hands. 'You're right. Sorry. I know you're both trying to protect me, but spending time with Eric just makes it harder to get over him.'

Beth carried her matching breakfast to the table. 'It shouldn't. He understands you're not in love with him. But I think it's great that you two remained friends.'

Kate opened her mouth, but closed it quickly. Setting the record straight would be pointless. Instead she picked up her fork and started to eat. 'This is really good, Bethie. Stick with this, along with toaster pancakes and blueberry jam. Then the new bride will have breakfast covered.'

'Thanks. Since Michael and I grab lunch on the run, as long as I make dinner the husband's domain, we'll be set.' Beth winked.

'Perfect. But I wouldn't mention the dinner part until *after* the honeymoon. Maybe you two can do it together.'

'That's what you can buy as a wedding present – a cookbook.'

When Kate and Beth reached the Westin residence in Gulf Breeze, the cleaning lady said Mr Westin wasn't in, but Mrs Westin was out by the pool. Instead of leading the way, the woman hooked her thumb in the general direction.

Such must be the difference between a cleaning service employee and a full-time housekeeper. But as trained investigators they had no trouble finding the tanned young woman swimming laps. They waited patiently until Kim surfaced at their end of the pool.

'Mrs Westin? Kate Weller and Beth Kirby. Could we talk to you, please?'

Kim reached for a towel and dabbed her face. 'Sure, have a seat and I'll be right there.' While they headed for a table in the shade, Kim climbed out of the water and dried off. Not bothering with a robe or cover-up, she took the only seat at the table *not* under the umbrella.

'Aren't you afraid of skin cancer?' asked Beth.

'Not until later when my waterproof sunblock wears off.' She combed out her silky hair and reapplied lipstick. 'Robert won't be home until one o'clock. He had a doctor's appointment.'

'That's fine,' said Kate. 'We just have a few more questions about Agnes Westin. I'm sure you know her as well as your husband by now.'

Kim's nostrils flared. 'That woman is as unpredictable as a rattlesnake crossing your path. And twice as mean.'

Beth leaned toward Kim. 'I hope you don't mind an off-topic question, but I'm getting married soon . . .'

Kim tilted her head. 'Best wishes to you, Beth. Ask me whatever questions you want.'

'How do you keep your mascara and eyeliner perfect while swimming? If I wear eye makeup in the pool, I come out looking like Rocky Raccoon.'

'This is permanent makeup.' Kim pointed helpfully at her eyes. 'The eyeliner is sort of like a tattoo, but not so painful. You simply *must* get this before the wedding. They have permanent lipstick too, but I prefer the high gloss of the real thing.' She puckered her lips to make sure they appreciated the effect.

Beth jotted something down on her tablet, while Kate leaned in to admire. 'Your makeup looks wonderful. Did you have that done before your marriage to Robert?'

'Yes, Robert said he would cover any pre-wedding expenses, so I pulled out the stops – permanent makeup, all new clothes, and weekly appointments for hair and nails. Plus I hired a massage therapist and a personal trainer to come to the house.'

'The results are extraordinary.' Beth's eyes rounded, which Kate knew was not part of any act. 'Wow, what do you do now?' Beth asked.

'Do you mean during the day? Let's see . . . soon I'll fix lunch for Robert, then I have a poolside massage at three.'

'No, what kind of *work* do you do? You have the perfect hours.'

Kim giggled like a child. 'Oh, I don't work. While Robert trades stocks on the computer, he prefers me home. We usually eat lunch together and then he'll join me for an afternoon swim when he's done.'

Beth's deer-in-the-headlights expression remained fixed. 'Did you *ever* work?'

'Of course. I worked at the gym Robert joined after his divorce. That's where we met. It was my job to teach the clueless how to use the machines.' She rolled her eyes.

'I see plenty of those people at my gym.'

'You're not kidding! Once this lady asked me how to turn *on* the exercise bike, as though it had an electric motor.' Growing more animated, Kim picked up her glass of water and took a drink. 'Uggh. That's warmer than pool water.' She jumped to her feet. 'I'll get us three cold bottles from the fridge. Say, why don't you two join us for lunch? Making two extra turkey sandwiches wouldn't be any trouble.'

Kate answered first. 'No, thanks. But a bottle of water sounds great.' As soon as Kim disappeared into the house, she hissed under her breath. 'Bringing you was a bad idea. We're not here to discuss permanent makeup.'

'Bringing *weapons* was a bad idea,' Beth replied. 'That spoiled brat is getting on my nerves.'

'Then go take a walk in the flower garden.' Kate pointed a finger. 'I need you to control your jealousy and hold it together.'

Without another word, Beth did as ordered. And with both of them gone, Kate fulfilled her objective for the visit. When their hostess returned with three bottles of water, everything looked perfectly normal.

'Oh, that will really hit the spot.' Kate grabbed one and drank deeply. 'While Beth admires your flowers, tell me who you think knocked off the first Mrs Westin?'

Kim wrinkled her nose. 'It could have been Lainey. Doubtlessly, the bulk of the estate will go to her after Robert is paid off. Can't blame her really. Could you imagine Agnes as your mother?'

Kate merely clucked her tongue, since no answer came to mind.

'Between you and me . . .' Kim glanced over her shoulder to make sure they were alone. 'I'm not sorry Agnes alienated daughter against father. Given time, Lainey will probably turn into a mini-Agnes. It's better this way.'

'What's better this way?' Beth asked, returning from the garden.

Kate shot her partner a warning look. 'Kim was about to share her opinion as to who killed Mrs Westin.'

'As I was saying, if it wasn't Lainey, then I'd put my money on one of Agnes's boyfriends, accent on the *boy* part considering the age difference. That woman always accused Robert of infidelity, which wasn't true, but you know the old saying about people who point fingers.' Kim nodded her head knowingly.

'They're guilty of the accusation?' asked Kate.

'Yep.' Kim leaned in close. 'Agnes was the female counterpart of a "womanizer."'

'I sure didn't see that coming,' murmured Beth.

Kate rose and pulled Beth to her feet. 'We've taken up enough of your pool time. Thanks, Mrs Westin, for sharing your insight.'

'And thanks for the beauty tips,' added Beth. 'Soon as I get my hands on my fiancé's credit card, I'll put your ideas into motion.'

'You're welcome. Next time you come, don't forget your swimsuits.' Kim smiled with the traditional hospitality of a southern belle.

They found their own way out, but Kate held her question until inside the car. 'You're not really going to run up Michael's credit card, are you?'

'Of course not, but why did we leave so fast? You couldn't possibly have gotten what you needed.'

'I didn't want to run into Robert. Besides, I got exactly what I came for.' From her bag Kate withdrew the water glass from the patio table. Kim's lipstick was clearly evident through the heavy-duty plastic bag.

'Wow. You stole one of their glasses? I'm in awe.'

'It's just cheap glass, not crystal from a place seating. I doubt it will be missed. I'll tell the detective to run DNA. As long as Kim isn't the killer, I'll get the glass back and sneak it into their patio. I'm no thief.'

'And if Kim is the killer? You've messed up the chain of evidence. Buckley won't be pleased.'

Kate frowned. 'Oh, dear, I was hoping to rule her out.'

'My money's on Kimmy. That lazy gold-digger is in too big a hurry to get a hold of Robert's settlement.' Beth turned on the AC full blast. 'But at least she'll get a new plastic cup in prison.'

'And now that we know Agnes Westin was dating, we have a new lead for the male luncheon guest. We got plenty in a short time.'

'You're finally getting the hang of this PI stuff.'

'Thanks, Beth. Let's just hope Buckley sees it that way.'

Beth pulled out her phone. 'I'll Google the choices for lunch. Of course, I liked the idea of getting a free turkey sandwich made by the Queen Bee.'

'Remember, nothing in the world is ever free. You taught me that. And with the new Mr and Mrs Westin, I don't want to lay out all my cards on the table.'

After Kate dropped Beth off at the hotel for her afternoon swim and siesta, she headed to the yacht club. According to Lainey, the *Arrivederci*'s captain hung out in the office whenever he wasn't out on a charter. And according to Roger Holcomb's Facebook page, he was still available today for an afternoon sail, or a sunset cruise along the barrier islands of Gulf Islands National Seashore. Many people would be surprised how much information was available on Facebook, even if you weren't 'friends,' unless you used the maximum privacy settings. But then what would be the point of having a Facebook business page?

Kate lucked out for the second time that day when she found the captain polishing the brass on the *Arrivederci Sorrento*. 'Ahoy, there, Captain,' she called from the dock. 'May I come aboard? I'm Kate Weller and I work for Lainey Westin.'

A fiftyish man with thick silver hair and darkly suntanned skin peered up. 'I haven't heard anybody say that in years. Have you been watching cartoons, young lady?' Holcomb's laugh was hearty, his smile genuine.

'Not for a long time, and that's a shame,' Kate grinned back.

'Climb aboard, matey. If you work for Lainey you have as much right being here as me. Agnes won't be taking anymore moonlit sails.' His smile slipped a notch.

Slipping off her hard-soled shoes, Kate stepped barefoot onto the yacht. 'I'm the private investigator Lainey hired. Would you mind answering a few questions?'

'Ask anything you want, but I need to keep working. Lainey is paying me to maintain the *Arrivederci*, assuming it will soon be hers.' Holcomb added more polish to his cloth.

'She is a beauty. Does she have a wood hull?'

Holcomb's hand paused on the railing as he stared at her. 'Did you just step out of the nineteenth century?'

Kate felt a little foolish. 'I don't know much about sailboats. I read on the website she had been made in Europe . . .'

'Okay, I get it – medieval castles, moats, flying buttresses, the old gondolas of Venice.' The wrinkles around his mouth deepened as he laughed. 'No wood hull. This beauty was made in the Netherlands at one of their exceptional shipyards. How about a beer, matey?'

'No, thanks. And you shouldn't drink *anything* from this boat.'

'Don't worry. The police already took anything consumable away to run tests. I brought my own cooler.' Holcomb popped the top and held out a can.

'I guess one won't hurt, thanks.' Pulling up a plastic chair, Kate took a sip. 'The Netherlands? Why didn't Agnes have the ship built by her own company, the one founded by her grandfather? Then she could've overseen every detail during construction.'

'You need to be brought up to speed, now that you're in the right century.' Holcomb wiped his hands on a rag. 'The Cook family builds American luxury yachts, small ocean liners, and racing craft. You know . . . go-fast boats. Nothing with masts or sails.'

'I noticed that on their website, but I thought they might have made an exception for Mrs Westin.'

'Nah, sailing vessels require totally different engineers.' Holcomb took a gulp of beer. 'Agnes spotted the *Arrivederci Sorrento* while honeymooning with Robert in Europe. It had been commissioned by an Italian duke from Sorrento, hence the name. Since her christening in Amsterdam thirty-five years ago and her maiden voyage to the Mediterranean, she's had a colorful history. Unfortunately the duke and his wife divorced and she was then sold to a French playboy from Nice. He had quite a reputation along the Riviera. The story goes that he lost everything in Monte Carlo at the gaming tables, including the *Arrivederci*, which had been put up as collateral. His beautiful wife of six years divorced him shortly thereafter. Apparently, she didn't like living in a peasant's cottage in the French countryside. When Miss Agnes spotted the *Arrivederci* for sale in a Monte Carlo marina, she bought her on the spot. Robert tried to talk her out of it. After all, the Clark family didn't build their reputation on sailboats. But, of course, Robert didn't want to tell his blushing bride *no*, and Miss Agnes usually got her way. It didn't take long for him to fall in love with the ship too.'

'What a romantic story. Did the newlyweds *sail* back to Florida?' Kate asked.

'It is very romantic. And from what I've heard, those two were madly in love at first.' Holcomb gazed at the horizon, momentarily distracted. 'But no. Miss Agnes got seasick in rough waters. Since crossing the Atlantic guarantees bad weather at some point, the Westins hired a captain and crew to sail her back while the newlyweds flew home as planned.'

'During the divorce, Mrs Westin managed to keep the *Arrivederci*.' Kate added her own assumption.

'Yep, no surprise there.' The captain opened a second beer. 'Like I said, she's used to getting her way.'

'Robert probably missed not being able to take her out for a sail.' Kate watched his face for a reaction. His expression was a dead giveaway.

'He sure would have been sad without being able to sail.' The captain winked.

'Don't leave me in suspense. Tell me what you mean.'

'I guess it can't do any harm now that she's gone.' He took another swig. 'As much as I liked Miss Agnes, I felt sorry for Robert. He was a nice, all-around guy. So every now and then I took him out for a sail. I also taught him how to captain, so sometimes he took Miss Kim out, but always with a crew. The *Arrivederci* wasn't a boat you could single-hand, not even as an experienced captain.'

'Didn't Agnes find out?'

'Nope. It was only when I knew she would be out of town. She still loved to vacation in Europe. Once when she went to Paris for a month, I let Robert and the missus sail down to the Bahamas for five days. I could have lost my job over that one.' Holcomb wiped his forehead with a handkerchief.

'That must have been when he hid the gun in the galley,' Kate mused.

'I don't know anything about a hidden gun, but Robert was definitely afraid of pirates in the Caribbean. If someone found a gun, that's probably when he brought it aboard. The crew probably carried their own weapons if they were heading to the Bahamas.' Holcomb set the beer into a holder. 'Is there anything else, Katey-Matey? I need to finish up here.'

She smiled at the moniker. 'One more thing, and please understand I ask this solely for professional reasons. I'm not out to besmirch anyone's reputation.'

He scratched his head. 'That's good to hear. I liked Miss Agnes. She didn't have many friends, but she was always kind . . . and generous to me.'

Kate leaned closer. 'Did Miss Agnes have any . . . boyfriends, lovers, or whatever women her age call them?'

Holcomb tilted back his head and laughed. 'Of course she did. She loved men, and why shouldn't she have male *friends*? She was single and had a lot to offer.'

'Was she dating anyone special lately?' Kate chose her words carefully.

'Didn't Miss Lainey tell you?' Before Kate had a chance to answer, the captain continued. 'No, of course she didn't. Miss Lainey wanted to believe her mother sat around knitting socks for future grandchildren.' He picked up his bottle of polish and rag and headed for the bow of the ship.

'His name, Captain?' Kate called.

'Oh, yeah. His name is Mark Harris. I don't know where he lives.'

She waited for more information, but when the captain got

lost in polishing brass, Kate walked off the *Arrivederci* and drove back to her hotel. *Mark Harris.* The perfect name for an under-the-radar murderer.

After yesterday, Eric didn't know if his taking Kate to the prison was a good idea or not. But now that Beth had bowed out and insisted he take her place, he had little choice. The last thing he wanted was to make things worse with Kate. So Eric sucked in a breath and knocked on her door promptly at nine o'clock.

'Good morning,' he said when she opened the door.

'Hi, Eric. I'm ready to go. Just let me grab my purse.'

'At least the rain stopped. Looks like we'll have a nice day for our trip.' Eric usually resorted to benign comments about the weather when at a loss for the right thing to say.

'It won't be much of a trip. Milton is only an hour away.'

'Just the same, should we take my car?'

'No, we'll take mine. Just in case.'

Just in case my vehicle explodes into bits and pieces? Eric decided not to ask for clarification. 'Look, Kate, I'm sorry Beth blindsided you into helping me look at properties.'

'No, I'm the one who should apologize,' she said once they reached her car. 'My friends are only trying to help. From now on I plan to act like an adult. Actually, I'm glad Michael is coming to spend the weekend with Beth. As long as you're not mad she maneuvered you into babysitting, I appreciate your company.'

'And in return, I'll try not to make you uncomfortable.'

'Look, Eric, that's not the reason I've been avoiding you.'

'Then what is?'

'Because I don't want you to end up dead!' Kate's words echoed around the small car. 'Besides, I thought you were starting your new job.'

'I don't start until Monday. So in the meantime I can take an old friend to visit her brother!' His words resonated as loud as hers.

'Fine!' she snapped.

'Fine!' he repeated. Then they both burst out laughing.

Along the way to Santa Rosa Correctional, she described

what they would find and explained the difference between maximum security and medium. Eric sat back and listened, but also watched the rearview mirror for suspicious cars. Since he'd been raised in a tight family, it was hard to fathom not seeing your brother in sixteen years, but he kept his opinion to himself.

'Will they let me visit Liam with you?' he asked once they turned into the prison parking lot. 'I'd love to meet the guy.'

'No, I'm sorry. You have to be already on the approved visitor list. Anyone not immediate family gets vetted carefully. I can't bring Liam anything from home either. I can only buy food at their commissary at their prices.'

'American capitalism at work,' he said.

'That's one way to look at it.'

'What does your brother look like? I can't picture him.'

'Believe it or not, he kinda looks like me. Funny how that sometimes happens with adopted siblings.' Kate turned off the car and stared at the plain gray building. 'If you want to drive around Milton for a while, be back in two hours.'

'Nope. I'll wait right here.' Eric pulled a dog-eared paperback from his back pocket.

Kate opened the door and climbed out. Then she stuck her head through the driver's window. 'I'm glad you came with me. You're not half as annoying as Beth.' Her lips drew into a smile.

'Good to hear. Now get going. Time's a-wasting.'

Right now, Eric was happy with even an off-handed compliment like that, just as long as she stopped avoiding him. That made life a lot easier all the way around.

Kate purchased food at the commissary, signed in at the window and, at the appropriate time, she and the other women, children, and a few older men were herded into the fenced courtyard. Liam was sitting at the exact same picnic table as before. She supposed that's what inmates did – tried to establish familiarity both for themselves and their families.

'Hi, Liam.' She sat down on the opposite bench.

Liam glanced around uncomfortably. 'I don't know why you're here,' he hissed. 'I tried to get a message to you not to come. You should never come again.'

'And a good day to you too,' she said sarcastically.

'There's no point, Kate.'

'Well, I did bring you goodies.' She set the bag on the table. 'Now can I stay for ten minutes?'

Liam ignored the sack of food. 'I told you it's not safe. I wish it were different, but it's not. So please . . . go before someone sees you and reports back.'

'Reports to whom?' she demanded.

'I don't know who pulls the strings in here,' he whispered with equal vehemence.

Kate leaned as close as she could. 'I'll go as soon as you tell me the truth. Who shot that guard? Was it you?'

'What difference does it make? I was part of the plot to rob that armored car. Look it up, sister. All conspirators share the guilt if somebody ends up dead.'

'It makes a difference to me.' Kate reached for his hand, but he yanked it back.

Liam straightened his spine and looked her in the eye. 'Since you insist, I shot him. Sorry, but your only living relative is nothing but a cold-blooded killer.'

'I don't believe you.' Kate felt hot tears rush to her eyes.

'I don't care what you believe. I confessed. It's a done deal and I'll pay my dues until the parole board deems me fit to re-enter society.' Liam's features hardened into the face of a stranger. 'Now get on with your life and forget about me. Stop meddling in the past. It's not healthy for either of us.' Abruptly, Liam jumped up. 'Guard,' he called, 'we're done here. I'm heading your way.'

Kate stood on shaky legs. 'I know you didn't kill him. You weren't even there when that guy died.'

Her brother wheeled back around as all color drained from his face. '*You're* the one who wasn't there! I kicked you out of the car ten blocks back.'

'I was there. You got stopped behind every red light in Pensacola.'

Suddenly the guard tapped Liam's shoulder. 'You done or not, Weller?'

'Sorry, Odell, I changed my mind. Give me ten more minutes with my sister.'

Kate waited until Odell sauntered back to his post before continuing. 'I ran after your truck and hid behind telephone poles so you wouldn't see me.'

Liam slumped back down on the bench. 'You never could mind your own business. Always spying, always eavesdropping. I guess that prepared you for your line of work now,' he sneered.

'Yeah, it did. I saw that guard already on the ground when you joined your friends. You didn't shoot anybody.'

Liam's haughty attitude melted before her eyes. 'Please go home, Katie. I can't protect you in here.' This time he reached out a hand.

But she ignored the gesture. 'I don't want or need your protection. What I want is the truth. Call it my relentless nosiness. Which one of your friends pulled the trigger?'

He shook his head sadly. 'That's where you're wrong – you have no idea who you're up against. As for the guard . . . I have no idea who shot him. When I got there, everybody was talking at the same time. I asked what happened, but they kept yelling at me for being late. The job was a done-deal. One of them held up the bag of money. Then someone hit me hard from behind and knocked me out cold. When I came to, the police were everywhere and the gun was in my hand. Paramedics were loading a body bag into the back of an ambulance.'

'And your pals were gone, along with the money,' Kate added.

'Yeah, they were gone all right. I guess they couldn't carry me and a half-million dollars in cash.'

'*That's it?* Split four ways – five hundred k wouldn't have amounted to much.' She imbued her words with plenty of scorn.

'Maybe that's why they wanted me out of the picture.' Liam shrugged. 'The take should have been much more. Somebody got bad information, but that doesn't matter now.'

Kate glared at him. 'It doesn't matter that only you went to jail?'

He gazed up with his exasperatingly cool eyes. 'Luck of the draw. Like I said, it makes no difference who pulled the trigger.'

'What happened to the second guard?'

Another shrug. 'Rumor has it he ran off when bullets started to fly.'

'Which one of your *friends* knocked you out and stuck the gun in your hand?'

'If I had to guess, I would pick our little ringleader. That guy always did have a screw loose.'

Liam chuckled with such nonchalance that Kate lunged across the table and grabbed him by the shoulders. She shook him so fiercely that the guard started moving in their direction.

'Settle down!' Liam thundered. 'Or they'll throw you out of here.'

Kate smiled sweetly at Odell and sat down. 'If you really want me to go away and not come back, you'd better start making sense. Or I'll keep coming back and kicking up a fuss.'

'That would be reckless.'

'My co-worker found out you changed your plea at the last minute and confessed. Why?'

'If I changed my plea the DA said he would take the death penalty off the table. Think about it. The news media was screaming for justice and I was the only one caught. Anyway, I'll be eligible for parole in a few years.'

'But your fellow conspirators had all this time to live their lives, besides one hundred sixty-seven thousand each to spend.'

An angry look flashed in Liam's eyes. For a moment Kate thought she would be shaken like a ragdoll. 'You think I don't know that? They set me up to take the fall. If any of them land in here, they won't make it to their first parole hearing.'

'Well, well,' she murmured. 'Liam Weller is alive and well, after all. Not that I condone an eye for an eye, but I thought someone had taken possession of your body.'

Liam glanced at the clock on the wall. 'Time is almost up, dear sister. You'd better go.'

'Why don't you request a meeting with the Escambia County DA? If you identify your co-conspirators, he might move up your first parole hearing.'

Utter sadness filled his face. 'You're still the same, sweet, country girl, aren't you?'

'This isn't about me,' she snapped.

'Oh, but it is. It's *always* been about you, Katie-girl. According to that attorney I fired, if I didn't confess, an eyewitness was ready to step forward and testify I shot the guard. Then I got a message that my sister would be in for a world of hurt if I snitched on my pals. They planned to keep tabs on you for the rest of your life.' Liam leaned across the table until he was nose to nose. 'And since you're here, pestering me again, I know they've done exactly that. So I said nothing to the DA back then and I've got nothing to say now. Somebody's watching you out there, and somebody's watching me in here. Drop this or we'll both end up dead.' Liam sat back. 'If we play our cards right, I'll see you in a few years.'

'There must be something—'

'No!' he shouted. 'Now get out of here and don't come back! I have nothing more to say.' Liam pushed to his feet and, for the second time, strolled out of her life without a backward glance.

SEVEN

It took Kate the distance between the prison's visitation park and her car before the full impact of Liam's revelation sunk in. When it did, she took one look at Eric and burst into tears.

'What happened inside?' He placed a hand on her shoulder.

Sobbing, Kate leaned close enough so Eric could put his arms around her.

'Was Liam mean and nasty? Did he hurt your feelings?'

She shook her head.

'Did you wait all this time, but he didn't show up?'

Another negative head-bob.

'Talk to me, Kate. We're friends, remember?' Eric tightened his grip on her shoulder.

Kate pulled away and leaned against the headrest. 'All these years Liam spent locked up in jail—' her words broke into a shaky staccato – 'were because he was protecting *me*. It was exactly like I saw under hypnosis. Liam didn't shoot that guard. The guy was dead before my brother arrived. Liam took the blame, along with a maximum sentence, because his cronies threatened to hurt me. That's why he never ratted out the men who set him up.' Tears streamed down her face unchecked.

'And that's who's been watching you.' Eric's hands balled into fists as he scanned an almost empty parking lot.

Kate tried to rein in her emotions. 'Someone's been watching Liam too. When he requested a new lawyer, that's when they blew up your car. It was a warning not to start digging up the past.'

'What are we . . .' Eric hesitated. 'Sorry. What are you going to do?'

She started the ignition. 'Give me an hour to think. By the time we get back I'll give you my answer.'

Eric did exactly what Kate asked. For the next sixty minutes, he fiddled between stations or stared out the window at the rural Florida Panhandle. The moment they turned into the Vacation Inn and Suites parking lot, he switched off the radio. 'Well, what's the plan?'

Kate focused on a family unloading the car after a day at the beach. 'If I hadn't moved back home, you wouldn't be here looking at restaurant locations.'

'You sound mighty sure of yourself, Weller. Ever consider I might prefer the Gulf of Mexico over the Atlantic Ocean?'

'Baloney, you're not a beachy kind of guy. Tell me the truth – is there anything I can say to make you go back to Charleston?' She still couldn't meet his eye.

Eric rubbed his jaw with the back of his hand. 'Can't think of a single thing. Friends stay loyal through thick and thin, remember?'

'That's what I thought.' She swiveled around to face him and pointed at a red, turbo-charged Charger. 'See that sports car over there?'

'Yep, that is one sweet ride.'

'It belongs to Michael Preston – Beth's partner and fiancé. Michael is here to spend the weekend. When he returns to Savannah, I want Beth going with him.'

'Aren't they getting married soon?'

'In two weeks, unless Beth postpones it *again*. And I don't want her doing that. If I'm still alive and kicking, I'm her maid of honor. If Beth got hurt while babysitting me, I couldn't live with myself.'

'And this is where I come in?' Eric asked, lifting an eyebrow.

'Yes, but only because you're too stubborn or too stupid to stay away from me after someone blew up your car!' Kate crossed her arms.

'It was just a car, Kate. Look around. Cars are everywhere, unlike beautiful women who really know how to sweet-talk a man.'

It took her a moment to realize he was mocking her. 'Look, Manfredi. I don't want anything bad happening to you either. But if I send Michael and Beth home, you're all I've got. Nate's wife just had a baby, so I can't ask my boss for help.'

'Ahhh, you're at the bottom of the barrel.' Eric released his breath with a whoosh. 'And that's your best offer?'

She cringed at her poor choice of words. 'You're *nobody's* bottom of the barrel, but I know that beneath that cool sophistication is a man who can handle himself in dangerous situations. So let me rephrase: Eric, will you help me track down a killer who's gotten away with his crime for sixteen years? Keep in mind he'll do anything to stay out of jail.'

'I thought you'd never ask. I accept.' Without warning, Eric took hold of her chin. 'You're right – I can take care of myself. And nothing will happen to you, not on my watch. I'll see that you make it to Beth's wedding on time and in one piece.' Releasing her chin, he pulled out his cell phone. 'Let me call my new boss and back out of the *sous chef* position.'

Kate pulled the phone from his hand. 'No. That's where we've gone wrong. I've been too obvious – stomping up to Santa Rosa Prison, demanding my brother tell me who pulled the trigger, without a thought as to who might be listening. Today, Liam put on a good show when he sent me away. But if I go everywhere with a six-foot-four-inch bodyguard, no one will believe Liam's ruse.'

Eric shook his head. 'But if I'm not with you, what help can I be?'

'Tomorrow is Sunday. You and I will go to the beach like other friends on vacation. If anyone is watching me, they'll see nothing they don't like. Then, on Monday, you report to the restaurant as planned. Then after your shift, I'll pick you up. I promise not to do anything suspicious until we're together.'

'No, Kate. If Beth and Michael go back to—'

She didn't allow him to finish. 'Any investigating I do will be on my case for Nate. Remember? I still work for a living, so you might as well too. If that's really why you came down to Pensacola . . .'

'Yeah, it's why. You're *not* that irresistible, Weller.'

'Good to hear. Now let's break the news to Beth and Michael.' Kate opened the car door, but Eric grabbed her wrist.

'No, why not wait until Sunday night to tell them? Otherwise, Beth will pester you all weekend.'

'Wow, a smart man who can cook. What *a catch* you are, Manfredi.' She imbued each word with sarcasm.

Eric stretched to his full height next to the car. 'Don't mess with me. I'm way bigger than you.' He headed across the parking lot.

Kate ran to catch up. 'What are your plans for tonight? Why not stop in and meet Michael? You already know Beth. You two have been conspiring behind my back.'

He stopped in his tracks, his face unreadable. 'Who's the smart one now?'

She pulled open the door. 'I'm sure your accomplice would like you to meet him.'

'Lead on. Why don't we all have dinner tonight? And not down by the pool. I'd like to treat Beth and Michael to celebrate their engagement.'

'Fine by me, but let's see what they think.' Kate pushed the button for the elevator, feeling oddly disconcerted, as though she'd just been outwitted.

Once they entered her suite, Beth practically bowled her over. 'Kate! I'm so glad you and Eric are back from Milton. Michael tracked down Mrs Westin's boyfriend on social media. He is . . . or rather he *was* an avid poster of their romantic liaisons on Facebook and Twitter.'

'Hi, I'm Michael, Beth's fiancé and a fellow co-worker at Price Investigations.'

'Eric Manfredi, Kate's landlord from Charleston and trusted confidant, much to Beth's dismay. A pleasure to meet you.' The two men shook hands.

Beth stepped in front of Kate. 'Only initially dismayed. I judged you based only on size. Big people intimidate me.' She stood on tiptoes. 'But I was charmed the moment I tasted your cooking. Michael had better hurry up and walk me down that aisle.'

'You're the one holding up the three-ring circus, missy.' Michael slipped an arm around her waist. 'Don't feel bad, Eric. Beth totally despised me for the first few weeks.'

'And in your case, height had nothing to do with it.' Beth batted her long eyelashes up at Michael.

Feeling neglected, Kate stepped forward. 'Eric invited us

out to dinner, but I'm sure you lovebirds would prefer to be alone.'

'Not in the least,' said Beth. 'We'll soon be stuck with each other for eternity. Thanks, Eric. We cordially accept.'

Kate rolled her eyes. 'Tell me what you found out about Mrs Westin's lover.'

'Come look at these photos Mark Harris posted on Instagram the day Mrs Westin died. It shows the two of them on the *Arrivederci Sorrento*.'

'No thanks. I prefer not to see anything sleazy.'

'Sit,' Michael ordered. 'There's nothing X-rated.'

Kate sat and, with Eric peering over her shoulder, she gazed at two smiling people at a bistro table with champagne glasses in hand. A picnic hamper was open at their feet.

'From the angle, it was probably a selfie taken by Harris.' Michael tapped a few keys and the photos rotated like a slide-show. 'All the shots are equally benign: just two people having lunch and then sunbathing on deck. Notice there is no staff present in any of the pictures.'

Kate waited to comment until she studied the final shot of Harris climbing the main mast, obviously taken by Mrs Westin. 'The boat appears to be docked so Captain Holcomb wasn't necessary. And you don't need a waiter to serve sandwiches and fruit salad.'

'True,' Michael agreed. 'But that means there were no witnesses during their final rendezvous.'

'Except for dozens of people in the marina if the boat was docked.' Beth passed around a bowl of pretzels. 'Who's to say the *Dancing Fool* wasn't having its own dockside party?'

'That's what I'll find out when I talk to Mark Harris, among other things.'

Beth rubbed her hands together. 'I can't wait. We'll uncover the true motivation behind this May–December relationship.'

Kate exchanged glances with Eric. 'We'll have to discuss that later, Beth.'

'Doesn't anyone want to see the video of Mark and Agnes?' asked Michael.

'Not me. I'm going to hit the pool before dinner.' Beth marched into the bedroom and closed the door.

'I'll pass too. I need to Google a special place for the engaged couple to have dinner.' Eric dug his hands into his pockets.

'I'll view the video in private. Send it to my laptop,' said Kate.

'Will you please relax?' Michael asked, sounding exasperated. 'It's just two people snorkeling around the marina. There's absolutely nothing vulgar about it and they seem genuinely fond of each other. Although it could've been dangerous if a speedboat didn't notice their snorkels.'

'I get that, but I need to talk to Beth in private,' Kate said softy. 'I want her to go home with you on Monday. Eric will fill in as my bodyguard and investigative assistant. You two can concentrate on your wedding and the case Nate assigned you.'

'Sounds good to me, and we do have a case to work in Savannah. But Beth isn't going to like it.'

'I know. That's why she and I need some girl-time, in case it turns into fisticuffs.'

'Could I stand by with my video camera?' asked Michael, to Eric's great amusement. 'It would really break the ice at my bachelor party.'

'Absolutely not!' Kate snapped

'I'll leave you to thrash out the details and call later.' Eric sauntered toward the door. 'Michael, you're welcome to spend the night on my couch instead of theirs. Then you won't have to fight two women for the bathroom. I'm in 308.'

'Sounds good, thanks.' Michael waved over the computer. 'I'll finish my background check on Harris and stop over later.'

With Eric gone and Michael's nose buried in his laptop, Kate slipped into the shared bedroom.

'Are you coming down to the pool?' Beth asked. She was already in her swimsuit and was busy applying suntan lotion. 'Isn't Eric sweet? I can't believe he wants to take Michael and me out for our engagement. Do you think he'll pick someplace fancy?'

Kate sucked in a deep breath. 'Yes, I would love a dip in the pool. Yes, Eric is very sweet. And yes, I'm sure it'll be the fanciest place in a three-county area.'

Beth stopped in mid-swipe, her fingers full of lotion. 'What's going on? You usually ignore my run-on questions.'

'You and I have something important to discuss.'

'Don't even think of backing out of the wedding now. No one else can fit into that hideous bridesmaid dress.'

Kate swallowed down a laugh. 'No, and the ridiculous dress has nothing to do with it. I can't wait for your wedding.'

Beth wiped her palms on her knees and plopped down on the bed. 'This sounds serious.'

Kate sat next to her. 'Tonight we'll celebrate and have a good time. Tomorrow Eric and I will spend the day at the beach. You and Michael are welcome to join us if you like.'

'O-kaay, that sounds good. I love swimming in the Gulf. Now get to the point.' Beth's eyes narrowed.

'I can't be so obvious when I'm poking my nose into Liam's misguided past. So you're going home with Michael on Monday. I already spoke with Nate. He agrees with my decision.'

Beth arched her back like a startled cat. 'I'm not going anywhere. With Michael here, we can wrap up the Westin case and devote our full time and attention to Liam. Don't you understand the danger you're in? Someone who killed before will kill again to prevent the truth from coming out.'

'It's you who doesn't understand. Michael is here because you asked him to come and he adores you. But I refuse to endanger your life anymore. Eric can help me track down whoever is targeting me.'

'Why is it okay for Eric to risk his life but not okay for me?' Beth's face knotted with confusion.

'Because he's single, same as me. No one is counting on him to walk down the aisle in the immediate future.'

'Sounds like you're just using the man. I think that stinks. Besides, I'm a heck of a lot more qualified to protect you.'

Kate shot back in anger. 'I care very much about Eric, even if we have no future. I tried sending him away, but he refuses to leave. Please, Beth. Why must you always have your way?'

Her best friend's face grew pale. 'I guess I don't. Just

promise you'll call if you need me. Savannah is only . . . nine hours away.' Beth slid off the bed.

'Don't be angry with me.'

Beth turned to face her. 'I'm not mad. I get it. I just wish there was more I could do. Leaving right now . . . feels so final.'

But Kate couldn't think of a single thing to say.

Since he had no calendar, Sunday was the only thing breaking Liam Weller's days into measurable weeks – no work, extra yard time if he had no visitors and better food in the mess hall. Liam shouldn't have any more visitors since he ordered his little sister to stay away. Liam's usual routine was to eat breakfast, attend the non-denominational church service, then work out in the yard. On rainy days he would read in his cell, away from the loud-mouthed bullies who picked the TV shows in the common room. The library had a decent selection of dog-eared and censored fiction and non-fiction self-help books. A man could learn anything, from hooking up electronics, raising vegetables in pots on the patio, or how to make lasagna with only five ingredients. After years of eating inmate-prepared meals, Liam intended to learn how to cook before he was released. The library also contained a law section, which Liam would steer clear of since Kate had a target on her back.

Katie-girl. Why would she want to help a loser like him? A man who'd caused nothing but grief since the day their parents died. Even if he never learned to grow vegetables or hook up a computer, he hoped to live long enough to make this nightmare up to her.

After the chaplain finished sharing practical examples of how to turn the other cheek – a popular topic for incarcerated felons – Liam headed toward the library.

'Hey, Weller, where ya going?' The voice of Darius Gage, the nastiest guard in the cellblock, stopped him in his tracks.

Liam turned. 'Library. Fixing to get me a book written during the current millennium.'

'Forget 'bout that. You got yourself a visitor, inside, since it's raining cats and dogs outside.'

The tiny hairs rose on Liam's neck. *No way would Kate come back this soon, not after how he treated her.* 'Who is it?'

Gage sighed like life was way too exhausting before he checked his clipboard. 'Signed the sheet as John Henry Holliday. Says he's your cousin from Atlanta. Let's go. I've got better things to do than track down your sorry butt.'

'I don't remember no cousin and there's no John Henry Holliday on my visitor list.' Liam fought to make sense of something niggling in the back of his brain.

'Look, Weller. Since you don't get many visitors, I approved the request this morning. Maybe some long-lost relative croaked and left you a fortune. You can spend it at the prison commissary.' Gage cackled like a hyena.

Suddenly, Liam's fog cleared. John Henry Holliday was the famed gunslinger known as Doc, sidekick to Wyatt Earp, who practiced dentistry in Atlanta. The ringleader of their merry band of thieves had idolized the on-screen version played by Val Kilmer in *Tombstone*. The guy must have watched that movie a dozen times and could mimic Kilmer's accent perfectly.

'Well?' demanded Gage impatiently. 'You wanna see him or not?'

'Sure, I remember that cousin now. On my mother's side. Thanks.'

Grunting, Gage led him to the indoor visitation space, a near duplicate of the outdoor area, minus the fresh air. When Liam sought a familiar face among the visitors sitting alone, he almost didn't recognize their former fearless leader. The brash, blustery punk who loved fast cars, redheads, and Mexican food looked much older than he was. His once fleshy frame had deteriorated into angular bones covered by jaundiced skin and stringy, thinning hair. The man's life on the outside certainly hadn't included health clubs, good hygiene, or nutritious meals.

'Charley Crump . . . as I live and breathe,' murmured Liam as he sat down on the opposite bench. 'John Henry Holliday from Atlanta, Georgia – what a clever touch.'

'I thought you would appreciate that.' When Crump smiled, he revealed an appalling lack of dental work, which would have dishonored his chosen namesake. 'Look at you, Weller, all bulked up. Must be doin' some serious weightlifting.'

'Weaklings don't live long in here.' Liam folded his hands on the table. 'To what do I owe this rare pleasure after sixteen years?'

Crump's grin faded. 'Thought I should pay you a little social call.' He glanced nervously around the room at families and inmates, all minding their own business. 'Rumor has it your airheaded little sister has been comin' round.'

Liam's hackles rose. 'That little *airhead* finished college with honors. If my memory serves, you never got past the tenth grade.'

'If she's so smart, she'd know it ain't safe sticking her nose into other people's business.' Crump's sneer gave him a rat-like appearance.

Liam grabbed his shirt, tearing the worn fabric without effort. 'You the creep bothering my sister?'

Crump tried to pull away but only widened the tear. 'Hey, you ripped my shirt. You owe me ten bucks. Let go, or I'll yell for the guard.'

Liam released his hold. 'Stay away from Katie. I have people on the outside who will happily tear your face to match your shirt.' It was a lie, but he didn't have many motivational options.

'You got this all wrong. I ain't the one threatening Katie, and I sure didn't blow up anybody's car.' Crump dropped his voice to a whisper.

Liam's blood turned to ice water in his veins. 'You knew about the car blowing up?'

'Heard through the grapevine. I guess it belonged to her boyfriend. Exploded right in front of them in a public parking lot. But I had nothing to do with it.'

Liam's fingers itched to wrap around Crump's throat. But solitary confinement wasn't a place he yearned to experience. 'Then who? Jimmy Russell?'

'Man, you're really out of touch in here. Jimmy Russell is dead, some kind of freak hunting accident. Who's stupid enough to clean their rifle in a deer stand and blow their own head off?' Crump shook his head, as though disappointed with Russell's final act on earth.

Liam had no answer to that. 'Doug Young?' he asked.

'*Doug Young*?' Crump's expression changed to confusion. 'Haven't heard that name in years. That coward was too scared to even show up that day. No way could that guy rig a car bomb. He'd blow himself up instead.'

Liam stretched his large callused hands across the table. 'Tell me who did or I'll snap your neck before that guard gets halfway here. Might as well make a life sentence worth my while.'

Crump scooted his chair back. 'Would you take it easy? I don't know. Who did you tell about *me*?'

'Nobody. If I were gonna spill my guts, I would've done so long ago. Then I wouldn't be so lonely in here.'

'That's what I thought, but somebody's been parked outside my apartment a couple times a week. Maybe some friend of your sister's? That boyfriend of hers is probably pissed off about his car.'

'I just told you. I didn't drop your name to Katie or anyone else. And I never met her boyfriend.' Liam was rapidly losing patience.

'This ain't good.' Crump glanced around the room, growing more agitated by the minute.

'Break me out of here and I'll help you figure it out.'

'I'm serious, man.' Charley tried to snake his fingers through his hair but caught a nasty tangle instead.

'At least you've had sixteen years of freedom to spend your one hundred k. More, since I never got my share.'

Crump laughed. 'That's what you think? All I got for the biggest mistake of my life was twenty k, along with a major headache. I spent most of it on my mother's nursing home. I couldn't stand that dump the county stuck her in.'

'Why only twenty? Weren't you the one divvying up the take? It should have been a lot more than that.'

Crump's unhealthy complexion blanched to paper white. 'Look, I can't sit here rehashing the past all day. Trust me – I ain't got no secret bank account in the Caymans. Just tell Katie to mind her own business. And if I were you, I'd watch my back. Prisons like this probably have as many weapons as your neighborhood dive bar.' Charley sprang from his seat so fast his chair fell over backwards.

Liam watched the shell of a man disappear through the reinforced steel door, unsure if their former leader had just issued a warning . . . or a threat.

EIGHT

On Saturday night at the engagement dinner, Beth had been atypically quiet, while Michael and Eric happily made up any conversational deficit. The two men had hit it off immediately, with Michael promising Eric a personal invite to the nuptials, and Eric promising to keep Michael up to date on developments in Pensacola. Kate had no doubts both would take place.

Sunday, Beth and Michael accompanied her and Eric to the beach on Santa Rosa Island. Even though Michael had wanted to go to the zoo, Beth refused to give in two days in a row. Instead she perched on a stool, watching anything that moved in three directions. Liam's enemies would have to stage their hit by sea for any success. Michael pretended to be reading a *People Magazine* until Kate announced she was heading to the waves. Then, suddenly, everyone wanted to cool off in the surf.

Once they returned to the hotel, Eric volunteered to cook his speciality – pasta Bolognese. How he managed to already have the necessary ingredients for the complex recipe was beyond Kate. But it tasted wonderful, even if the dinner felt like a last meal for the condemned.

Today, while Kate watched Beth pack her suitcase, she had to bite her cheek to keep from crying. But it was all for the best. Someday they would look back and laugh at the high drama.

It just wouldn't be today.

Eric sauntered outside just as Beth and Michael loaded their suitcases into the trunk of Michael's car.

Beth angled a ferocious glare at Eric. 'And I thought you wouldn't have the guts to show up and say goodbye.' Begrudgingly, she extended a hand to him.

'A handshake? No way.' Eric pulled tiny Beth into a bear hug.

'You'd better take care of my bestie,' she said. 'I'll need her for bridesmaid duty in a couple of weeks.'

Kate stomped her foot. 'Will you please stop? Can't you trust that you trained me well?'

'I trust my training, just not your learning.' Beth ducked her head into the car. 'Call me every day.'

Michael turned to Eric. 'Is a handshake okay from me?'

'For now, yes.' Eric shook vigorously. 'Just don't forget to send my wedding invitation. I don't trust Kate to include me as her plus-one.'

Kate didn't bother to argue or stomp her foot a second time. She was too caught up in the emotion of her co-workers leaving.

'Where to, boss?' Eric asked, once they disappeared from view.

'I thought you started your new job today.' She swiped at her eyes with a sleeve.

'They don't need me for lunch. I don't report until three o'clock, which gives me plenty of time to watch your back while you work your case.'

Kate pulled her gaze away from Main Street traffic. 'Good, we'll take your car. Nobody knows that one yet. I'll take a quick shower and meet you in thirty minutes. I won't get in until I'm certain I'm not being watched.'

'Ten-four, Agent Ninety-Nine.'

'Please, no more jokes. You need to take this seriously,' she called over her shoulder.

Half an hour later, Kate climbed in Eric's car after checking the lot for suspicious characters.

'Now will you tell me where we're going?' he asked.

'To see Mrs Westin's former lover. Mark Harris is a fairly common name, so I studied the postings of every Mark Harris on social media in the area and narrowed our search down to two.' Kate tapped the screen of her phone to bring up a map. 'Turn left and follow the signs for Route 98 and the Bay Bridge. The first address is a warehouse in Gulf Breeze that was converted into condos ten years ago. Most of the units have water views. Sounds like a romantic kind of place, no?'

Eric kept his eyes on the road. 'It does. Where does the second Mark Harris live?'

'In a high-rise apartment on Gulf Breeze Parkway. But it's almost in Navarre, which seems too far away from Mrs Westin's house.'

'I agree.' While Kate programmed his GPS, Eric plugged in his iPod, apparently preferring music to idle chatter.

So Kate studied Harris's Facebook page, even though she'd practically memorized the details last night. When they arrived at the first building, she pressed the buzzer next to his name and waited.

'May I help you?' said a male voice.

'Mr Harris, this is Kate Weller and her associate, Mr Manfredi. We're private investigators, but we're unsure if we have the correct Mark Harris. Are you acquainted with Mrs Agnes Westin?'

'Yes, Agnes and I were friends,' he said.

'Then may we come up and ask a few questions? We work for Lainey Westin.'

'All right. I'm in 1002.' After a brief pause, the security door swung open.

In the elevator, Eric pressed the button for the top floor. 'Thanks for a promotion my first day on the job.'

Kate peered up at him. 'Don't get too excited. The pay remains the same – nothing. Harris might have wondered why I brought my former landlord along. Mainly you're here to keep your eyes open. If Harris is the killer, who knows what he has up his sleeve. But you may only ask three questions, so choose wisely.'

Harris's front door opened only the length of his security chain. 'May I see identification, please?' he asked.

'Of course.' Kate passed her PI ID, along with Eric's driver's license, through the opening. 'My partner is still in training. That's why he only has a driver's license.'

Satisfied, Harris allowed them to enter. Although the unit was nowhere near as grand as Lainey's, the furniture was expensive and the view of Santa Rosa Sound spectacular.

'Lovely condo. Do you own it, Mr Harris?' asked Kate.

'I do not. I rent. Please have a seat.' He pointed at the white leather couch.

'Thank you. May I ask what you do for a living?'

'I'm a graduate student pursuing an advance degree in art history. Although obtaining my doctorate is most likely out of the question now. I also work part time at the museum in town.'

'What kind of career expectations does one have with a doctorate in the fine arts?' Eric asked, burning off question number one.

'I hope to become curator at one of the world's major museums. My dream job would be to work at the National Gallery in London or the Metropolitan Museum of Art in New York.'

'Do you live here alone?' Kate asked, bringing Harris back to present time.

'I do. Would you like coffee or tea?'

Eric shook his head, while Kate spoke for them. 'No, we're fine.' Her gaze drifted around the room. 'Times certainly have changed. When I was a student at the University of Florida, I lived in a walk-up with three other women. It was a dump compared to this.'

'Let's not beat around the bush, Miss Weller.' Harris sat on a leather chair. 'My rent was being paid by Mrs Westin. Lucky for me she paid six months in advance. So I'll have a chance to find another place before I'm booted out. Ask me whatever you like. I have nothing to hide.'

You know what they say about people who make that claim. 'How did you two meet?' she asked.

'At the museum. It was opening night for the new wing – black tie, open bar, fully catered. My invitation was because I work there. I had to rent my tux. Mrs Westin paid a thousand dollars for her ticket. And I assure you she neither rented her gown nor her jewelry. As you know, Agnes was a knowledge-able patron of the arts.'

'Were you surprised by Mrs Westin's interest in you?' asked Eric. 'Considering the rather large age difference.'

'Not at all. Despite the fact I earn only slightly more than minimum wage, I know a lot about art and art history. Most of our benefactors know little about the masterpieces they're helping to support . . . and have no desire to learn.' Harris crossed his legs. 'I don't mean to sound ungrateful, but most are simply looking for a fashionable tax write-off.'

'And Mrs Westin?' Kate couldn't help but notice his expensive watch.

'Agnes began studying art in college and never stopped. She knows as much as me, if not more. Just not about the pieces we had recently procured abroad. When Agnes approached me with specific questions, I was happy to provide a private tour while the other guests proceeded to the buffet and bar area. We began seeing each other regularly after that night.'

'Forgive my impertinence, Mr Harris. But do you also date women your own age?'

'No, I don't. As a student, I have no money to wine and dine women, unless they would be content with food off the dollar menu and watching a movie that I recorded. And, believe me, women my age are not. Perhaps Mr Manfredi can back me up on this.'

Eric offered a nod, along with a small smile.

'In the beginning, my relationship with Mrs Westin was platonic. We visited museums, galleries, and private collections throughout the panhandle, plus Mobile, Jacksonville, and St Augustine. She always bought lunch and dinner. Later, when she realized I might not finish my degree without a benefactor, she insisted on taking care of the tuition, along with my rent and utilities. Art was that important to her, and she enjoyed my company. In exchange, she had a young man on her arm for her numerous fundraisers and as a travel companion.' Harris described the relationship without an ounce of embarrassment.

'Talking about this doesn't bother you?' asked Eric, exhausting his quota of questions.

'Not in the least. Women have had sugar-daddies for years. Why shouldn't the privilege work both ways? And that's how I thought of my relationship with her – a rare privilege.'

'I gather your relationship advanced beyond platonic status.'

'That detail, Miss Weller, is none of your business.'

'I beg your pardon.' Kate lowered her gaze to the expensive Mexican floor tiles.

'Neither of us had any delusions that our liaison would be anything but temporary. We agreed that her support would end when I graduated next year. I planned to move from this plush condo and return the *rented* furniture. But, in the meantime, Agnes had arranged to take me to Europe this summer: One month in Paris at the Louvre and the National Galleries, one month in Italy, and a final month at the Rijksmuseum in Amsterdam. It would have been an art lover's dream come true.' Harris's eyes darkened. 'In case you're wondering, that trip is out of the question. I'd also signed an agreement drawn up by her attorney that our relationship wasn't a common-law marriage. Upon her death, the money will go to Lainey or to charity, as specified in her will. So, as you see, I had no motive to kill her.'

'I didn't mean to imply—'

Harris held up his hand. 'I'm not offended. You need to cover all bases, and I want Agnes's killer caught.'

'You're assuming she was murdered. Suicide hasn't been ruled out.'

'Agnes never would have killed herself. She was too content with the life she'd created.'

'According to your Facebook page, you had lunch with Mrs Westin on the day she died,' said Kate. 'Most likely you were the last person to see her alive.'

Sadness filled his face. 'Yes, I posted a lot of photos that day. If I were the killer, that wouldn't have been very smart of me.'

'Can your tell us anything about that day – how you spent your time, what you ate and drank? You never know what might be helpful?'

Harris walked to the window overlooking the Intracoastal Waterway, where pleasure boats bobbed in the calm waters. 'We ate chicken salad sandwiches on sourdough bread. And she had broccoli salad. I hate broccoli and I'm allergic to walnuts. Her housekeeper always puts in walnuts anyway, probably because she doesn't like me.'

Kate jotted down notes while Harris patiently waited for her.

'We drank bottled iced tea and white wine,' he continued.

'Agnes loves a sparkling Riesling with lunch, but I don't remember the brand.'

'Did you supply any of the food or drinks?'

He laughed. 'Agnes was very discerning. Her housekeeper, Luisa, always prepared the hamper and filled a cooler for her outings.'

'Were any of the bottles already opened?' Kate interrupted.

'No, I opened the tea and popped the cork on the bubbly. Her fingers were usually too stiff.'

'According to your posts, you two sunbathed on the bow, read books, and snorkeled around the marina. Any other activities?'

Harris pushed his glasses up his nose. 'Any others would fall in the "none of your business" category.'

Eric cleared his throat to mask his chuckle.

'We're trying to solve a possible murder, nothing more.'

He sighed. 'If I thought anything else would be helpful, I would tell you. As I said to Detective Buckley, I left her around three o'clock and went to work. Agnes was in a good mood and feeling fine. Nothing we did that day endangered her health.'

Kate decided not to mention snorkeling in the vicinity of speedboats with sharp propellers.

'She was in such good spirits that she asked me to pop the cork on the second bottle before I left.'

'Didn't you find that strange since you were leaving?' asked Eric, overstepping his quota by one.

'Not really. I'm not much of a drinker. Two glasses is my limit, but sometimes Agnes enjoyed a third glass and called a taxi to get home. She wouldn't climb behind the wheel.'

'Do you think she might have been expecting another guest?'

He shrugged. 'Maybe Lainey stopped by. Those two preferred the *Arrivederci* for their shouting matches instead of arguing in front of servants.'

Kate tried a long-shot. 'Any idea what their favorite point of contention was?'

'Sure, Agnes hated Lainey's boyfriend . . . excuse me – fiancé. She would do anything to keep that marriage from taking place.'

As she rose to her feet, Kate exchanged a look with Eric. 'Thank you, Mr Harris, for your candor. If you can think of anything else, please call me.' She laid her business card on the glass coffee table while Eric shook hands.

'What was your impression?' she asked him in the elevator.

'I liked the guy. Sure didn't seem like a heartless killer to me. Someday he'll write a kept-man's how-to guide and make a million bucks.'

'I'll buy you a copy. In the meantime, I intend to verify every word he said, especially the part about not inheriting a dime from Agnes. I wonder if the will has been filed in Probate Court yet.'

'Is that the only thing that piqued your interest upstairs?' he asked. 'Don't forget, I'm your partner now.'

'I'd also like to know how much alcohol was in Mrs Westin's blood.' Kate ticked off on her fingers. 'And if she had another guest after Harris on the *Arrivederci*. And why Lainey hadn't mentioned a fiancé when Beth and I talked to her. I never knew an engaged woman who didn't drop *that* tidbit into conversation every chance she got.'

Eric rubbed his palms together as they climbed in with Kate behind the wheel. 'I'm going to love my new job.'

Kate cocked her head to one side. 'Your new *job*, Mr Manfredi, is *sous chef* at Henri's out at the seashore. We should get back to town so you can go to work on time.'

'Oh, yeah. I almost forget. Too bad, I was really starting to enjoy myself.'

'All right,' she said, not wanting to dampen his enthusiasm. 'I'll call Detective Buckley so you can listen, but no butting into my conversation.'

'You have my word.' Eric placed his hand over his heart.

Eric had his own reasons for eavesdropping on Kate's phone conversation with the detective in charge of Mrs Westin's death. He had truly enjoyed himself during the interview of Mark Harris today. Most likely Kate assumed he wanted to keep her in his sights, protect her from Liam's former cronies, which of course he did. But ever since she'd risked her life in Charleston to keep his father out of prison, he'd developed a passion for crime-solving.

Wasn't that why he'd gone to law school – to bring potential felons to justice? But during his internship in the prosecutor's office, Eric had learned justice wasn't dispensed fairly in this world. Those with deep pockets could handpick juries sympathetic to their plight, while the poor were stuck with overworked public defenders who could barely pay their rent, let alone hire a professional jury consultant. By the time Eric graduated, he'd lost all desire to take the Bar exam. He wasn't sure what he wanted, but it wasn't prosecuting the down-and-out while fat-cat criminals received immunity for testifying against bigger fish.

Opening a restaurant had been his grandfather's dream, and Ernesto Manfredi's primary reason for immigrating to the United States. The small, humble bistro his *nonno* started was now a four-star restaurant in a sophisticated city known for its adventurous, upscale cuisine. His parents no longer lived in the upstairs apartment like his grandparents had. They owned a mini-mansion in the suburbs, while Eric's condo was fully paid for, thanks to Bella Trattoria.

Although his dad loved inventing new dishes and preparing every sauce from scratch, cooking had never been Eric's passion. He'd joined the family business after law school because he had nothing else to do, and his sister needed help with the operation's practical side. Although his decision to follow Kate to Pensacola had nothing to do with evaluating possible second locations for Bella, Eric might have found the career he'd been looking for.

'You gonna make that call, or not?' he asked, halfway back to the hotel.

At the next red light, Kate punched in the number for the police department and asked for homicide. 'Remember, you listen and learn while I talk to Buckley, no interrupting. Save your questions for when I'm off the phone.'

'Yes, Miss Weller,' chimed Eric, mimicking a schoolboy.

'Detective Buckley?' she asked when someone picked up the other end. 'Kate Weller, the investigator working for Lainey Westin. I have you on speaker. Eric Manfredi is here, serving as my bodyguard for the day.'

'*A bodyguard?*' Buckley hooted. 'Who have you irritated to the point of bodily harm?'

'The list could be lengthy, sir, but specifics aren't pertinent to my professional case. I'm curious if the ME finished his autopsy yet.'

'He has, Miss Weller. But no, you may *not* have a copy of his report.'

'Could you at least tell me if he's ruled out both natural and accidental causes?'

'Let's just say I've been officially assigned to the Westin case.'

'What about the DNA on the wine glasses from the yacht? Was the tumbler I provided any help?'

'Only so far as to rule out the *new* Mrs Westin as one of Agnes's luncheon guests. It wasn't a match.'

Kate met his gaze and frowned. 'According to Mark Harris, he spent the afternoon alone with Agnes.'

'Yes, that's what he told me too. Have you been following me like a bloodhound? The state of Florida considers stalking a serious crime.'

'Absolutely not. Captain Holcomb of the *Arrivederci* provided the name of Mr Harris. I was simply doing my job, sir.'

'See that you don't overstep the line. Turns out the victim's DNA was on *both* wine glasses. The boyfriend, Mark Harris, voluntarily provided DNA during questioning. It matched the DNA on one of the water glasses.'

'Only the water, not the wine? Harris told me he drank two glasses of Riesling that afternoon.'

'Gee, PI, I dunno. Maybe Harris left some in the glass and Mrs Westin didn't want it to go to waste. Perhaps she wiped the rim before finishing it off. Women can be so odd at times.'

Eric burst out laughing, while Kate scowled.

'Were you aware, Detective, that Harris didn't eat any of the side dish? He's allergic to nuts, and the broccoli salad contained walnuts. So the poison could have been in there.'

'Hold on. Nobody said anything about poison, Miss Weller.'

'True, but if it wasn't a natural death from stroke or heart attack, no head trauma from a fall, and there were no gunshot or knife wounds, what else could it be?' This time Kate winked at him.

'She might have been bitten by a rare Jamaican yellow blowfly, instantly fatal, while the toxin leaves virtually no residue in the blood.'

'Are you serious?' she asked. 'Does such an insect even exist?'

'Do your job, Miss Weller.'

Eric pulled out his phone for a quick Google search.

'Did the ME's report include a full toxicology screen?'

'It did, which you may not have a copy of. Is there anything else, because I really need to get back to work?'

Kate ignored Buckley's question. 'I assume you checked with marina security, which keeps video on the cars entering and leaving the yacht club. Could you at least tell me if Mrs Westin had a visitor after Mark Harris left for work? Harris thought maybe Lainey had stopped by.'

'Hmm, let me think about it . . . Nope, can't tell you that either,' Buckley said after a few moments. 'But a clever girl like you could charm her way into seeing that video. The security guard let me see the tape without a court order. So much for the privacy of the rich and infamous. Gotta go, Miss Weller. Remember what I told you about not overstepping.' Buckley laughed and hung up.

Kate dropped her phone in her purse. 'Well, he was less than helpful.'

'But now you have me,' said Eric. 'From my cursory research of the Calliphoridae species, I found none called the Jamaican yellow blowfly, rare or otherwise. However, since blowflies inhabit most continents and islands, one would assume they live on Jamaica. And because blowflies thrive on rotting flesh, they definitely could transmit dangerous pathogens to humans or livestock. But I found none so toxic that one bite could kill a woman. In other words, Buckley was pulling your leg.' He slipped his phone into his pocket.

'Thank you, Eric.'

'You're welcome. And may I say you handled yourself beautifully!'

Kate rolled her eyes. 'How so? I failed to find out the alcohol content of Mrs Westin's blood, or anything else from the tox screen. Buckley neither confirmed nor denied poison as the cause of death.'

'I thought your conclusion was a good one.' Eric patted her shoulder.

'Baseless assumptions can lead a PI off-track, and that's what my conclusion was. Plus we still don't know whether Agnes had any other guests that afternoon.'

'Think about what you did learn.' With goose bumps forming on his arms, Eric rolled down the window.

'And what would that be?' Kate turned up the AC.

'Although he didn't say so, it didn't sound like Buckley considered Harris a suspect. That confirmed your own conclusion. Now, can we compromise with the AC?' Eric rolled up the window.

Kate switched the control to low. 'Lack of motive goes a long way. Harris had no reason to kill Mrs Westin.'

'And Buckley steered you toward the marina security guard.'

She smiled. 'That's true, Manfredi. Not bad for your first day, but it's time for you to go to your real job.'

'I've got a better idea,' he said. 'Don't cross the Pensacola Bay Bridge.'

Kate pulled off the road. 'What are you up to?'

'I know you'll head to the yacht club to watch the video as soon as you get your car. Then you'll probably want the tumbler back from Buckley so you can sneak it back to Kim Westin's patio. So why not drop me off at Henri's? I only have to work four hours tonight. You can pick me up later and we can have supper together. Think of all the time and gas you'll save.'

Kate thrummed her fingers on the steering wheel. 'That makes sense, but we won't be dining at Henri's. They're too expensive.'

'We can eat anywhere you like.'

She watched her rearview mirror for a chance to turn around. 'Just don't get the notion you and I are joined at the hip. I'm capable of taking care of myself.'

'I don't doubt it for a minute,' he said.

But actually, Eric doubted it plenty. Although she should

be fairly safe at police headquarters and while scaling the privacy wall at the Westins', he didn't like the idea of Kate returning to the marina alone – a place she'd already been and might have been followed. After Kate dropped him off at Henri's service entrance, the next four hours passed interminably slowly. The owner and head chef was a nice enough guy and the staff reasonably pleasant, but his duties as the second-in-command allowed too much time for him to worry about Kate.

Although rather pricey for a beach community, Henri's menu was a mixed bag of Italian, French, American, and what he called bar food. Most of the seafood was served fried, instead of grilled or blackened as he preferred. However, since he was here for a legitimate reason to remain close to Kate, he would work hard with his eyes and ears open and keep any criticism to himself.

When Kate picked him up four hours later, she was grinning from ear to ear. 'How did your first day go?' she asked.

'Well, the head chef yelled at me only once and nobody sent back any of the food I made.' Eric held up his hand for a high-five.

'Way to go.' Kate slapped his palm before peeling out of Henri's parking lot. 'Did the owner know of any restaurants for sale?'

'I didn't ask, not on my first day. I was being trained on their style of food prep, so I kept quiet on my true motives. What did you find out?'

'My lips are zipped until I'm sitting with a cold beer in front of me.'

'In that case there's a pizza shop that serves great antipasto quarter-mile on the right.'

Kate slowed down as they turned into the crowded lot, but refused to talk until the waitress delivered two cold beers. 'Ah, that's better,' she said after the first swallow. 'The security guard at the marina was just as pliable as Buckley described. It only took five minutes of sweet-talk, plus a double mocha latte to view the video for the day Mrs Westin died.'

'Only five minutes? You little minx.' Although Eric definitely preferred wine, he sipped his beer to be sociable.

'It was mainly the latte. That guard might not be big on privacy, but he knew everyone who passed through his gate. If he didn't recognize an owner or frequent guest, he jotted down names, license numbers, and who they were visiting. He knew exactly when Mark Harris left and he was certain no one else visited the *Arrivederci* until Captain Holcomb showed up late that evening.'

'Everything points to the man without a motive. Harris was alone on the boat, with access to food and drink, and plenty of time to slip poison into the broccoli.' Eric picked up his fork the moment the waitress delivered their salads.

'Everyone thinks broccoli is supposed to be so healthy.' Kate took another gulp of beer. 'But I can't see Harris as a murderer. He had too much to lose and nothing to gain. Unless he was lying about Agnes's will.'

'We'll need to see a copy of that will. How did it go at the police station?'

Kate waved a forkful of romaine at him. 'That stinker, Buckley, left the tumbler in a brown bag at the front desk. He knew I'd pester him to look at the autopsy face-to-face.'

'Hiding from women is always easier than saying no.'

'Sounds like something you learned from Mark Harris. Tomorrow I'll visit Lainey again. I want to know more about her mystery fiancé, and whether or not she's Agnes's sole beneficiary.'

Eric shook his head. 'No, we'll pay a social call to Lainey together.'

Kate lifted one eyebrow. 'What about your job?'

'For the next week I only work four hours during the dinner rush.'

'Don't you need to scout properties for sale? Or was that just a ruse right from the beginning?'

'I'll look online in the morning. The internet saves plenty of legwork. Besides, you promised Beth you'd let me babysit.'

'Fine,' she said, 'but Lainey might wonder why I have so many *partners*.'

'Tell her Beth was fired because she annoyed too many clients, something I don't ever intend to do. Who wouldn't believe that?' Eric leaned back as the waitress placed a pizza in the center of the table.

'I'm the one you don't want to annoy, Manfredi.'

Kate had tried to sound bossy, but Eric had seen a look of relief when he insisted on coming with her. And that suited him just fine.

NINE

The hotel room seemed oddly empty the next morning. Without her roommate, Kate had the bathroom to herself, full control of the remote, and wouldn't have to worry about someone eating the ice cream, then replacing an empty container. Just the same, Kate missed Beth. But Beth could be reckless, which Michael didn't need this close to the wedding.

Eric would work out just fine as a bodyguard – a fact that both pleased and scared her. With so uncertain a future, she didn't need to get emotionally wound up in a man.

After two cups of coffee and a quick shower, Kate punched in a familiar number. 'Good morning, Eric. I hope I didn't wake you.'

'Are you kidding? I'm already down at the breakfast bar. Wow, this is a veritable banquet.'

'Generous praise, since you're a gourmet chef. The hotel usually serves scrambled eggs covered in melted cheddar, fried potatoes, and white toast.'

'Something wrong with that, Weller?'

'Not a thing. I'll be right there.' On her way down, she punched in Lainey Westin's number.

The wealthy heiress picked up on the first ring. 'Hello, Miss Weller.' She had apparently programmed Kate's number into caller-ID. 'I wondered when I'd get some kind of case update.'

Although Kate sent the boss, Nate Price, regular updates, keeping her client informed hadn't occurred to her. 'I would love to do exactly that. May I come by your house this morning?'

'I'm on my way out the door for Pilates, then an appointment with my financial adviser. Give me the short and sweet over the phone.' Lainey sounded like she was eating while talking.

Kate organized a concise answer in her mind. 'Let's see:

Since you weren't on the yacht that day and didn't see your mother that morning, I don't think the police still consider you a suspect. For the same reasons, they have ruled out your father and stepmom as well.'

The sound of munching ceased. 'What did you say?'

'Your father and stepmom,' Kate repeated the words innocently.

'Kim Westin is my father's second wife – nothing more, nothing less. Do we understand each other, Miss Weller?'

Kate hadn't been dressed-down so thoroughly since middle school by her least favorite teacher. 'Absolutely, I won't make that mistake again.'

'Thank you. Now that I'm no longer a suspect, I'm curious as to who the police think did kill my mother.'

'Most likely no one has been officially eliminated, but I think Detective Buckley is looking at Mark Harris, your mother's . . . art history friend.' Kate wasn't about to make the same mistake twice. 'Mr Harris admits to having lunch with her on the *Arrivederci* that day, and to the best of my knowledge, your mother had no other guests on the boat.'

'Mom had asked me to stop by, but I was in no mood for one of her temper tantrums. I made up an excuse and didn't go. I'd say I dodged a bullet.'

Kate wondered if the pun had been intended. 'Were you acquainted with Mark Harris? If so, how would you describe your relationship?' she asked.

'Yes, we've met. Basically, we stayed out of each other's way. At least with Harris to keep my mother amused, she left me alone. What have you learned from the police? Was my mother poisoned?'

'I believe so, but the police won't release the toxicology report to me. And I can't force them to.'

'I need to know! I read that poisoning is a horrible way to die.' Lainey's voice was filled with anguish.

'Some poisons can cause respiratory failure, which can be painful, but others simply cause someone to fall asleep and not wake up. Since we don't know how she died, you shouldn't torment yourself like this.'

'You're right. Thank you, Kate.'

'You're welcome. When can we get together?'

'Meet me at her house later,' Lainey said after a brief hesitation. 'I need to pay the staff and clarify their duties. Right now the housekeeper doesn't know what to do with Mom's mail, and the cook is afraid to clean spoiled food out of the fridge. Plus that creepy Mr Chapman won't cut the grass or whack the weeds until he gets paid. It's a state of confusion over there.' She sighed wearily, as though no one understood the woes of the rich. 'Jot down her address. I'll get there as soon as I can. I'm sure the housekeeper will let you wait inside. Luisa lets everyone else in.' Lainey provided an address with a few directions and hung up.

When Kate finally entered the breakfast area, Eric had almost finished eating. 'What took you so long?' he demanded.

Kate fixed a small plate of eggs, grits, and fried potatoes. 'I called Lainey to make sure she'd be home. We are to meet her at her mom's house in Oriole Beach. Apparently, Mrs Westin's staff hasn't known what to do since she died.'

'What kind of staff did Agnes have?' Eric spread jam on his last piece of toast.

'A housekeeper, a cook, and a gardener who refuses to work until he's paid. We'll know more once we get there.' Kate started eating as though the building were on fire.

'What's the big hurry?' Eric asked.

'I want to question the staff before Lainey arrives. We might learn more if their new boss isn't around.'

'Smart thinking. I'll fill two to-go mugs with coffee.'

Kate took two more bites of food and met him at the door. Although the distance to Mrs Westin's beautiful home wasn't far as the crow flies, heavy traffic heading to the shore stretched the trip into thirty minutes.

'Looks like the gardener has a better work ethic than Lainey gives him credit for.' Eric pointed at a middle-aged man in a broad-brimmed straw hat clipping roses in the garden. He didn't even glance up when their car doors slammed in the driveway.

'Good afternoon,' Kate greeted. 'Are you Mr Chapman, the gardener?'

He peered through thick-lensed glasses. 'Well, it sure ain't the butler out here getting stuck by thorns.'

Kate smiled at his sarcasm. 'I take nothing for granted these days. I'm Kate Weller and this is Eric Manfredi. We're investigators working for Lainey Westin and we'd like to ask you a few questions.'

'Ask all you want, but that don't mean I'm gonna answer.' Like a well-oiled machine, Chapman snipped three stems with his right hand, caught the spent blooms in his left, then tossed them into a bushel basket. But, even at his brisk pace, the hundred or so bushes would take all afternoon.

'Have you worked here long?' Kate asked.

'Almost fifteen years. That long enough for you, missy?'

'See here, sir. There's no need to speak—' Eric began.

But Kate interrupted. 'That's all right, Mr Manfredi. I'm sure Mr Chapman is still upset by Mrs Westin's passing.'

That stopped the snipping and tossing in its tracks. 'You think I'm hot under the collar because the boss is dead?' he asked.

'Aren't you?' Kate rocked back on her heels.

Chapman muttered a rude expletive. 'I'm mad because nobody's paid me in two weeks. I got bills same as the next guy.'

'Lainey Westin will be here soon to settle up. She told me so this morning.'

''Bout time that worthless daughter came around.' He resumed clipping.

Apparently Eric didn't like those who spoke ill of the dead. 'If you didn't like Mrs Westin, why have you stayed fifteen years?' he asked.

'I'll tell you why, sonny.' Chapman waved his clippers under Eric's nose. 'Miz Westin paid well, if she thought you were worth it. She had the best rose garden in the Pensacola Garden Club, so she paid me well. The new boss-lady better not cut my salary.'

Eric pushed his clippers to the side. 'Was Mrs Westin displeased with anyone in particular here?'

'Miz Westin had some trouble with Luisa a while back, but that conniving housekeeper is still around.' He gestured toward the house with his tool. 'And the cook has been here longer than me. She always got along fine with the boss.'

'Was that it – just the three of you?' asked Kate.

Chapman pondered for a minute. 'Miz Westin used to have two maids but fired them long ago. Now a cleaning service comes in once a week, and Luisa takes care of the laundry. Is that all your questions, missy? I need to concentrate on my work.'

'No, it's not,' Kate answered flatly. 'I just found out that Lainey was engaged to be married. I'm curious what Mrs Westin thought about her future son-in-law.'

Chapman's face contorted with anger. 'How would I know that?' he snapped.

'I'm thinking a gardener spends a lot of time trimming hedges, pulling weeds, and clipping flowers right underneath windows. And we both know Mrs Westin wasn't soft-spoken.'

'Even if I did hear a few things, like I said, she paid me well. I got no reason to spread malicious gossip.' He resumed clipping.

'Will this loosen your tongue?' Kate pulled a twenty-dollar bill from her wristlet and dangled it over his shoulder.

Chapman uttered a foul word. 'Twenty bucks – keep it! You probably need it more than me.'

Eric reacted before Kate could reply. 'How about now?' Over Chapman's left shoulder, Eric dangled a hundred-dollar bill.

Reacting quickly, the gardener stuffed the larger bill in his shirt pocket, then turned to face them. 'Now that's more like it. Agnes hated that guy at first sight. He never stood a chance. He was their favorite bone of contention, although over the years there have been many.'

'And his name?' demanded Eric.

'Steve Rivera,' Chapman said. 'But Agnes always called him Esteban just to irritate her daughter. They both loved to throw salt in open wounds.'

Kate shrugged. 'I'm not following you. Isn't Steve Esteban in Spanish?'

Chapman shrugged. 'Miz Westin said Rivera was trying to hide his heritage by calling himself Steve, like he was putting on airs or something. That's all I know, no matter how much money you throw at me.'

'Thanks, Mr Chapman,' said Kate. 'I'll make sure Lainey talks to you while she's here.'

'Oh, yeah? Talk is cheap,' he yelled as Kate and Eric walked around the house. 'Tell her to bring her checkbook.'

'A hundred bucks? What got into you, Manfredi?' Kate asked the moment they were out of earshot. 'Don't think for a moment my expense account will reimburse that! Twenty, yes, but not a hundred.' She stuffed her twenty into Eric's shirt pocket.

'I have a new job with money to burn. Besides, you refused to let me take you someplace nice for dinner.'

'Not until we have something to celebrate,' she muttered, climbing the front porch steps.

'We now have the fiancé's name and how Agnes felt about him.'

'We could've gotten that from Lainey and saved a hundred bucks. I want you to keep a low profile. You're not a trained PI.' She thumped his chest with her finger.

'Fine.' Eric knocked on the front door.

A few moments later, the door swung open, and before them appeared a small dark-haired woman wearing an old-fashioned dress. 'May I help you?' she asked.

'I'm Kate Weller. I work for Lainey Westin. This is my assistant. May we come in?'

'Did Miss Westin say it would be okay?' she asked.

'She did. I talked to her before her Pilates class. She'll be stopping by later. Are you Luisa?'

'I am.' The housekeeper blinked and stepped to the side. 'You might as well wait in Mrs Westin's office with Mrs Collier. I have plenty of work to do if Miss Lainey is stopping by.' She pointed down a long hallway, then meandered away in the opposite direction.

'Should we draw your gun?' Eric whispered as they walked down the hallway. 'This Mrs Collier could be dangerous.'

'This is why you're a chef and not a private investigator,' she hissed under her breath. 'You never know when to take something seriously.'

'Point taken.' He mimed closing a zipper across his lips. 'I intend to listen and learn.'

'Good.'

As they passed two bedrooms, Kate switched her footfalls to tiptoes so as not to alert Mrs Collier. Her ploy worked. As Kate and Eric arrived at the next doorway, they startled an attractive, fortyish woman rummaging through a desk drawer. 'Hi,' Kate said. 'Are you Mrs Collier?'

'Yes . . . who are you?' The woman's hand halted mid-rummage.

'Kate Weller. I work for Lainey Westin. Luisa said I should wait for Lainey in here with you.'

'Lainey is coming *here*?' The question left no doubt as to how Mrs Collier felt about the news.

'Yes, most likely this will be her house now. May we help you find something?' Kate utilized her most youthful and naïve tone of voice. 'Sorry, this is my partner, Eric.'

Suddenly, a smile filled the woman's face. 'Oh, don't bother. I'm sure another member has our most recent roster.' She stretched out her hand. 'How do you do? I'm Martha Collier, vice president of the garden club. We're all still *reeling* from Agnes's passing.'

'My sympathy for your loss,' murmured Kate, shaking hands. 'Was Mrs Westin a member?'

'Agnes was our esteemed president. Now I must assume her duties, and my roster of members is woefully out of date.' Martha fluttered too-thick-to-be-real lashes. 'Since Agnes was my best friend, I knew she wouldn't mind me looking in her desk for it.'

'The new president needs a roster,' Eric said sympathetic-ally. 'How do you do, ma'am. I'm Eric – Kate's boyfriend. We're just here to make sure the staff gets paid.'

Kate bit the inside of her cheek, while Eric pumped Martha Collier's hand.

'Good idea,' said Collier, closing the desk drawer. 'If Lainey wants a quick sale of this white elephant, the house and garden should be properly maintained.'

Kate decided to play along. 'If it turns out another member doesn't have the roster, should I ask Lainey about it?'

'Oh, no, that won't be necessary.' Collier's drawl was thick enough to be sliced like bread as she moved toward the doorway. 'Lainey has more important things on her mind than the garden club.'

'Mind if we ask you something before Lainey arrives?' whispered Kate, glancing down the hallway. 'We'd love to know what Agnes really thought about that Steve Rivera.'

To be sure, the question caught Mrs Collier by surprise. 'What would that have to do with paychecks for the servants?'

'Not a thing,' Kate giggled, taking another glance down the hall. 'But the gardener mentioned that Lainey and her mom fought all the time about her choice of boyfriends. I'm just being nosy.'

Kate waited to be put in her place, to get her second dress-down of the day. Instead Mrs Collier shut the office door. 'You're not kidding they fought about Lainey's fiancé. Agnes Westin was the world's biggest bigot. It didn't matter that Rivera came from plenty of money, or that his ancestors were some kind of Cuban royalty, Agnes despised him. Know what she confided in me?' Collier asked with conspiratorial inflection.

Kate leaned closer. 'No, what?'

'That if Lainey married this wetback, she would be cut out of her will.'

'What an awful thing to say! Agnes couldn't possibly mean that. Lainey was her only child.'

Collier pulled down her glasses with one finger. 'Are you really this naïve? Agnes did her best to ruin Rivera's Lexus dealership. She filed fictitious reports with the Better Business Bureau, and paid some kid to smear their Facebook page until Lainey figured out who was doing it.'

'Steve Rivera owns a Lexus dealership?' asked Kate, wide-eyed. 'Those are really nice cars.'

'Not just one dealership. The Rivera family owns a chain of them throughout the Sunshine State. I'd say that's hitting below the belt.' Collier glanced at her watch.

'Do you think Agnes went through with it? Do you think she cut her daughter out of her will?'

'Who knows? I personally can't wait until the will is made public. I think there'll be more than *one* surprise. Agnes not only hated anyone who wasn't lily-white – if your ancestors stopped at Ellis Island like mine did, you were also second-rate.

Didn't she know the Quakers who landed on Plymouth Rock were also *immigrants*?'

'Actually, those who arrived on the *Mayflower* were Pilgrim Separatists, not Quakers,' Eric corrected.

'What difference does it make, young man?' Martha snapped.

'None whatsoever, ma'am.' Eric bobbed his head respectfully.

'I gotta run.' Collier yanked the door open. 'Let's just keep everything said and done here between us, okay? Lainey would probably demand a court order to release the garden club roster.'

'Absolutely,' Kate readily agreed.

Collier smiled at Kate, but offered Eric only the barest of acknowledgements.

'I don't think she liked me,' Eric said after the woman hustled down the hall.

'You could be right. But did you see how guilty she looked when we walked in? My guess is she was looking for a copy of Agnes's will, not the roster of garden club members.'

'My, Miss Weller. You're not half as naïve as you look.'

Kate smiled. 'Let's get something to eat and then go back to the hotel.'

'Wait a minute. Aren't we waiting for Lainey?'

'I'll leave her a note that I had an emergency. I'd rather first learn what I can about Steve Rivera on the internet. We can always question Lainey later.'

'What about pay for the staff?' Eric persisted.

'I'll put that in the note too. Let's go!'

'Okay, while you're researching Rivera, I'll look into lawsuits or complaints filed by their Lexus dealerships – anything that has become public record.'

'No, Eric. After we grab lunch at a drive-through, you need to get ready for work. You can't be late on your second day of work. After all, you're already down a hundred bucks today.'

Several hours later, Kate felt a twinge of guilt as Eric climbed into his SUV and left for work. She didn't like lying to Eric. And it wasn't because he was her temporary protector now

that Beth had gone home to Savannah. She liked the guy . . .
a lot, and got the feeling that he seldom lied to her. Eric
Manfredi was straight as an arrow, but she couldn't have him
following her around as though she were a bumbling idiot.
She might not care what Martha Collier thought of her, but
she yearned for Eric's respect. Maybe she was shallow,
but she wanted him to report back to Beth Kirby that her
protégée could take care of herself.

But that wasn't the only reason she'd led Eric to believe
she'd be staying in to research Steve Rivera. She'd rather not
let him know she had a seven o'clock appointment with a
hypnotherapist. Like Beth, Eric didn't have a very high opinion
of the 'fringe' sciences. He suspected the vast majority were
frauds, out to separate fools from their money. And that was
probably true in most cases. But Kate knew Leslie Faraday
was for real. Under hypnosis, she had seen a bit of her past
that had been locked in an inaccessible corner of her mind.
So Kate was going back until she remembered everything from
that horrible summer night.

When Kate arrived, Mrs Faraday was chatting with guests
on the front porch of Sweet Dreams Bed and Breakfast.
Everyone stopped talking when Kate climbed the porch steps.

'Ah, Miss Weller, you're right on time. Shall we go to my
office?' Faraday asked, opening the screen door.

'Are those two on their honeymoon?' she asked. 'They look
so young.'

'They married right after high school. Very few couples
do that anymore. I blame video games and the high price of
rent these days.'

Unsure if the hypnotist was joking or not, Kate just smiled.

But once she closed the office door, Faraday became all
business. 'Frankly, I was shocked when you called me for a
second appointment.' She pointed at the sofa while taking her
position in the upholstered chair.

'Why were you shocked?' Kate sat down in the exact spot
she'd occupied before.

'You were very upset when you left here. Often when
patients relive something distressing from the past, they don't
return.' Faraday opened a spiral notebook.

Kate chose her words carefully. 'I wasn't distressed. I was shocked . . . and scared. That's why I wanted to stop the session. And that's why I ran out of here like a banshee.'

She nodded. 'Okay, what is it you want from me today?'

'I want to go back. I want you to put me under.'

Looking confused, Faraday flipped through a few pages of notes and skimmed the page. 'As you were emerging from the regression, you said and I quote, "Liam didn't shoot that man. He was already lying on the ground." Then I asked, "What happened next?" And you told me that you didn't know because you ran away.' Faraday stopped reading and met Kate's gaze. 'I don't know what else you aim to learn.'

Kate swallowed hard. 'I lied to you. I didn't run, because I was too scared to move from my telephone pole. Please, Mrs Faraday, I want to see what happened to Liam and his friends.'

The hypnotist pursed her lips. 'This isn't like rewinding a videotape. Who knows if I can get you back to that precise moment in your past? Hypnosis is not an exact science.'

'Can we try, please? My brother's life may be at stake.'

'Very well.' Still sounding unsure, Faraday walked around the room, dimming lights and closing blinds. 'First of all, I want you to verbalize what you hope to see under hypnosis. What do you hope to learn? Sometimes, if we focus on a question such as where we last saw our cell phone, right before we fall asleep, the answer will come to us in the dream state. We might trigger a regression in the same way. Tell me what you hope to learn.'

'I want to see what happened to Liam,' Kate said quickly. 'And I want to see what his friends looked like and which one of them knocked Liam out,' she added after a few moments.

'Very good.' Faraday rolled over her chair and turned on her tape recorder. 'Sit back comfortably, Kate, and close your eyes. Relax the muscles of your neck . . . your arms and legs . . . and your back. Take three very deep breaths. Draw the air in through your nose and breathe out through your mouth. Imagine you are standing on the beach, watching the waves lap the shore. It is a warm summer day and you are ten years old. Can you feel the warm sun on your face and hands?

'Please don't nod your head. Instead, speak every thought

that comes to mind. Now, can you see yourself standing on the beach in your shorts and T-shirt?'

'Yes.'

'Very good.' Faraday spoke softly in an almost melodic voice. 'Remember, Kate, these are memories and nothing from the past can hurt you.'

'Okay.'

'As you listen to my voice, your mind forms a picture of that summer day when your mom worked the night shift and Liam was supposed to watch you. Do you remember that day, Kate, when Liam made plans to go out with his friends?'

'Yes, Liam was very mad at me. He gave me a Coke and a bag of chips and told me to watch TV in my room all night. I asked what if I gotta go to the bathroom. He said stop being such a baby!'

'Is that what you did, Kate? Did you stay in your room all night?'

'No, I climbed out my window and hid under a smelly tarp in his truck.'

'And Liam didn't know you were there until you came up for air. What happened then?'

'He got real mad.' Kate's child-like voice rose in agitation.

'Don't worry; Liam loves you. He just wants to keep you safe.'

'He made me climb out of the truck and then he drove away. I started crying.'

'But you were very brave. You followed him several blocks through downtown Pensacola, until he parked by the curb. What did he do when he got out of this truck?'

'He walked over to his pals. They were standing in the middle of the street.'

'What do you see in the middle of the street?'

'A car accident – a shiny black van and a smashed-up red car. And there's a man lying on the ground. He's not moving. Everybody is yelling. Liam is yelling too. He's real angry.'

'Why is he so mad, Kate?'

'Liam is mad at his friends. He said a bad word and points at the ground. Then he said, "This wasn't supposed to happen."'

'Who's he talking to, Kate?'

'A skinny man and a chubby man with a beard.'

'Do you know their names?'

'No.'

'What does the chubby man say?'

'He called Liam a bad word and says, "This is your fault, because you can't get anywhere on time." Then Liam grabs the man's shirt and says, "You were supposed to wait till we're all here."'

'Tell me about this chubby man. What color is his hair?'

'Brown. And his hair looks dirty. He wears glasses.'

'Then what happens to Liam and his friends?'

'Somebody hit Liam on the head.' Tears began to stream down Kate's face.

'Remember, nothing here that can hurt you. Was it the chubby man with the beard who hit Liam or the skinny man?'

Kate shook her head. 'No, it was a different man. He came from behind the black truck.'

'Tell me what this man looks like. Is he tall or short?'

'I don't know.'

'Is he a white man or a black man?'

'I don't know.'

'All right, tell me what happened after this man hits your brother.'

'Liam falls on the ground by the man with blood on his shirt. And the skinny man starts yelling, "What did you do that for?" Then the chubby man says, "Shut up. He's been nothing but trouble right from the beginning." Then I heard sirens in the distance and somebody yelled, "The cops are coming!"'

'What did everyone do then?'

'The chubby man picks up a duffle bag and the skinny men says, "This ain't right. We can't just leave him like this." He points down at my brother. Then the man who hit Liam says, "Shut up and get moving. We ain't got much time. Or maybe you want to end up down there with your pal?"'

'Now can you see the face of the man who hit Liam?'

Kate shook her head. 'No, his back is to me. But he's wearing a red plaid flannel shirt.'

'What happens next?'

'The chubby man and skinny man run away with the black bag. Then the other man squats down next to Liam.'

'What did he do?'

'I couldn't see. Maybe he was saying sorry. Then he went into the dark building.'

'He didn't run away like the others?'

'No, he went inside the building.'

'What did you do, Kate?'

'I just stood there behind the telephone pole. I wanted to see if Liam was okay, but the flashing red and blue lights were too close. I was scared the police would tell Mom I snuck out of the house. So I ducked into the alley behind Liam's truck and ran until I was far away.'

'Did you see police cars on the next street?'

'Yes, but I hid behind a trash can when one drove by.'

'Then you walked back to Highway 29 and hitched a ride to get home. Once you were home, nobody was there, right?'

Kate nodded. 'I hid under the covers and pretended I was asleep.'

'That's where you are right now, Kate. Safe at home in bed where nothing can hurt you. But the sun is shining, so it's time to wake up. As I slowly count back from five, you are going to wake up. Five,' said Faraday.

Kate's closed eyelids fluttered.

'Four,' she said, slightly louder.

Kate's shoulders twitched.

'Three.' As she spoke in her normal voice, Kate shifted on the sofa.

Faraday moved to stand above her patient. 'Two.'

Kate's entire body spasmed.

'One.'

As Kate opened her eyes and shook off the last vestiges of sleep, Faraday handed her a second notepad.

'I want you to jot down everything you can remember, Kate. Don't bother with spelling, punctuation, or complete sentences. Keep writing until you can't remember anything else that you saw or heard. Just like a dream, the longer you're fully conscious, the less you'll be able to remember of our session.'

Kate started writing and didn't stop until her hand cramped painfully. 'That's it. I sure hope you tape-recorded our session.'

'I did. Between my recording and your notes, you should have an accurate picture of the events that night.'

Kate reached for several tissues and dabbed her damp face. 'I don't know if these are tears or sweat from exhaustion. But I feel like you made me run around the block, carrying a twenty-pound weight.'

Faraday laughed, then handed her a new memory stick. 'That's a normal response. Feel free to rest for as long as you need. I have no other patients tonight.'

Kate pushed to her feet. 'I appreciate the offer, but I need to beat someone back to my room.'

'Are you kidding? That's exactly like what you described in your regression.'

'Yes, but now it's a hotel room and a boyfriend I need to beat instead of my mom.' Kate pulled out her checkbook and paid for the session.

It was not until she was inside her car that she realized what an endearing term she'd just used for Eric Manfredi.

TEN

No matter how Kate referred to Eric – her partner-in-training, bodyguard, or boyfriend – she did not beat him back to Vacation Inn and Suites that night. Eric was sitting on a kitchen chair in her doorway when she stepped off the elevator. She would either need a battering ram or stick of dynamite to get around him.

'Where have you been, young lady? The street lights have been on for half an hour!' Playing the role well, Eric tapped his toe on the tile floor.

'What are you doing here, Manfredi, and how did you open my door?'

'Don't change the subject.' He rose to his full six feet four inches and crossed his arms over his chest. 'You told me you were staying in to research Steve Rivera.'

'I did, until I learned all I could from the internet.' Kate tried to squeeze past him, but he parried to the left and right. 'Okay, I'll confess if you let me inside.'

'Don't even think of jumping from the balcony.' Eric stepped to the side.

Kate walked into her suite, which seemed naked without her roommate's junk. 'By all means, Eric, make yourself comfortable.' Her voice oozed with sarcasm.

'I'm waiting for a full confession.' He moved his chair back to the table and bolted the door.

'I had an appointment with my hypnotherapist tonight for a second session. I went alone because you don't think much of the pseudo-sciences.'

Eric blinked. 'I don't care if your appointment was with Aladdin on his flying carpet. Spend your money however you choose. But until we find out who shot that guard, I don't want you going anywhere alone.'

Kate grinned at his analogy. 'Do you have Aladdin's number? I'd like to give him a call.'

Eric took hold of her shoulders. 'Stop joking around, Kate. You're not safe in Pensacola.'

She shrugged off his hands. 'I know that, but tonight we got one step closer to finding out who pulled the trigger. Sit down and I'll tell you the whole story. But first I need something to drink.' She headed for the refrigerator, then halted midstride. 'No, *first* you're going to tell me how you got in here. Beth gave me her key card when she moved out.'

'Not until after Beth had an extra copy made for Michael. He was originally planning to sleep on your couch, remember?' Eric stretched out comfortably in the recliner.

'And Michael gave the copy to you instead of me?' Kate pulled two Cokes from the vegetable crisper.

'Yep, he figured if I had to come to your rescue, a key would come in handy.'

She chose not to comment on Michael's faith in her abilities. Instead, Kate handed Eric a Coke and launched into a summary of the hypnosis session. She omitted the details about entering and exiting the subconscious state and concentrated on the new information she'd learned.

Eric gazed up at the ceiling. 'So, under hypnosis, you saw Liam's two cronies and will be able to describe them to your brother.'

'Yes, but neither of them knocked out Liam. There was a third guy Liam didn't know about.'

'Could he have been the other armored car driver?'

'No, this guy had on a plaid flannel shirt – red, to be exact. The guards wear uniforms – white shirt with an insignia on the pocket, and black pants.'

'Chances are your brother will know who their ringleader recruited at the last minute.'

'That's what I'm hoping, especially since he probably got Liam's share of the loot after framing Liam to take the fall.'

'Sounds like you got your seventy-five bucks' worth. What do we do now?'

Kate tipped up the can and finished her drink. 'We can't talk to Liam until Saturday. And in the meantime, I've got my bread-and-butter case to work tomorrow. Let's go meet Steve Rivera, the lucky fiancé of a soon-to-be very wealthy woman. I need to track down the nearest Lexus dealership.'

'One step ahead of you, boss.' Eric sat upright in the recliner and pulled a piece of paper from his pocket. On it was the name and address of a dealership.

'Aren't you a handy man to have around? Speaking of paying jobs, how did your second night at Henri's go?'

He scrunched his nose, as though whiffing something foul. 'I need to find a suitable location to open another Bella. The owner accepted a delivery of fresh fish, just caught in the gulf yesterday. And what did he tell me to do with it?'

'I'm assuming you grilled it as the daily special.'

'That's what a sane chef would do. But my boss had me dip it in heavy batter and drop it in the deep fryer.' Eric closed his eyes to the painful memory. 'And we served it with fries and coleslaw.'

Kate had to hold her hand over her mouth to stop laughing. 'A restaurateur must cater to his or her clientele. This is the beach. People want ice cream, hot dogs, and stuff fried. Me, I love fried flounder under a thick blanket of tartar sauce, with creamy coleslaw, Cajun fries, and lots of catsup.' She rubbed her belly in a circular motion.

Eric stood and lifted his chin with imperious dignity. 'With that comment, Miss Weller, I'll take my leave. I'll meet you in the breakfast bar at eight-thirty.' He opened the door and closed it none too quietly behind him.

But before he reached his suite, Kate hollered down the hallway, 'See you then, my favorite hash-slinger. Just don't expect eggs Benedict or crème brûlée.'

Kate laughed herself silly as she bolted the door. But, if she was being honest, she liked Eric keeping tabs on her and sleeping only twenty feet down the hall. With Beth and Michael gone and her brother in jail, she was alone in the town where she grew up. She could call her last foster mother, but what could a fifty-something woman do with three teenagers still in the house? Having someone who looked out for her – especially someone who cared – helped her to fall asleep and remain asleep until morning.

At first her dreams were filled with tubs of fresh fish being battered and deep-fried by someone chained to the stove. But they ended with a handsome knight just returning from the Crusades, a knight who just happened to ride a white horse.

When Kate joined Eric at breakfast the next morning, he was eating plain toast and drinking black coffee.

'What . . . no ham and eggs with cheesy grits today?' she asked.

'No, I had a plate of fried fish after my shift yesterday to see why it's so popular, and I still have heartburn.' He nibbled his piece of toast.

'Different strokes, my friend,' Kate said. 'I'm not hungry either, so let's get going. The closest dealership is almost in Mobile. Luckily, that's the one where Steve Rivera works.'

While Eric drove west along I-10, Kate updated the Westin case file on her laptop. Eric seemed a million miles away today, so she steered clear of small talk. Once they arrived at a showroom filled with upscale automobiles, Eric popped out to open her door.

'Always the gentleman. I'm glad I brought you, Manfredi.' Kate exited the vehicle carefully in her snug sheath dress and high heels. High-end cars warranted the most expensive clothes in her closet which, in her case, hadn't been very expensive at all.

'You look very nice today, boss,' he said, offering her his hand. Eric must have had the same idea regarding apparel. He was dressed in pressed chinos, a starched shirt, and a linen sport coat.

Kate took his arm but muttered under her breath. 'Thank you, but you should curb those kinds of comments. Since temporarily I am your boss, there are federal laws against sexist behavior in the workplace.'

'I'm not allowed to say you look nice?' Eric looked bewildered.

'You may not.' Kate smoothed down her dress with one hand. 'Let's just pretend we're in the market for a snazzy car, at least until we're face to face with Mr Rivera.'

Once inside the lavish showroom, they were approached by not one but two sales professionals. Eric smiled at one, while Kate greeted the other. 'Good morning,' she drawled. 'I'm

Kathryn Weller. A friend of ours recommended this dealership and told us to ask for Steve Rivera.'

'Yes, ma'am, sir,' said the female salesperson, nodding at them. 'I'm so sorry, but Mr Rivera is out ill today. But I'd be happy to help you . . . or perhaps Mr Prentiss?' She gestured to her cohort. 'He has twenty-two years in the luxury car business.'

Kate smiled demurely. 'As far as I'm concerned, you both look quite competent. But our friend insisted that we deal directly with Mr Rivera. Could we wander around and narrow down our choices? Then we can make an appointment after Mr Rivera returns.' Kate kept grinning until she thought her face might crack.

'Absolutely!' chimed Miss Stokes, according to her name-plate. 'Take all the time you need. Our customer lounge has coffee, tea, soft drinks, snacks and high-speed WiFi – complimentary, of course.' She pointed a well-manicured hand toward a doorway.

'Come on, honey.' Eric grabbed Kate's hand. 'Let's get started. I can't wait to drive one of these beauties.'

'Just remember, dear, we're not buying anything today.' Kate let Eric drag her to a sleek sports car.

'Five-liter V-8 engine, 471 horsepower, ten-speed automatic transmission.' Eric read off an impressive list of features. 'Let's check out the interior.' While Kate climbed in the passenger side, he slid in behind the wheel. 'I have fallen in love.'

'You'd better be talking about the car.' Kate leaned back in the most comfortable seat ever and closed her eyes.

'Of course, I am. Glass top, heated and ventilated seats, heated leather-trimmed steering wheel. Too bad I just bought my Expedition. But maybe it's time we traded in yours.'

'Have you totally lost your mind?' she whispered. 'We are *not* a married couple, shopping for an expensive car. We're supposed to be working. Besides, I drive a Price Investigations' vehicle and Nate would never lease one of these. He's seen how I parallel-park.'

'Too bad, because this is one gorgeous set of wheels.' Eric smoothed his hand across the dashboard.

'Please focus on why we're here.' Kate elbowed him in the ribs.

'Yes, ma'am, but I don't think we'll learn much from Rivera's employees. Why would they discuss a media smear campaign with perspective car buyers?' Eric adjusted the seat to accommodate his long legs.

'That's a good point. We should visit Rivera's competition in the area. Maybe they'll dish whatever dirt Agnes Westin put in motion.'

Eric shook his head. 'That won't work either. Spreading negative press would make them liable in a slander lawsuit.'

Kate swiveled around to face him. 'Look at you – putting your law school background to good use. But you're right. We need to pay Lainey's fiancé a visit and ask him outright. Rivera's reaction alone might tell us plenty.'

'Good idea, but first let's test-drive this beauty.' Eric gripped the wheel with both fists. 'We could open her up on Route 10. Zero to sixty in less than five seconds – can you imagine?'

'What I imagine is a long string of speeding tickets. On so many levels, Manfredi, you're even worse than Beth. I'll call Michael for Rivera's home address. That guy can find it faster than us.' Kate climbed out of the car.

'While you do that,' said Eric, climbing out too, 'I'll take a quick peek under the hood.'

Kate shook her head and pulled out her cell phone.

Ten minutes later, when Miss Stokes approached, Eric still had his head under the hood.

'From your smile, may I assume you like our luxury coupé, Mr Weller?' asked the sales rep, making a natural assumption regarding his name.

'I do indeed, but my wife reminded me that, with her delicate condition, we should probably look at sedans or SUVs.' Eric mimicked rocking a baby in his arms.

Luckily, Miss Stokes had already pivoted on one stiletto, so she didn't see Kate's murderous expression. 'Oh, that's wonderful news. Over there we have our LS or the LX, every bit as luxurious, but more practical for a growing family.'

'Goodness.' Kate pressed a hand to her still flat stomach. 'I'm not feeling so well. I believe we'll come back another day to continue our search.' She sighed as though the troubles of womanhood were too much to bear.

'Of course. Feel free to drop in any time or call first to make sure Mr Rivera is here that day.' Miss Stokes's smile could rival a pageant contestant's in the final round of competition.

'That's what we'll do.' Eric wrapped his arm around Kate's shoulders and walked her out of the building.

Kate allowed this to continue until they reached his car. 'Are they still watching us?' she demanded.

Eric glanced over his shoulder. 'Mr Prentiss is. I think that man has a crush on you.'

'Let me know when he turns around.' She hissed through gritted teeth. 'Because I fully intend to shoot you in a non-vital organ.'

Eric threw his head back and laughed with abandon. 'Now for sure I've reached Beth Kirby's level of partnership. She told me you two wanted to wrestle in the alley most days.'

'That's the truth,' said Kate with a chuckle. 'But Beth always got the job done. She put the job before mealtime, leisurely pursuits, and even mud wrestling. Keep that in mind, Manfredi.' She set the GPS for the address provided by Michael and stepped on the gas.

While she drove, Eric checked his email and called his sister for an update on the family restaurant. From how often he told his sister, 'We'll discuss that some other time,' Kate assumed everything wasn't running smooth-as-silk back in Charleston. As Eric spent more and more time helping on the Westin case and serving as her personal bodyguard, the less and less she believed he was here to scout new restaurant locations.

She had already convinced herself she wasn't in love with him back in Charleston. This time it wouldn't be so easy. Eric Manfredi was a nice guy. He was loyal, steadfast, and true. But unlike a cocker spaniel or Labrador retriever available at any pound or rescue organization, Eric was also handsome, competent, and cooked food that made a diet look like a silly notion. Plus he *wanted* to be near her. For the first time in Kate's life, she was someone's first choice. And that made falling in love with him hard to resist.

When they arrived at Steve Rivera's condo, they found him

not only home but in sweat pants and drinking a can of ginger ale. Feeling under the weather hadn't been a ploy.

'Mr Rivera? Sorry to bother you, but could we ask you a few questions? I'm Kate Weller and this is Eric Manfredi, my business partner.'

Rivera's forehead furrowed with confusion. 'Are you the Mr and Mrs Weller who were at my showroom looking at the LC? I don't normally sell vehicles from my home.'

For some reason, Kate hadn't anticipated Miss Stokes or Mr Prentiss calling their boss. 'I'm sorry. I owe you an explanation. I . . . we work for Lainey Westin. We're investigating her mother's death, not shopping for a car.'

Rivera's expression didn't change. 'Come in and have a seat. I'd wondered which pair of newlyweds would demand that *I* sell them one of our top-end vehicles.'

They followed him into a tasteful living room, but nowhere near as chic as Lainey's condo. 'I apologize for the subterfuge, sir. I thought the least invasive place to ask a few questions would be at your place of business.' Kate sat on an overstuffed sofa.

'So when I called off sick, you made up a wild tale?' Rivera leaned against a floor-to-ceiling bookcase.

Eric answered before Kate had a chance. 'I'm responsible for that. I've wanted to climb into an LC for a long time and today I got my chance. What an impressive machine.'

Rivera's eyes lit up with the praise. 'In that case, you're both excused. The LC is an engineering marvel. Now what can I help you with, Mrs Weller?'

'Kate, please. We heard a rumor that Agnes Westin wasn't fond of you and didn't want you to marry her daughter. Was this true?'

'Unfortunately, it was. She hated my Latin background and did everything in her power to make trouble.' Rivera swept his hair back from his forehead. 'Funny part was Agnes always called me "Esteban," thinking it would annoy me. Esteban just means "Steve" in Spanish. That's what my grandparents called me. So why would it annoy me?'

'I also heard troubling gossip that I'd like you to confirm or deny. Did Agnes Westin attempt a negative publicity campaign against your Lexus dealership?'

Rivera pushed off the wall of books and settled in a chair. 'She did. Up until then, she'd kept her vitriol on a personal level.'

'What exactly did she do?'

'Agnes posted on Facebook that she'd bought a car that was a lemon. *What does that even mean?*' Rivera's dark eyes could bore a hole through concrete. 'I don't sell used vehicles, and the manufacturer's warranty is one of the best in the industry. Any problem with one of our cars would have been immediately corrected to the customer's satisfaction.'

'So the post wouldn't have had much effect,' Eric murmured.

'Correct. Few people in our target market are even on Facebook. And, if they are, they're not looking at automobile recommendations. Then Agnes filed a fictitious complaint with the Better Business Bureau. Since that organization investigates every allegation, I became aware of my future mother-in-law's chicanery.'

'You had to be hoppin' mad,' Kate said.

'I certainly was, but before you jump to the wrong conclusion, I wasn't angry enough to murder her.' A muscle tightened in Rivera's jaw.

'What did you do?'

'I called Lainey and told her. She's had years of experience dealing with an irrational woman. Lainey told dear old Mom she'd better withdraw her complaint and remove those Facebook posts or she would personally start her own smear campaign. Agnes has plenty of skeletons in her own closet. She took down the posts and contacted the bureau immediately.'

'Would any of those skeletons be helpful in her murder investigation?' Kate asked.

Rivera gazed at the ceiling before replying. 'Agnes is gone. Nothing will bring her back. But I plan to be married to Lainey for the rest of my life. I won't be the one divulging any family secrets.'

Personally, Kate respected his answer. Professionally . . . not so much. 'Were you aware that Agnes threatened to disinherit Lainey if she married you?'

A vein in his neck began to throb. 'I wasn't aware, but I'm not surprised. Lainey told me a lot about growing up with her mother. Agnes threatened to cut Lainey out of her will many times. She wanted her daughter to be exactly like her and used any manipulation to get her way.'

'You see where this puts *you* in the murder investigation?' Kate tried to look sympathetic. 'Agnes tried to ruin your business reputation, something that probably took you years to build. Plus, she threatened to disinherit your bride-to-be.'

'Actually, I don't see. My grandfather and father established the business's reputation for integrity years ago. I come to work each day holding my head high. It would take more than one bitter woman's lies to ruin me.'

From the corner of her eye, Kate saw Eric smiling, but Steve Rivera was by no means done.

'Regarding Agnes's estate, which you seem to think dangled like a plum in front of Lainey's nose?' He laced his fingers across his chest. 'Lainey had already inherited a fortune from her grandfather. Grandpa had established a trust when Lainey was still a child. Maybe he was aware of his daughter's recklessness. Regardless, she and I will be fine financially. Lainey isn't marrying a poor man. If you don't believe me, I'll show you my investment portfolio.' Rivera's words chilled the room by ten degrees.

'That won't be necessary,' murmured Kate. 'And I beg your pardon. Lainey hired me to find her mother's killer, not insult her future husband.'

'Apology accepted, but I must ask . . . isn't finding the killer a job for the police?'

'Yes, and they're working hard on the case. But your fiancée wanted to make sure no stone went unturned.'

Rivera released a hearty laugh. 'That sounds like her. Her relationship with Agnes was a love–hate conundrum.'

Kate rose to her feet. 'We've taken up enough of your time, Mr Rivera, especially since you're not feeling well. But could you think of anyone with a major grudge against Mrs Westin?'

'I'd look at those who worked for her. Behind her back they called her everything from "Wicked Witch of the South" to names that even made a grown man blush.'

'Why wouldn't they find work elsewhere?' Eric asked as they walked to the door.

'According to Lainey, Agnes paid twice the going rate. It's probably the only way she kept any help at all.'

'I've spoken to her gardener and he said the cook got along fine with Mrs Westin. I guess that leaves the housekeeper?' Kate held out her business card.

'I don't wish to sic the dogs on anyone.' Rivera tucked her card in his pocket.

'Understood.' Kate pulled open the door. 'Thank you again and best wishes on your upcoming marriage.'

Eric extended his hand. 'Forgive me for asking, but why did your employee think she and I were newlyweds?' he asked while they shook.

'Miss Stokes said you two were acting lovey-dovey, plus your first child was on the way. Was all that part of your subterfuge?'

Kate answered quickly. 'It certainly was.'

'Actually, only the part about the baby,' Eric amended as he closed the door behind them.

The moment Kate dropped off Eric and he disappeared into the hotel, she turned her car around and drove in the opposite direction. Although she hadn't lied to him, she also hadn't corrected his wrong assumption. Eric thought she was planning to visit Julian Buckley, the detective in charge of the Westin homicide. Had he known she was on her way to the Escambia County Sheriff's Department, he would have insisted on coming along. And, whether or not Eric needed to work for financial reasons, she wanted to talk to the detective who'd investigated the armored-car robbery alone.

Computer-savvy Michael Preston had sent her a file of everything he'd found on Liam's criminal past, which wasn't a whole lot. But at least the robbery–homicide detective who'd caught the case agreed to talk to her. The investigation had been closed shortly after Liam's confession, so no one should be watching. Nevertheless, Kate took a roundabout way to the station in case she was being followed.

'Miss Weller?' A deep voice startled Kate from her perusal of *Southern Living Magazine*. 'Hi, I'm Detective Tony Mendez.' A pleasant smile lifted his average features into the handsome category.

'Thanks for agreeing to see me on such short notice.' Kate extended a hand in need of a manicure.

'We can talk privately in here.' Instead of leading her back to his cubicle, Mendez opened the door to a small conference room off the busy lobby. 'Coffee, water, anything?'

'No, I'm fine.'

He took a chair at the table. 'You said on the phone you wanted to talk about your brother, Liam Weller. I couldn't place him, so I checked the database. Your brother is serving twenty-five to life after pleading guilty to aggravated homicide. Do I have the right Liam Weller?'

'You do. But recent information has come to light that suggests Liam never shot that security guard.'

Mendez shrugged. 'It makes no difference which one pulled the trigger in an armed robbery. All conspirators share the same degree of culpability. So, even if a new witness stepped forward, the new evidence would have no bearing on Liam's conviction.'

'I understand. But if the parole board heard that Liam wasn't even there when the guard died – that he had no intent to hurt anyone – they might grant parole on his first attempt.'

'I made a call after talking to you. Your brother has been a model prisoner. As long as that doesn't change, he already has a good chance at parole. So why are you really here, Miss Weller?'

Kate wasn't prepared for Mendez's bluntness. She paused, then stammered, then raked a hand through her hair. 'This is why I don't play poker,' she said.

The detective smiled as he waited for her explanation.

'I was ten when my brother was locked up. After that I had nothing to do with him, yet someone has been keeping tabs on me for years. They wanted to make sure I didn't remember that night.'

'You were *there*?' he asked, skepticism evident in his tone.

'Rumor has it.' Kate launched into an abbreviated version of the events. 'But I never had any desire to remember. As far as I was concerned, my brother was a loser who deserved to be in jail.'

'You'll get no argument from me. What changed your mind?'

'Despite the fact I had no contact with Liam, the phone calls continued during high school and college – not often, maybe every six months or so. A man would call and say, "I haven't forgotten you, Katie-girl" and then hang up.'

'Wait a minute.' Mendez scratched at his ear. 'You're saying someone has bothered you for years, yet you never went to the police?'

'No actual threats were ever made. I thought the police would consider them prank calls from a rejected boyfriend.'

'So when did things change?' he asked, not refuting her assumption.

Kate inhaled a deep breath. 'I'd been working for Industrial Commission as an investigator. In other words, spying on claimants who aren't as *disabled* as they profess. But I left that job and went to work for a PI firm out of Mississippi. I have since received weapons training, along with my license to carry.'

'And your stalker became nervous,' he concluded.

'It would seem so, even though my career change had nothing to do with Liam.'

'So what happened? I'm assuming the prank calls escalated into something else?' Mendez pulled a tablet from his drawer.

'Yes, if you agree that a blown-up car is an escalation.'

'Your car?'

'My boyfriend's SUV. Someone called and warned me at the last minute, which saved Eric's life.'

'And you think this car bomb is connected to a sixteen-year-old robbery you witnessed, but don't remember.' Mendez pressed his fingertips to his eyelids.

'I know it is.' Kate spoke with utter assurance. 'Now that I've answered your questions, I want to know why you never tracked down Liam's accomplices. Why was he the only one prosecuted for that fatal robbery?'

He fixed her with a glare. 'Rest assured it wasn't my idea to close the case. Your brother confessed to being the triggerman and the mastermind. We found zero evidence at the crime scene that identified the others involved. When Liam took the plea deal and refused to identify his co-conspirators, the DA at the time told me to shelve the case until new evidence surfaces. We never have a shortage of unsolved homicides to work. I'm not the boss so I'm forced to follow orders.'

She nodded. 'So you never found out who they were.'

Mendez huffed out a breath. 'I know exactly who they were, or at least a ninety percent hunch. It wasn't too hard to figure out who Liam hung out with at the time. But, as I mentioned, no evidence connected them to the crime, and without evidence I can't request an arrest warrant.'

Kate stared at him with her mouth open. 'Was one of them dark-haired and -eyed, wears glasses, and doesn't see the value of a daily shower?'

'That would be Charley Crump, who I believed to be the mastermind, not your brother.'

'And the other man very skinny with kind of reddish hair?'

'That was Jimmy Russell, someone Liam met when he went to Juvenile Hall. How would you know that if you have no memory of that night?'

'Let's leave that alone for the moment. You knew who they were but they still went free?'

'As I said, Miss Weller, I didn't have a shred of evidence connecting them to the hold-up or the shooting. And neither of them spent copious amounts of money in the years since. If they robbed that armored car and got away with it, what happened to the half-million dollars that went missing?'

Kate exhaled through her nostrils. 'I have no idea. Maybe it's in some offshore account. Which one of them do you think has been my stalker?'

'Well, it definitely isn't Jimmy Russell. He shot himself while hunting three years after the hold-up. The coroner listed the shooting as an accidental death, but I always thought it a suicide. Maybe he couldn't live with himself after killing that guard. And that could be why he never spent all that money.'

'Then it must be this Charley Crump. If he masterminded the robbery, he's probably the one who's afraid I'll regain my memory.'

'Doubtful. Charley Crump doesn't have the mental where-withal to rig a car with an explosive device. Even an armored car robbery was way out of his league. He's your average smash-and-grab kind of criminal.'

Kate sat silently for a moment. 'Then it has to be the third man in a red plaid flannel shirt, the one who knocked out Liam.'

Mendez's chin snapped up. 'What on earth are you talking about? Your brother was the third man. One of his pals knocked him out and he took the fall for them.'

Knowing there was no way around it, Kate told the detective about her two sessions with a hypnotherapist and then waited for him to break into hysterics. That never happened.

'I heard about hypnotic regression to restore suppressed memories, but they've never helped me solve a cold case.' He pushed his glasses up the bridge of his nose.

'I had my doubts, too, until you confirmed the two men I saw were Charley Crump and Jimmy Russell, two of Liam's cronies. If I accurately described those two, then the third man – the one who knocked Liam out – wasn't a figment of my imagination either.'

'What did he look like?' Mendez leaned forward in his chair.

'That's just it. I listened to the recording the therapist made several times, and I just plain didn't get a good look at him. All I can tell you is he was average size and wearing a red plaid flannel shirt.'

'Was he with Crump and Russell in the stolen car that crashed into the armored car?'

'I hadn't arrived on the scene yet. Neither had Liam.'

'And your brother didn't see who hit him?'

'No. When he came to, the gun was in his hand and everyone else was gone.'

Mendez pulled the case file towards him. 'So this fourth gang member probably took the loot and instilled serious fear in the other two. He, most likely, is your stalker and the mad car bomber.' He rummaged through the papers. 'Looks like my cold case is officially reopened. I'll go have another chat with Charley Crump and ask someone to look at the Russell shooting with fresh eyes.'

'What about the other armored car driver – the one who ran off? Could he have been in on it?'

'I spent hours keeping an eye on him. After the heist he

took a short medical leave, but was back on the job two weeks later. The guy has no police record, married to his high-school sweetheart with two kids, lives in Ensley, and goes to church every Sunday. I ran a check on his financials for years, but no windfalls of cash ever surfaced.'

'So what can I do to help, Detective?' Kate asked.

He stared at her. 'Find a safe place to stay until this is over with and don't let *anyone* near your car. This is a job for the police, not a private investigator.'

'But I could—'

'No, Miss Weller. You've already helped by telling me about the fourth man. Although let's hope I never have to testify in court as to how I came by that information. Juries usually aren't open-minded about things like hypnosis, past-life regressions, and out-of-body travel.'

'It was a present-life regression. I don't believe in reincarnation and I certainly never left my body.'

'Whatever, you get my point. Do you need to be placed in protective custody?'

'That won't be necessary. I have a bodyguard provided by my pals at the agency. I ditched him to come here alone.'

Mendez stood and handed her his card. 'Take this and call me if you get any more threats. And, in the meantime, no more ditching the bodyguard. You'll need him until this is over.'

'If I'm not safe, neither is Liam. Bad things happen all the time in maximum security prisons.'

'I can't move him to a safe house, but I'll check into the situation. Right now, I'm walking you to your car to make sure the undercarriage is clean.'

Kate left the Escambia County Sheriff's Office with a bad feeling deep in her gut. She'd had this sensation before. It was fear. But this time it was for Liam, a brother she'd all but given up on.

ELEVEN

When Kate got back to her hotel room, Eric was sitting on her sofa. 'Did you get fired already, Manfredi? Some master chef you are.'

He didn't so much as smirk at her joke. Instead Eric picked up his phone and tapped a few keys. 'Good evening, Miss Weller. Pour yourself something to drink and make yourself comfortable. I just sent Beth a text. She will be calling you in a few minutes.'

'Why would Beth be calling me now?' Kate asked, glancing at her watch. But she already knew the answer.

Eric fixed her with a cool stare. 'Business was slow tonight, so when the boss told me I could leave early, I had the waitress ring up two shrimp dinners, which I then cooked. I thought we could eat supper down by the pool. But when you weren't here, I realized that me being your bodyguard wasn't working.'

'So you alerted Beth and Michael?' Kate perched on the arm of the couch, her drink forgotten.

'Yes and not just them. I called your boss too,' Eric muttered through gritted teeth. 'I care about you, Kate. Since that means nothing to you, I called the other people who care about you. Maybe you'll listen to one of them.'

Kate felt her cheeks grow warm as her eyes stung with tears. 'I care about you too.'

'You sure have a strange way of showing it.'

'I went to see Tony Mendez, the detective who investigated Liam's robbery–homicide sixteen years ago.'

Eric dropped his face into his hands. 'You're even more reckless than I thought.'

'What I *am* is embarrassed by this whole business with my brother. You already got caught up in this once. I won't have you killed because of my family.'

Eric sat for a minute, immovable. Finally, he stood and

walked toward the door. 'Maybe Beth can talk sense into you, because I'm done here. Not everything is your decision, Kate.' Then he was gone.

Kate felt frightened and nervous. Not for her safety, but because she had pushed Eric to the edge. It had only been a matter of time. There was good reason why she'd never had a serious romantic relationship at her age. If her phone hadn't rung, she would have cried herself silly.

Picking up her phone, she held it a couple of inches from her ear. 'Hello, Beth.'

'Don't you "hello" me. Did someone drop you on your head as a baby? What's the matter with you?'

'There are too many things to list. Let's cut to the chase, shall we?'

'All right then, let's. Why won't you let Eric back you up while you're gallivanting all over Pensacola?'

'*Back me up?* Eric doesn't even carry a weapon.'

'Actually, he does.'

'You gave him one of your guns, a gun he doesn't even know how to use? How totally irresponsible.'

'No, Kate. I didn't give Eric anything. He brought his own weapon from Charleston and knows exactly how to use it. Now, I'm going to talk while you listen.' Beth paused to see if she had the guts to argue, but Kate did not. 'You agreed to work with Eric or Michael and I never would have left. We're up to our eyebrows on a new case and can't drive to Florida until Friday, at the earliest. As much as I don't want to, you've left me no choice but to ask Nate to fire you. You don't know how to be part of a team.'

The sincerity in her friend's tone turned Kate's blood to ice water as the one thing she wanted more than anything evaporated before her eyes. No, make that two things – her job and Eric, because he was as good as gone too.

'I won't stop seeking the truth about my brother's case,' Kate said feebly.

'I realize that, but without Price Investigations footing the bill for your expenses, you'll be forced to get another job and only investigate on your free time. I'm still willing to help on the weekends, except for the one I'm getting married.'

If Beth had been trying to make her feel guilty, she couldn't have done a better job.

'Please don't call Nate. I'm willing to change, if you give me one more chance.'

Beth sighed with exasperation. 'Will you work strictly on the Westin homicide *with* Eric and leave everything else until Michael and I get there?'

'I would, but Eric has already washed his hands of me. He stormed out of here ten minutes ago.' After her true confession, Kate burst into tears.

'You'll get no pity-party from me, girlfriend. You had that coming.'

'I know,' Kate wailed. 'Could you talk to him? Please, Beth? Eric will listen to you.' She sat for a full minute, listening to the icemaker replenish cubes, while noise from the pool dwindled to one country music station.

'I could, but I won't. If you want to salvage whatever it is you have with that man, walk down to his room and beg for mercy. Do it tonight before he checks out and heads back to his sane life in Charleston.'

Kate hiccupped. 'I'm going right now. Will you still be awake if I call you later?'

'You think I could sleep while your entire life implodes?' Beth screeched. 'Yes, call me later. And good luck.'

Kate heard the click as her call to action. Without washing her face or refreshing her makeup, she blew her nose and marched out her room, not bothering to grab her key card. At Eric's door she knocked with conviction. When no one answered, Kate knocked again, fully prepared to keep knocking until the door opened or the manager appeared with an eviction notice.

'Okay, okay, hold your horses.' The door opened a few inches, revealing Eric in sweat shorts and a T-shirt. 'Can't a guy heat up his dinner?'

'Not unless he has enough for a neighbor who's lost her two best friends in the whole world,' Kate said meekly.

Eric crossed his arms. 'That would be Beth and Michael?'

'No, Michael thinks I'm a crazy-woman. That would be Beth and you.'

'I also think you're a crazy-woman.'

'No argument here, but hopefully you'll let me apologize while we eat shrimp and rice.'

The door remained at six inches. 'I need to know exactly what you're sorry about.'

'For going back on my word to you and Beth.' Kate hesitated, finding the second part harder to say but far more important. 'And for letting my personal baggage keep you at arm's length. I swear I don't want to do that anymore.'

'I'm not looking for commitment, Kate, only the assurance you'll let me help you.' Eric spoke softly, but with the clarity of a man who knows his mind.

'I understand. I want your help on the Westin case and with my brother's mess. And most of all I want your friendship.'

'All right. First we'll eat, then we'll call Beth. We'll have a four-way discussion of what you learned tonight from the detective and how she and Michael think we should proceed. Do you agree?'

'I do, with my whole heart.'

Then the door, along with her second chance, swung open.

After eating dinner on his balcony, Kate punched in Beth's number and put her phone on speaker. Beth did the same for Michael's benefit. Kate filled everyone in on what she learned from Detective Mendez, including his decision to reopen the cold case. Next she reassured Beth and Michael that Eric would accompany her everywhere except to the ladies' room and brought them up to date on the Westin case.

'So Lainey's fiancé struck you as an upfront kind of guy?' Beth asked after Kate finished.

'Yes, apparently Agnes had threatened to disinherit Lainey many times over the years. This was nothing new. Plus Lainey inherited a big chunk of cash from her grandfather.'

'And Steve Rivera told us he has plenty of money,' Eric added to the conversation. 'Although I'd like Michael to verify that if he gets a chance.'

'No problem,' Michael interjected.

'So who does that leave?' Beth demanded.

'Okay, let me review,' said Kate. 'Kim Westin had plenty

of motive, but no access to the house or boat that day. Mark Harris had tons of access but no motive. In fact, Agnes's death seriously crimps his future plans. If it turns out Rivera is as loaded as he says, we need to look at the household staff. According to Rivera, one of them had a problem with Agnes in the past – the housekeeper. She could still be carrying a grudge.'

Eric took control. 'Kate and I will return to the Westin home first thing tomorrow. The house sits empty, but the staff is maintaining the property until after probate. Hopefully, Lainey paid them while she was there.'

'Kate, do you agree with this plan?' Beth asked.

'Yes, of course I do. I will go nowhere without Eric.'

'He has our blessing to duct-tape you to a chair if necessary, including a wide piece over your mouth.'

'You've made your point, Beth.'

'Good. We'll try to get there Friday night. Now turn off the speaker, hand the phone to Eric, and walk away, Kate.'

Kate couldn't hear a single word being said, but she could see Eric's face from the bathroom doorway. He listened, then smiled, then laughed; then finally all the color drained from his face.

That evening they swam in the pool and watched an old movie on TV, but Kate didn't have the guts to ask about Beth's final instructions.

Eric volunteered no information, not that night nor on the way to Mrs Westin's in the morning. To pass the time, Kate called Lainey with a case update and to make sure she'd paid the hired help. She had. Once they pulled into the driveway, Eric was first to break the silence.

'Who should we question first? We still haven't talked to the cook. She's still on the payroll and would've had access to the picnic hamper that day.'

Kate climbed out of the car. 'True, but I doubt that she's here today. Who on earth would she be cooking for? Plus the cook got along well with Mrs Westin, according to the gardener. Let's talk to him again and then track down the housekeeper.'

'He sure had a bug up his nose. You take the lead, boss,' Eric added.

They found the horticulturist in a tidy cottage behind the garage, sharpening his shears and clippers with a grinding wheel. Seeing the array of sharp objects didn't imbue Kate with extra confidence.

'Excuse me, Mr Chapman, Kate Weller and Eric Manfredi. Could you spare us a few minutes?'

Frowning, Chapman turned around with a scythe in his hand. 'I remember who you two are.'

'Wow. I've only seen one of those in old movies.' Kate pointed at the tool. 'What on earth do you cut with it?'

'Nothing, not for a long while. But I want to be ready if the neighbor lets his yard turn into a pasture again. I won't have every kind of varmint nesting close to my roses. Now what do *you* want?' he snarled.

'First, you're going to put down that tool,' said Eric. 'Then you'll lose the bad attitude. We had enough of it two days ago. Then you're going to answer this lady's questions, either the easy way or the hard way.' Eric loomed over the gardener like a storm cloud.

'Fine, no need to get huffy.' Chapman placed the scythe on the workbench. 'What do you want to ask?'

Kate choked back a smile. 'First, tell me about the blowouts you had with Mrs Westin. After all, the woman wasn't easy to get along with.'

Chapman squinted, peering from Kate to Eric. 'Don't know who you been talkin' to, but I *never* argued with the old lady. She paid so much better than the rest, I just said "yes, ma'am" and "no, ma'am" to any cockamamie request she had.'

Eric resumed his benign posture. 'Then tell us who did have a grudge.'

Chapman glanced down at his dusty boots. 'Man, I don't like stirring up trouble.'

Kate poked his shirt with her index finger. 'You don't have much choice. Start talking.'

He lowered himself to a stool. 'Mrs Westin overheard Luisa – she's the housekeeper – talking to Betty – she's the cook – that her son couldn't find work as a carpenter. And that if he didn't find a job soon he'd have to go back to Mexico. Well, Mrs Westin butts in and offers Luisa's son a job as a handyman. She had a long list of repairs she wanted done around this place.'

'What kind of work?' asked Kate.

'Everything from painting all the bedrooms, to cleaning gutters, to adding on to the sun porch. Mrs Westin asked to see his work visa because she didn't want trouble with the INS and Luisa gives her a photocopy.' Chapman pulled off his cap and ran a hand through his gray hair. 'Mrs Westin saw that it had expired, so she calls the Immigration office. She thought since Miguel had a job, there wouldn't be a problem getting the visa renewed.'

'But there was a problem,' Kate murmured.

'Yeah, a big one. On Miguel's first day on the job, immigration officers arrived and hauled him away. They detained him for three days to make sure there were no warrants out for his arrest and then deported him back to Mexico.'

'And Luisa became upset with Mrs Westin,' Eric concluded.

'Upset isn't the word for it. Luisa believed Agnes purposely made trouble for her son, which wasn't true. Mrs Westin was an old woman. She didn't understand how the world works. She asked Luisa, "What's wrong with Miguel going home for a few months? Your family probably comes from a sweet little *pueblo*."' Chapman slapped his cap against his pant leg. '*A pueblo*. Agnes probably learned that word from an old Clint Eastwood movie. You know the kind – men wearing big sombreros, strumming guitars in the shade.'

Kate felt a jolt of fear for two people she'd never met. 'That would be an inaccurate description?'

'You've got no idea. The Gonzales family is from Matamoros in the state of Tamaulipas, an area well known for cartel warfare. Miguel probably had been pressured to join one faction or the other. That's why he came to the US in the first place. Where he comes from, young men aren't allowed to be conscientious objectors.' Chapman kept glancing at the door, as though fearing an invasion of gun-wielding thugs.

'How long ago was this?' Kate pulled out her notepad for the next round of questions.

'Six or seven months.'

'Did Miguel apply for another work visa?'

'Of course he did, but it ain't that easy. Especially since he didn't dot all his i's the first time around.'

'And Luisa was still angry with Mrs Westin?' asked Eric.

'Wouldn't you be? Miguel went right back to a war zone.'

'Why couldn't Mrs Westin speak to Immigration on Miguel's behalf?'

'She did, but it did no good. You gotta follow the rules. By the time her attorney filed an appeal, Miguel was back in Mexico. Mrs Westin even contacted her congressman to intervene with the Mexican government, but all that bureaucratic red tape takes time.'

'Does Luisa know about this?' asked Eric.

'No, Mrs Westin didn't want to get her hopes up until her son re-entered the States. I suppose *that plan* will fall by the wayside.' Chapman turned his grinding wheel on. 'Is that it, Miss Weller? I gotta get some work done.'

'Only a few more questions, I promise.' Kate switched the grinder off. 'Since Luisa still works here, I take it things went back to normal after their initial blow-out.'

He thought long and hard before replying. 'Only on the surface. I asked Luisa why she's still here. She said she wanted to stay close to the *she-devil* in case something happens to Miguel. Then she would make sure Mrs Westin suffered the same kind of pain.'

Eric straightened his spine and fixed the gardener with a glare. 'I hope you're not fanning the flames, Chapman. We've got no reason to believe something happened in Matamoros.'

'No, we don't,' he snapped. 'But Luisa always heard from her son every Sunday. Miguel would call like clockwork to check on his mother. And she hasn't heard from him in a month. Make of that whatever you will.' The gardener pulled off his gloves and stomped out, thus ending their interrogation.

Kate and Eric walked from the airless potting shed into the sunshine as Chapman disappeared around the corner of the house.

'What are you thinking, boss?' Eric asked. 'Should we go question Luisa? I bet you're eager to search her room.'

Kate thought for a few moments while sweat pooled on her upper lip. 'As enticing as that sounds, anything she admits or anything we find in her room wouldn't be admissible in court. I need to call Detective Buckley. If Luisa is our poisoner – assuming that was the cause of death – we need to follow the letter of the law. Lainey and her mother deserve justice. Let's call from the car where there's air conditioning.'

Detective Julian Buckley was not only in his office, but he picked up on the first ring and listened without interruption. 'Is that it?' Buckley asked after Kate recounted their conversation with the gardener.

'Isn't that enough?' Kate asked, flummoxed.

'It's enough if I'm only interested in chatting with a Mexican housekeeper. That's not even close to being enough to obtain a search warrant. Do you know for sure that Miguel Gonzalez is dead?'

'No, but he always called his mother on Sundays.'

'My mom lives in Jamaica. She'd be happy to give you an earful as to how many times I disappointed her.'

'But Luisa had access to the picnic hamper on the day Mrs Westin died,' Kate said.

'Yes, I made that connection five minutes ago. But it's still not enough for a search warrant.'

Kate sucked in a deep breath. *What did her mentor, Beth Kirby, always say?* If you smell smoke, chances are there's a fire nearby. 'What if we had permission to search the house?' she blurted. 'If the housekeeper has a room somewhere in the house, wouldn't the owner have legal access to it?'

'Good point, Miss Weller. The owner maintains full access to the home, unless the housekeeper has a signed affidavit that grants private quarters. However, being that the owner of the house died, she can't give us permission to search.'

'According to Agnes's will, Lainey Westin owns the house and has assumed responsibility by paying the wages of the household help.'

This gave the homicide detective something to consider. 'Lainey has paid Luisa Gonzalez as the heir apparent?'

'Yes, she paid her on Tuesday.'

'And you think Lainey would let the police search her mother's house?' he asked.

'In a heartbeat. She wants her mother's killer caught.' Kate tossed her conjecture up into the air, hoping it was true.

'I would want Miss Westin here, giving us permission to search in front of witnesses. If we find anything – which we probably won't – it could be tossed out of court on a technicality otherwise.'

'I'll text her and insist she meet us here ASAP.' Kate chanced a glance at Eric. He seemed to be biting the inside of his mouth.

'All right, Miss Weller,' said Buckley. 'Text me if anything changes. Otherwise I'll be at the Westin house in twenty minutes with a couple of cops.' The detective hung up before Kate could rethink her plan or hedge the anticipated outcome.

'Want me to step out while you call Lainey?' Eric asked softly.

Kate shook her head. 'No, you watched me crawl out on a limb. If it breaks, I want you to witness my destruction.'

But lo and behold, Lainey did not refuse her request. When Kate explained she had good reason to suspect someone on the household staff, Lainey drove straight from a late lunch with college pals to the mansion. She brought along a copy of her mother's will, which her attorney had just filed in Probate Court. The house was hers. Thus, as new owner, she sent Luisa on an errand to pick up her dry cleaning. Once Luisa left, Lainey gave Detective Buckley permission to search the entire house in front of Kate, Eric, and Betty the cook, who was cleaning out the pantry.

Buckley didn't mess around with basement cubbies or seldom-used trunks in the attic. He and two uniformed officers worked their way systematically through the housekeeper's quarters, while Kate and Eric made small talk with Lainey in the hallway. Since the furnishings were sparse and housekeepers weren't usually known for expansive wardrobes, the search didn't last long.

'Take a look at this, Kate,' Buckley called, using her given name for the first time. With gloved fingers he pulled a bottle from a shoebox labeled 'important papers,' and held it up for everyone to see.

Although Kate didn't recognize the brand-name of rat killer, the warning label was quite obvious. Warning: toxic substance – fatal if ingested. Not to be sold in the US or Canada. 'Well, I'll be,' she said.

'She didn't buy that at the neighborhood hardware store,' said Eric.

One of the cops held open an evidence bag for Buckley. 'No, she did not. Get this to the lab right away,' Buckley said to the officer. 'Most likely it's the poison that killed Mrs Westin.'

'Will that be enough to convict her?' Lainey asked, stepping from the hallway shadows. The elegant woman looked a little green around the gills.

'It's certainly enough for an arrest warrant, Miss Westin.' Buckley softened his expression. 'We'll take things one step at a time. Forensics will compare this to substances found in your mother's blood sample.'

Kate took hold of Lainey's arm. 'You need to sit down. You look ready to faint.'

'I can't believe someone hated my mother enough to kill her.' She clung heavily to Kate all the way to the kitchen.

Eric filled a glass with water and handed it to her. 'Would you like us to call someone – your fiancé, perhaps?'

Lainey drank half the glass. 'No, Steve is still homesick. I don't want him driving here. I just need a few minutes, then I'll be fine.'

Buckley barked orders to his officers and radioed for backup, along with an APB with the make, model, and tag number for Luisa's car. 'Just in case she doesn't come back to work today,' he murmured to Kate and Eric. Then he left to get into position.

As soon as they were alone, Lainey gave Kate a hug. 'Thanks, Kate. I knew you wouldn't rest until the right person was in custody.'

'Thanks, but we're not done yet,' Kate said after returning the hug. 'Luisa's not in custody yet. And the police will need corroborating evidence.'

'Mrs Gonzalez could have been set up,' added Eric.

Lainey issued a dismissive snort. 'Luisa should have been fired long ago. Those people usually bite the hand that feeds them.'

'*Those people?*' Kate asked, feeling the little hairs on her neck stand on end.

'Domestic workers,' said Lainey. 'I don't care what their ethnicity . . . they all have the moral code of junkyard dogs.' She rose from the chair and glanced at her diamond-encrusted watch. 'Yikes. I need to meet my financial planner in thirty minutes.' Lainey flashed a smile on her way out the door. 'Send me a text when Vera Renczi is in jail. When this nightmare is over . . . you'll be getting a nice bonus.'

Kate and Eric locked gazes but didn't speak until they heard Lainey's tires squeal down the driveway. 'Who on earth is Vera Renczi?' Kate asked. 'And just between you and me, that apple didn't fall far from the nasty tree.'

Eric laughed. 'You're not kidding. I was hoping Little Miss Heiress turned out to be our killer. Some people just don't deserve a life of luxury.'

Suddenly, the apple-cheeked face of Betty appeared in the doorway. 'All right if I get back to cleaning out the pantry and cupboards?' she asked.

'I believe so,' said Kate. 'We're on our way out.'

Kate and Eric left through the front door just in time to see Luisa Gonzalez apprehended by eight members of law enforcement. The fifty-year-old housekeeper and murder suspect didn't resist arrest. They stayed long enough to see Luisa read her rights, handcuffed, and hauled off.

'Where we off to now, boss?' asked Eric the moment they climbed in the car. 'This day has sure taken an exciting turn.'

Kate started the engine. 'Back to the hotel. You need to get ready for work and I need to update my case file. Then I'm dying to jump in the pool.'

'Nothing doing. When I leave for the restaurant, you're staying locked in your hotel room. You'd make for an easy target swimming laps. You can swim tomorrow morning while I keep an eye out.'

Kate opened her mouth to protest the ridiculousness but remembered her promise. 'Okay, but what about dinner? Can I at least call for a pizza?'

'Definitely not. Who's to say the person delivering your

extra pepperoni, double-cheese calorie bomb isn't an assassin? I'll cook whatever you have a taste for after my shift.'

Kate decided against explaining the difference between a garden-variety killer and a trained assassin. 'I have my own personal chef just like Oprah?'

'Just like. Tell me your heart's desire.'

'Fresh grouper, grilled, with steamed broccoli and brown rice on the side. And since I'm being so healthy, I want bananas foster over vanilla ice cream, flambéed right at tableside.'

Eric rolled his eyes. 'You're an expensive woman to bodyguard.'

Kate smiled, thinking she might learn to like this after all.

Liam had spent plenty of time thinking about Charley Crump's visit. In fact, he'd been unable to think about much else. Charley had left Santa Rosa Correctional in a worse emotional state than when he'd arrived. Charley hadn't come to warn him or his sister. He feared for his own life. But who could Crump be afraid of if Jimmy Russell was dead and Doug Young hadn't shown up for the heist?

Why hadn't he known that Doug chickened out at the last minute? Why couldn't he remember those minutes before being knocked unconscious? And who had knocked him out?

With a dull ache behind his eyes, Liam stood in line for the payphone. He was tired of looking over his shoulder and tired of covering for the man who'd sold him out. He wasn't doing Kate any good behind prison walls and someone needed to provide the protection he couldn't.

Liam punched in the number for his new public defender and held his breath until someone picked up. 'I would like to speak with Mr Katz,' he said.

'I'm Julian Katz. What can I do for you?'

'This is Liam Weller, an inmate at Santa Rosa Correctional. I'd like you to arrange a meeting with the Escambia County District Attorney's office. I wish to give testimony regarding my accomplices sixteen years ago. There is no statute of limitations since someone died during the robbery.'

Liam waited while his file was located, then answered the anticipated questions: 'No, I'm not trying to obtain a new trial or overturn my conviction. I need protection for my family. I believe one of my co-conspirators is threatening my sister and her friends on the outside.'

Patiently, Liam explained the relevant particulars to save the lawyer time. And surprisingly, Attorney Katz not only sounded interested in his case but confident that he could get the DA there soon. Since attorneys were never denied access to their clients, Katz assured him he'd be in touch.

'You about done, Weller?' Darius Gage, Liam's least favorite guard, appeared behind him. 'Other men are waiting to use the phone.' The man swung his baton on a leather strap.

'Yeah, yeah, I'm done.' Liam hung up. He was so relieved to have taken a step in a positive direction he gave little thought to Gage's presence.

This particular guard never cared how long inmates talked on the phone or whether or not those in line ran out of patience and bashed in skulls. As long as he got his paycheck at week's end and the warden left him alone, Darius Gage was a happy man.

Unfortunately, he wasn't too happy at the moment. As soon as Liam re-entered his cell, Gage pulled out his cell phone and punched in a familiar number. 'Yeah, it's me,' said Gage. 'We've got a problem. Weller just asked his new public defender for a sit-down with the DA's office. He'd sell anybody down the river to keep his sister safe.'

TWELVE

After last night Kate thought she might enjoy having Eric around instead of Beth. The grilled grouper, herbed rice, and steamed broccoli in lemon butter tasted delicious. Yet they couldn't hold a candle to his Bananas Foster, which Eric had served poolside. With twinkling stars overhead and soft music drifting from the lounge, dinner would have been downright romantic if they were a couple. But they weren't.

Actually she wasn't sure what they were – business partners? Employer and employee? Captive and jailer? Their relationship defied description. Yet even without a defining label, they had eaten too much, laughed comfortably, and talked long into the night. Eric shared funny stories of growing up in a three-generation household with a grandfather who pretended not to understand English and a grandmother who didn't approve of her son's choice of a wife. Irena Manfredi, Eric's mom, hadn't been allowed to prepare anything other than salads in Bella Trattoria for years. Finally Alfonzo, Eric's dad, insisted that his wife be allowed to try her hand at the daily specials. Slowly, Irena won respect and acceptance from her mother-in-law.

Kate shared stories of the bizarre pets she and Liam had during their early years. When Eric's boa constrictor slipped its cage during one of the frequent escapes by Kate's gerbils, the siblings spent several frantic hours searching for the critters. In the end, her pet became dinner for his pet.

Despite how enjoyable dinner had been, Eric turned back into a professional bodyguard first thing this morning. Their pool time deteriorated into a shouting match. While Eric swam his forty laps, Kate called Julian Buckley for an appointment. Unfortunately the detective couldn't see her until late afternoon, and Eric's job was forty-five minutes away at the beach. Kate needed an in-person update on the Westin homicide, since it was much easier for the detective to decline information on the phone than if she were standing in front of him.

When Kate tried to explain this, Eric behaved like a stubborn mule. 'Call him back and ask for an appointment tomorrow morning.'

Kate stood her ground. 'That's ridiculous. Buckley is a busy man. If he can squeeze me in this afternoon, that's when I'm going. He'll think I'm a nutcase if I call him back.'

Eric boosted himself from the pool and reached for a towel. 'Who cares what he thinks? I'm more concerned about keeping you safe.'

'I appreciate that, but I care what he thinks. At least until the case is over.'

'No, Kate. We're going to the station together or you can conduct your business over the phone.' Eric tossed the wet towel over a chair.

'Excuse me? I agreed to accept your help, not take orders from you.' Kate pulled a long T-shirt over her head, feeling vulnerable in her swimsuit.

'What time can Buckley see you today?' Eric asked as a muscle jumped in his neck.

'Four o'clock.'

'Why don't I drop you off on my way to work? Then I'll pick you up after my shift and we can grab something to eat. How does that sound?'

'Sounds like you're making all my decisions. That's something I'm not used to.' Kate stuffed her three types of sunblock, hairbrush, and lip gloss into her bag.

Eric slipped on his flip-flops and followed her to the elevator. 'Every now and then we should let other people make our choices.'

Kate waited until the elevator opened to respond. 'That could be true, but it won't be today.' She stepped in but blocked his path. 'I'm driving to the police station and you're driving to the restaurant. I promise not to pick up hitchhikers.'

'You're a very stubborn woman,' he muttered under his breath.

'And you're trying to bully me!' Suddenly the elevator alarm buzzed.

'Could you let me in so we can discuss this like adults?'

But she didn't feel very adult-like. 'Nope, I'm going to my room. You can go back to the pool and soak your head.' As the door closed, she caught a glimpse of Eric's face. He looked more sad than angry, as though she'd just crossed some imaginary line in the sand.

After a long cool shower, she dressed in her most professional outfit, strapped on her holster, and drove to the station with one eye on traffic and the other on the rearview mirror. But no one had followed her – not any psycho-killer or trained assassin, and certainly not the man she was once in love with. And still was, if she was honest. She just had the hardest time showing it.

Inside the station, Detective Buckley seemed happy to see her.

'Miss Weller,' he greeted. 'Thanks for your patience. I had a few things to take care of this morning on the case. Let's go to the conference room where we can talk privately. If the other detectives find out I hang out with PIs, I'll lose my reputation as a hard-nose.' Buckley led her through a maze of cubicles where everyone seemed to be up to their eyebrows in paperwork.

'I appreciate you seeing me,' she said after he closed the door. 'Would you mind giving me an update?'

'After your phone call yesterday, it would be my pleasure. Have a seat.'

'Is Luisa Gonzalez still in custody?' Kate asked.

'Absolutely. Her bail hearing hasn't been set because she initially declined counsel. She refused a lawyer because she didn't want to get stuck with the bill. Once we explained in Spanish that an attorney would be appointed at no cost, she agreed. Now we're waiting for a bilingual public defender.'

'Do you think she'll get out on bail?'

'Not a chance. I'm asking the DA to charge her with capital murder. I'll talk to him later today. I believe we have enough evidence for the judge to set a trial date without presenting the case to a grand jury. This housekeeper is a piece of work. I talked to the cook after you and your partner left. Betty said Luisa always eavesdropped on Mrs Westin whenever her friends were over, and especially when she and Lainey had one of their legendary arguments. Luisa loved knowing Agnes's secrets. Maybe it made her feel powerful.' He shrugged.

'Did she say anything to substantiate her motive?' Kate asked.

'Plenty, and on video. After I explained she could have a free, Spanish-speaking attorney present during questioning, she said, "My English is fine. I don't need a lawyer – free or not."' Buckley leaned back and smiled. 'When I asked Luisa about her son, Miguel, I thought her head would explode. He's still stuck in Mexico. The government refuses to renew his work visa. They said he "abused the privilege," whatever that means, and won't consider any future requests.'

'Did you mention Mrs Westin had her congressman trying to intervene on Miguel Gonzalez's behalf?' Kate hoped it didn't sound like she was changing sides.

'I did, Miss Weller. I dotted the i's and crossed my t's. The last thing I need is an international media circus. I explained that Agnes had never meant for her son to be deported. Not knowing how bureaucracies worked, she only wanted Miguel's paperwork in order.' Buckley smiled again as though proud of himself.

'*And?*' Kate prompted.

'Luisa said that Agnes hated people "like her" and wouldn't do anything to help them. Her words, not mine.'

'Have you verified that Miguel is dead?'

'No, but I can't verify he's alive either. After landing in Matamoros, he seems to have dropped off the planet. I told her that just because we haven't located him yet, she shouldn't assume the worst. Then she said something in Spanish that didn't sound like "have a nice day." She also said she hoped the judge would deport her so her sister could visit her. I said it didn't work like that.'

Kate shook her head. 'The woman is truly clueless how the justice system works.'

'Before you go all softhearted, here's what we know according to the evidence. Number one – Mrs Gonzalez threatened Mrs Westin in front of witnesses, specifically that she would suffer like her son has suffered. Since she hadn't heard

from Miguel in a couple weeks, she believed him to be dead.
Number two – she packed the picnic hamper that morning
with food the cook prepared the night before and the cook
had that day off. Plus the tastiest morsel of all? The toxin
found in Mrs Westin's bloodstream exactly matched the rat
poison found in her closet. Since you can buy just about
anything online these days, including items not to be sold in
the US, I won't even include where the poison had been
manufactured.' Buckley leaned back in his chair. 'Before you
assume Luisa corresponded with flowery stationery and a
fountain pen, she had a laptop and ordered plenty of junk
online.'

'Did you log her computer into evidence?' Kate asked.

Buckley's grin was slow in coming. 'Yes, Miss Weller. I'm
not the rookie here. The techs are combing through it right
now, looking for anything I can use.'

Kate's chin snapped up. 'Don't you have enough already?'

'We'll let the District Attorney make that decision, but I've
got one small fly in the ointment. The forensic expert in the
ME's office couldn't find any poison in the remnants of Waldorf
salad. We believe that's where Luisa put it, since she knew
Mark Harris wouldn't touch the stuff. Luisa admitted that she
knew Harris was allergic to tree nuts including walnuts, even
after her lawyer advised her not to answer the question. Maybe
the poison was localized near the top and Agnes ate that part.'
Another shrug.

'Maybe there was another food Harris avoided,' Kate
suggested.

'Nope, I asked him and he said he ate everything else. Admit
it, Miss Weller. I've got a slam-dunk here.'

'Just about.' Kate jotted a few notes in her notebook. 'But
if it's just the same to you, I'm going to have another chat
with Mark Harris. Maybe he forgot to mention something.'

Buckley stood and pulled on his suspenders like an elderly
grandpa, instead of an attractive ex-Jamaican. 'Knock yourself
out. You get paid by the hour, along with expenses. Me? The
county pays me to collect evidence and then turn it over to
the DA to prosecute. I have lots of new cases to keep me busy.
I'll see you out the back door.'

Kate realized Buckley didn't want her walking past the other detectives' cubicles. 'I'm curious why you made time for me and also divulged pertinent information about the case.'

'Because I'm confident you'll use professional discretion and keep quiet about what we discussed. And because I'm grateful you made it easy to find the toxin during a legal search of Luisa's room. Another PI might have taken matters into her own hands and rendered whatever she found useless due to chain of possession.'

'I had a good teacher. My mentor trained me right.'

'Where's your car? I got a call from your new partner. He was worried, so I told him I would see you safely out of the parking lot.'

That Eric had called the Homicide Department didn't surprise Kate as much as the fact she couldn't remember where she'd left her car. After shading her eyes with one hand, her gaze fell not on her green Toyota, but a black Ford Expedition, parked on a side street. Eric's Ford Expedition – she would stake her life on it.

'Thanks, Detective, but that won't be necessary. I see my bodyguard parked across the street. He must have freed up his afternoon after all.' She flashed her prettiest smile at Julian Buckley, and for the one-time man-of-her-dreams? Kate curled her hands into fists and marched toward the black SUV with a nasty scowl. If it wasn't Eric Manfredi in the vehicle, the occupant would have feared for his or her life.

But, of course, it was.

Once Eric realized he'd been seen and that escape was impossible, he slouched down in the seat and hid behind today's edition of the *Pensacola News Journal*.

Kate yanked open the driver's door. 'You had better hope that restaurant owner doesn't fire you, because you're the worst PI in the world.'

Eric lowered his newspaper. 'Solo stakeouts haven't been covered in my training yet. You have only yourself to blame.'

'Eric, what are you doing here?' Kate asked softly, as though she didn't know the answer.

'I'm watching your back, partner. Beth bestowed the task

on me when she left town. And I honor my commitments.'
He lifted his chin defiantly.

'Seriously? You really think someone will shoot me in a
sheriff's department parking lot? Did you even bother to call
the restaurant?'

'Of course I did. I told Henri I had stomach flu. Believe
me, he'd rather I not spread viruses to his patrons. He told
me to come back when I felt better.'

'I can't believe you would risk your own career to sit in a
hot car all afternoon.' Beth rubbed the spot between her
eyebrows where a headache had begun.

'You were only in there for forty minutes. Besides, my
career is head chef back in Charleston. Henri's is a part-time
job to learn which properties are about to go on the market.'

Kate's patience was running razor-thin. 'Have you done
that, Eric? Have you learned about a single commercial
building about to be put up for sale?'

He focused his dark eyes on her. 'Low turnover in the
Pensacola area.'

Kate was in no mood to press the matter, not since she was
standing in the hot sun, surrounded by deputies coming and
going. But that time was coming . . . and sooner than Eric
would like. 'Fine,' she said. 'Since you're here, you might as
well follow me to Mark Harris's condo.'

Eric's forehead furrowed. 'Why? Isn't Luisa Gonzalez in
custody? Wasn't the poison a match to whatever killed
Mrs Westin?'

'Actually it was a match, but that doesn't mean someone didn't
plant it in her closet. Let's go talk to Harris a second time.'

He rubbed his chin. 'Now you have doubts, which you're
not expressing to the homicide department.'

'This isn't the best time for a PI lesson. Could you just
follow me to Harris's?' Like a petulant teenager, Kate marched
to her car and peeled from the lot.

By the time they reached Mark's high-rise, she regretted
her behavior. 'Sorry I yelled at you. It's nice that you want to
learn the ropes, but you already have a job.'

'Later we need to talk, Kate.' Eric gazed down from his
superior height.

'I agree, but right now let's see if Agnes's ex-boyfriend still lives here.'

Indeed, Mark Harris still lived there, but, from the looks of things, it wouldn't be for much longer. He immediately answered their knock, wearing a scruffy beard and even scruffier clothes.

'Miss Weller, Mr Manfredi, I didn't think I'd see either of you again.' Mark motioned them into a pared-down suite. 'Don't mind the mess. As you can see, I'm packing to move.'

'I thought Mrs Westin had paid the rent months in advance?' asked Kate, hoping her comment wasn't intrusive.

'She did, but I was offered an internship at a major museum in Chicago, part of a work/study program at the university. It includes a dorm room with a small living stipend. I'm jumping on the opportunity.'

'Good choice,' said Eric. 'May I carry anything down to your car for you?'

'That's very nice, but no. I'm staying for another couple days. What can I help you with?'

Kate didn't beat around the bush. 'Police have a suspect in custody for Mrs Westin's murder, but I'm not at liberty to say who the person is.'

Harris nodded while loading textbooks into a crate. 'There's just one minor detail I want to clarify before I close my case for Miss Westin.'

'Ask whatever you want.' Harris didn't look up from his task.

'I learned from the police that you're allergic to tree nuts and that Luisa Gonzalez was aware of this.'

'That is correct on both counts.'

'Then why, may I ask, did she pack Waldorf salad in the hamper that day? Or why didn't she at least omit the walnuts?'

'Luisa kept her well-paid position on the payroll by learning every nuance of her employer and those of her guests. She knew I preferred a light lunch but a substantial dinner. Agnes was just the opposite. Lunch was her favorite meal, then she ate like a mouse in the evening. Since I'm content with only a sandwich, Luisa made the salad how Agnes preferred it – loaded with walnuts. Usually Agnes could finish the entire container.'

'She didn't on the last day of her life.'

Harris met Kate's eye. 'I have no idea why not.'

'There could be a dozen logical reasons. Perhaps she lost her appetite because of the heat. Or she might have already been feeling ill. But I think there's something you're not telling me about lunch. Was there some kind of dessert that you didn't want? Maybe Agnes threw the rest overboard.'

Harris continued to pack books until Eric yanked the crate out of reach, forcing him to deal with Kate's question. With a weary sigh he plopped down on a fully packed box. 'There was something else I neglected to tell you or the police. I don't drink – never have and never will. My father was an alcoholic, so I vowed never to touch the stuff.'

'Why all the lies?' Kate asked. 'And why two wine glasses on the table?'

'Agnes was well on her way to becoming an alcoholic, if she wasn't one already. I told her several times I'd get her the help she needed discreetly, but she was still in denial. Appearances meant everything to her. So, until she was ready to dry out, I assisted with the subterfuge. Call me an enabler, but until a person is ready, intervention seldom works.'

'Who did Agnes not want to know about her drinking?' Eric resumed packing Harris's books.

'Her staff especially. She knew the household help gossiped about her behind her back and made fun of her. Agnes didn't wish to give them extra fodder.'

'Who else?' Kate asked.

'Her friends, if you could even call them that. These were her society peers from the garden club and numerous charitable foundations. They were the meanest, back-stabbing pack of jackals I've ever seen in my life.'

Kate and Eric exchanged a glance. 'You don't mince words, do you?'

'Actually I am, since I'm keeping my language G-rated. Most of these women were rich because they married powerful men. They resented Agnes because she came from very old money. So she was able to marry for love – as in the case of Robert Westin – or choose not to marry at all, like she pledged to do following their acrimonious divorce.

Agnes knew her friends were calling her names behind her back.'

'Any of these women stand out in your mind?'

'No. I didn't want her dwelling on them when we were together, so I changed the subject whenever she brought them up.'

'Who else knew about the heavy drinking, besides you?'

'Only the people Agnes trusted. Captain Holcomb knew, because he was very fond of Agnes and would never do anything to hurt her. And Lainey knew.'

'*Lainey?*' Kate and Eric parroted simultaneously.

'Yes, despite their frequent bickering, Lainey loved her mother and Agnes loved her. They just couldn't find a way to overcome their differences enough to get along. Lainey had also tried getting her mom into rehab once or twice. You can imagine how Agnes received those attempts.' Harris's eyes rolled back in his head.

'Why two wine glasses?' Kate prodded.

'Whether she and I were dining at her home or on the *Arrivederci Sorrento*, the table was always set with two wine glasses and two water glasses. I stuck to water and Agnes drank both wines, providing no other guests were present.'

'Makes perfect sense.' Kate offered her hand. 'Thank you, Mr Harris. Good luck in Chicago with the internship. You were a good friend to Mrs Westin, and it sounds like she needed all she could get.'

Harris's smile was bittersweet. 'Maybe we weren't *in love* with each other, but I loved Agnes Westin. I'll miss her and I'll never forget how good she was to me.'

While Eric stacked the box he filled, Kate wrapped her arms around the young man and hugged. 'I'm sure she loved you too.'

'Thanks. Please find her killer, Miss Weller. Agnes deserves justice.'

On the way to the car, Kate's eyes welled with tears. 'Wow, I hope one of *my* friends will feel that way about me.'

Eric wasted no time formulating a response. 'Two of them already do. You're just too thick-headed to realize it.'

When finally able to swallow her emotions, Kate cleared

her throat. 'I think we should head to Lainey's. I've got a few more questions for our favorite heiress.'

He looked at his watch. 'Nope, I'm starving. We'll call Miss Westin for an appointment for tomorrow morning. And it's time you and I had that little chat.'

Eric waited until Kate set up an appointment with Lainey before he asked her to make the first of many choices that evening. 'Should we go to dinner in your car or go back for mine?' he asked.

Kate slipped her phone in her purse. 'That depends on where we're going. It's your choice, Manfredi, and your treat.'

'Let's drive along the beach highway through the National Seashore. I'd like to eat in Orange Beach or Gulf Shores since I've never been to Alabama.'

'What?' Kate squawked. 'How can you have grown up in Georgia yet never been to "Bama."'

'I spent a sheltered childhood inside the city.'

'I'd heard Charlestonians lived a cloistered existence. Now I know it's true.'

'All I can remember is school and work, school and work. I started helping in Grandpa's restaurant when I was twelve. My parents' idea of vacation was taking a picnic basket out to Kiawah Island for the day.'

'What about spring break in college?'

'Panama City, Florida, close to Alabama, but no cigar.'

'In that case, we'll go to Orange Beach. Head back to the Bay Bridge.'

'Why don't we stay on 399? The brochure says the protected Gulf Islands extend into Alabama and Mississippi.'

'The national park extends, but not the road. We have to catch 182 in Warrington unless you have a boat in your pocket.'

Since he had no water craft, Eric followed Kate's directions back to the city. Along the way, Kate was content discussing Mark Harris and the Westin homicide, giving him time to collect his thoughts. Yet by the time they reached the small beach community, he still hadn't devised the proper approach. But the decision was soon taken from his hands.

'All right. Welcome to Orange Beach, Alabama. You're now

in the rocket capital of the world. There's a sign for a pizza shop in two miles. What exactly do we have to chit-chat about?' She thumped his shoulder.

'Let's stretch our legs. I see a path.' Eric parked the car on the wide shoulder and climbed out.

Kate took his hand as they picked their way between the dunes, careful not to step on plants trying to gain a foothold in the thin soil. Beyond the dunes, the beach stretched like an endless ribbon in both directions.

'I didn't think it would be so dark out here,' Eric said after stepping in a tidal pool.

'Homeowners keep back lights off to encourage sea turtles to nest,' she explained. 'The moon and stars are all we get. Now, shall I explain the life cycle of a turtle, or are you getting something off your chest?'

Shoving his hands deep into his pockets, Eric stared out to sea. 'I didn't come here to scout possible new locations for Bella.'

'I know, Eric. I figured that out long ago.'

He turned to face her. 'Why didn't you say anything?'

'I was waiting for you to come clean. Did you even get a job at Henri's, or was that part of your little charade?'

'I worked there. I told him I was looking for commercial property and asked if he could use a hand. He could, so I helped out in exchange for a few free meals.'

'You got supper and that's it? What's the matter with you?'

'I don't need the money, Kate, but I was curious how other restaurants handled certain protocols. I told the owner, Henry, the whole story on my second day.'

'His name is Henry, not *Henri*?' she asked.

'He said he could charge higher prices with a fancier name. Maybe I should use *Enrique*, like my grandparents called me.'

Kate chuckled, but then her smile faded. For a few moments, they stood on the beach, waiting for the other to speak. 'Since Henry knows the whole story, shouldn't you tell me everything too?' she finally asked.

'You're not going to make this easy, are you?'

'Nope. I want the facts spelled out for me, due to my deprived upbringing and all.'

'All right, I'll make this crystal clear.' Eric took hold of her chin. 'I'm in love with you. I have been for a while. I thought you felt the same until my car blew up. I never blamed you for that, yet you still ran away from me.'

She tried to interrupt, but he wouldn't let her. 'You wanted the truth, so here it is. What happened in Charleston is over with. Right now you're in danger. I came here to protect you. Not because it's my job, but because I love to. Once whoever has been stalking you is in jail, I'll go home and not bother you again. If that's what you want . . . but not until then.' Eric blew out his breath. 'There! Now what I want is something to eat.' He pivoted and started walking toward the car.

'Hey, crazy-man!' Something hit him in the center of his back. 'Don't I get a chance to talk?'

When he turned around, he spotted half a clamshell at his feet. 'I beg your pardon, Miss Weller. The floor is yours.'

Kate closed the distance in a few steps. 'I knew why you were here. I'm not as stupid as I look. But I didn't know you were in love with me.' She kicked sand in his direction. 'I feel the same way, but I'm not sure I can handle a real relationship. This isn't about me being coy. It's about me not having had much practice.'

Eric crossed his arms. 'In that case, we'll start over, just like Charleston never happened. We'll take things slow to see if we're remotely compatible.'

'Maybe I'll pick up a self-help book . . . *Relationships for Dummies.* In the meantime, what's going on with your family? How do they feel about you helping me with my case?'

Eric took her hand as they slogged through the sand to the path. 'That's not quite so easily explained. As much as I love my family, I don't want to spend the rest of my life as the head chef of Bella Trattoria.'

'But you love to cook,' she said.

'Yes, I love whipping up a batch of *pappardelle Bolognese* for my friends, but owning a restaurant consumes your life. I've worked at Bella before and after college and even worked part-time during law school. I would like to put my law degree to good use.'

'But you told me you didn't like the prosecutor's office and don't want to be a public defender.'

'I know that, but I also don't want to be a chef forever. I'm enjoying myself as a PI.'

'You've got to be kidding me. You went from possibly making the big bucks as a lawyer, to someday owning the best restaurant in the world's most popular tourist town, to being a *private investigator?* Do you have any idea how much I make a year?'

Eric felt the tension drain away as they both laughed. 'I have a good idea, but there's more to life than making money. A person should enjoy their job or each day becomes drudgery.'

'Is that what you feel when you're in Bella Trattoria?'

'For the last couple years, yes.' Eric could almost taste his shame and guilt. 'Like I said, I love my family and would never leave them in a bind. But while I'm here, I'd like to see if I have any talent at this. That is, if you'll let me.'

'Fine by me, as long as you realize you'll get the same pay as Henri's, but without the free meals.'

'Since I came to the Gulf Coast, I've put on a few pounds, so going hungry will do me good. However, tonight we're pulling out the stops with that pizza.'

Kate raced him to the car and won. But their good moods only lasted a short distance down the road.

'Liam?' she asked, answering her phone. 'Speak up. I can hardly hear you.' Kate tapped the button to activate the speaker.

Eric pulled into the pizza shop lot, switched off the radio, and leaned close to Kate.

'. . . wanted to tell you I did it. I talked to the district attorney about that night. I named my accomplices . . .' Then static obliterated several words. 'Jimmy Russell is dead. So that leaves Charley Crump. Doug Young never showed up, so he's off the hook for murder. Statute of limitations expired on conspiracy to commit robbery—'

'Liam,' Kate interrupted, 'if Doug Young wasn't there, who was the fourth man? I saw three men run away and you were on the ground.'

They listened to a buzz of static and then heard Liam

rambling about what the DA planned to do in the next few days. *Liam hadn't heard a word she'd said.*

'Liam,' she shouted.

'You need to—' Static obscured his words – 'Murphy here at the prison. He's the only one who can be trusted.'

Then Eric and Kate heard only static, followed by the ominous sound of nothingness. The line had gone dead.

Kate peered at him, her eyes glassy with moisture. 'Do you think someone saw my brother talking to the DA?'

Eric knew that lying wouldn't do any good. 'Nothing stays a secret for long inside Santa Rosa Correctional.'

'What should I do?'

'I'm going inside for a takeout pizza, in case we get hungry later. In the meantime, you call the warden. Tell him what's going on, and demand that he move Liam into protective isolation.'

She nodded. 'Good idea. Thanks.'

Walking into the familiar-smelling place, Eric could take little comfort from Kate's praise. As much as he loved working with her, investigating a family member took all the pleasure away.

THIRTEEN

Kate barely slept a wink after Liam's phone call. The warden had already left for the day when she called, but one of his assistants promised to deliver her message first thing this morning. Instead of going back to his suite, Eric slept on her couch after they talked for several hours. It had taken her that long to eat two slices of pizza . . . and fill in the blanks since their last honest, no-holds-barred conversation.

Today there wasn't much she could do other than her job. So Eric left long enough to shower and put on clean clothes, then they grabbed coffee in the lobby and drove to their appointment with the ultra-wealthy Miss Westin. They found Lainey poolside, sipping tea and reading the newspaper, but not looking particularly pleased to see them.

'Good morning, Miss Weller, Mr Manfredi. To what do I owe this unexpected visit? I thought the arrest of Luisa Gonzalez tied up my mother's murder with a bow.'

Kate forced a smile. 'In all likelihood, it has. But you're paying me well, so I intend to be thorough.'

'Please, sit.' Lainey gestured with her French-manicured fingers. 'Coffee, tea, something to eat?'

'No, thank you.' Kate and Eric spoke simultaneously as they took chairs under a striped umbrella.

'Rest assured,' Kate continued, 'Luisa is in jail and certainly won't be able to make bail, not with a capital murder charge. But I felt uneasy about something – something a clever defense attorney might be able to use should this go to trial.'

Lainey folded the newspaper and sat up straighter. 'I'm listening.'

'Your mother had been killed with the same poison that police found in the housekeeper's closet. Yet they found no poison in the container of Waldorf salad – the food we believed was used to kill her and not Mark Harris.'

Lainey wrinkled her nose. 'So what? Mom loved the stuff. She probably finished the container, destroying any evidence.'

Eric slapped his knee. 'That's what Detective Buckley concluded too.'

Lainey nodded indulgently at him before turning her attention back to Kate. 'But you think the poison was in something else.' It was a statement, not a question.

'On a hunch, I went to talk to Mark Harris again. The cold apple salad wasn't the only food he didn't partake of that afternoon.'

Westin's smile disappeared. 'What are you talking about?'

Kate dropped her voice to a whisper. 'Mark admitted that your mom had a drinking problem and that he didn't imbibe at all.'

'Why, that ungrateful little gold-digging—'

Kate wouldn't have repeated the rest of Lainey's colorful description under oath. 'Actually, Mark appreciated Agnes's support and was also very fond of her. He understood your mother's desire to keep her addiction private. That's why he agreed with the charade of filling two glasses and *never* betrayed her confidences.'

Lainey swept her blonde hair away from her face. 'Okay, Harris was an all-around great guy. Where are you going with this, Kate?'

'Maybe nowhere. Or maybe the poison was in the wine, not in the salad. To the best of our knowledge, Luisa didn't know that Mark didn't drink.'

Lainey drummed her long nails on the table. 'The police tested the wine and found nothing.'

Eric jumped into the explanation. 'They tested the red wine, which was missing only one glass. The bottle of white wine was empty and had already been rinsed out for recycling.'

'That's where the poison could have been.' Kate leaned across the table. 'Who else knew about your mother's over-imbibing besides Harris?'

'Only Captain Holcomb and me.'

'That's what Mark Harris said,' Kate agreed.

'But if you spent much time with Captain Roger, you'd

discover he was more loyal than a dog. He's been quietly in love with Mom for years.'

Kate nodded. 'That's the impression I got too. Plus, like Mark Harris, Captain Holcomb had nothing to gain by her murder.'

Lainey tented her fingers beneath her chin. 'Are you back to thinking I killed her?' Icicles could have formed on her words.

'Not at all.' Kate feigned surprise. 'I think someone else knew your mom would be the only one having wine on the boat.'

As Lainey considered this, her perfect skin furrowed with wrinkles. 'No, my mother would've died before she let the staff or her friends know the truth. She thought appearances were everything.'

That apple didn't fall far from her tree, Kate thought. 'Let's approach this in a different way. Did anyone stop by her house that morning?'

'I know how to find out. Follow me.' Lainey sprang from the chair, pulled on her cover-up, and stalked to the French doors in her high-heeled sandals.

Although Eric had no trouble, Kate practically had to run to keep up as they followed Lainey into the library.

'My mother was OCD about keeping to a schedule. She wrote down everything, even her weekly recurring appointments like massages and facials. I think she worried about getting forgetful someday.' Lainey pulled a date book from the desk drawer and flipped through pages at lightning speed. 'Here it is – the day my mom died.'

Kate held her breath as Lainey scanned the notations.

Lainey frowned, deepening the lines around her mouth. 'Beside lunch with Mark on the *Arrivederci*, only the executive committee of her garden club came by that day. And Mom never would have told those shrews.'

Kate exhaled with a sigh. 'Just the same, could you jot down the committee members' names?'

'Let's see . . . Mom was president. Then there was a VP, a secretary, and a treasurer.' Lainey pulled out an address book, wrote down three names and phone numbers and handed Kate the paper. 'Here you go, although I don't know what good these will do.'

'Like I said, I'm just covering all the bases. Most likely it was Luisa – retribution for her son's deportation. Thanks, we'll see ourselves out.'

Kate and Eric had just climbed into his SUV when Lainey rushed out the front door and down the steps. Panting, she reached Kate's window with a sprinter's agility, her stiletto heels long gone. 'I just thought of something. One member of the committee did stop by a few days before Mom died. The vice president loved to park in the back and walk into the kitchen like she owned the place. That annoying woman considered herself my mother's best friend. Mom would have been better off befriending a rattlesnake.'

Kate climbed out so that they were eye-to-eye. 'Why would you say that?'

'Once I spotted Marti Collier rolling her eyes behind my mother's back, but to her face she was always sugar-sweet. I *hate* two-faced women.'

'I couldn't agree more, but how would Marti Collier know Mark Harris didn't drink? Would she be so cruel as to risk poisoning an innocent man? And what could be her motive for wanting your mother dead?'

'As to your first question, like I said, Marti loved to enter the house without bothering to knock. Once she walked in during one of our arguments about her drinking. Of course, we stopped the moment we saw her in the doorway. But how long had she been eavesdropping before making her presence known?'

Kate bent down to make eye contact with Eric. 'Are you catching this, partner?'

'Loud and clear.'

Lainey glanced at her watch. 'As to your second concern, it's your job to figure it out. That's why I'm paying you the big bucks. Right now I'm late for my Pilates class.' She sprinted back to the house.

'Thanks, Miss Westin. We'll be in touch,' Kate called, climbing into the car. 'What do you think?' she asked Eric.

'I think your theory is a bit of a stretch.'

'Maybe, but I don't see Luisa as a cold-blooded killer. At least, not until she finds out for sure that Miguel is dead. In the meantime, let's see if any of Agnes's friends had a motive for murder.'

'Should we go back to the hotel to research the committee members?'

'No, I'll call Michael Preston. He can do that faster and better while you and I have a little chat with Charley Crump, the so-called ringleader of Liam's gang. Michael already found a current address for the guy.' Kate programmed Eric's GPS. 'Then tomorrow morning we'll head to Santa Rosa Correctional. How does that sound?'

Eric carefully backed down Lainey's driveway. 'I know better than to doubt one of your hunches.'

'Who says you can't teach an old dog new tricks?'

After an hour and several wrong turns, Kate and Eric arrived at Charley's last known address, in what had to be the worst neighborhood in Pensacola. Since his apartment building had a broken elevator, they hiked to the fourth floor and knocked on Crump's door. Then they knocked again, after no response.

'Old Charley doesn't seem to be home,' Eric observed.

'Lesson number thirty-eight: Only nice people with nothing to hide answer the door in this part of the world.' Kate raised her fist and pounded. 'Open the door, Crump. I know you're in there,' she shouted, even though she knew nothing of the sort.

A minute later the door swung wide. 'Who the blazes are you?'

Kate studied the dissipated creature standing in front of her with zero recognition. 'I'm Kate Weller. This is my boyfriend.' She hooked her thumb at Eric, but chose not to identify their vocation. 'Are you Charley Crump?'

'Little Katie?' he asked, his eyes growing round. 'Don't you recognize me? I came by your house a couple times when you were little. 'Course I used to be heavier and had more hair back then.' Crump snaked a hand through hair that hadn't been washed in days.

'Yeah, it's coming back to me now. Mind if we talk inside?'

Kate pushed her way past him with Eric at her heels. 'The dust in the hallway is making me sneeze.'

Crump's apartment was mainly one room, with a bathroom carved out of one corner as though an afterthought. One wall held the sink, stove, and fridge, while his bed, threadbare sofa, and television lined the other wall. Open on the unmade bed were two suitcases, the likes of which hadn't been seen in years.

'Packing to leave, Mr Crump?' asked Eric, pointing at the clothes hanging haphazardly from the suitcases.

'You got that right.' Crump returned to his bureau for another armload. 'If Little Katie was half as smart as her brother says she is, she would leave town too.'

Kate stepped into his path. 'Why? What do you know that I don't?'

Charley clutched the clothes to his chest. 'I know you've asked too many questions and stuck your nose into business that wasn't yours. Now you've made someone mighty nervous.'

'Have I made you nervous?' Emboldened by Eric's presence and the gun in her ankle holster, Kate yanked the clothes from Charley's grip and tossed them on the bed.

'*Me*? You thought I was the one in charge? Look around. Does it look like I got much from that heist? I'm not who you need to worry about, Little Katie.' Stepping around her, he stuffed clothes into the already full suitcases.

With the fluidity of a dancer, Eric put one hand on Crump's shoulder and spun him around. An easy enough task, considering Eric was six-foot-four-inches of muscles compared to the emaciated five-foot-eight-inch Crump. 'Then who is in charge?' Eric demanded.

'Ace is calling the shots now. He has been from the start, only Liam didn't know that. Ace didn't trust your brother. Turned out it was Doug Young who backed out at the last minute.' Crump sat on the suitcase in order to snap the latches. 'But that change of heart cost Doug dearly.'

'Meaning what?' Kate asked.

Crump glared at her with his watery blue eyes. 'All I know is that Doug Young disappeared from the face of the earth. Can you put two and two together, college girl?'

'Is that what happened to Jimmy Russell?'

Crump shrugged. 'Who knows? Like I said, nobody has found Doug yet. But Jimmy didn't *accidentally* shoot himself in the face sitting in a deer stand. That guy handled firearms better than anybody I knew.'

'So Ace killed Jimmy and most likely Doug. And he's why you're leaving town.'

'Bingo. I guess Liam was right about your superior intellect.' Crump set one bag by the door and returned for the other.

Kate plopped down on the other suitcase. 'You're not going anywhere until you tell us Ace's real name.'

'No way. Keep the clothes. I'll get more at the Salvation Army. Ace ain't the kind of guy you mess with.'

Kate jumped up and grabbed Charley's arm. 'Please help me. Liam talked to the district attorney about his accomplices, thinking you were the one threatening me.'

'You want my help after your brother just fingered me for a capital crime? Better find somewhere to hide, Katie girl. But there's no helping Liam, not in the joint. He never should have copped to the shooting.'

'Please, Charley. Stop at the district attorney's office and give a statement. Admit to being part of the robbery. The statute of limitations has expired for your crime. Say that you'd already taken off with the money when that guard got shot. For Liam to get out at his first parole hearing, I need someone to back up his testimony; something other than my suppressed memories through hypnotic regression.'

Charley stared at Kate. '*Hypnotic what?* You turned into one crazy lady. I'm not going anywhere near the DA's office. Ace's long arms can reach almost anywhere.'

Eric stepped between Crump and Kate. 'That's why you're not leaving here without giving us Ace's name.'

'Hey, buddy. I'm not the one who blew up your car. Aren't you two even listening?'

'I don't care about the car. It's Kate I'm worried about. Now what's the guy's name?' Eric drew his weapon and leveled it at Crump's head.

He sneered. 'You gonna shoot me, big guy? Go ahead.

At least I'll die quick, which is better than what Ace will do if he finds out.'

Kate gently pushed the gun barrel until it pointed at the wall. 'Fine, just tell me one thing before you leave.'

Charley retrieved his second suitcase. 'What's that, Katie girl?'

'Why did Ace knock my brother out cold? You could have all gotten away clean. Why did he shoot the guard?'

Crump's smile revealed chipped and yellowed teeth. Dental hygiene apparently ranked low on his list of priorities. 'That's two questions, so I'll just answer the first. Ace punched out Liam 'cause he was mad that Liam was late. You don't come tardy to a stick-up, so Ace decided to teach him a lesson.' Crump reached for the door handle then paused. 'I remember you always brought me a Coke whenever I hung out with your brother. That was real nice, Katie. So I'll think about stopping by the DA's, or at least giving the office a call.'

'Thanks, Charley. I would appreciate that.'

'You take my advice and find a safe place to hide. Until Ace gets his just deserts, he isn't someone to mess with.' Crump took a final perusal of the room. 'Hey, if you see anything you like, take it. Where I'm headed, I need to travel light.' Then Charley vanished out the door and down the steps, leaving Kate and Eric amidst the remainder of his earthly possessions.

Both of them gazed around the sad, dilapidated room. Kate walked to the windowsill and picked up a reasonably healthy pink geranium.

'What on earth will you do with that? You are living in a hotel room.'

She smiled. 'No clue, but it'll die if we leave it behind. Who knows when they'll rent this dump again? Plus, someday I might have a cool place to live again.'

'The suite above my family's restaurant is still available.'

'How would that work if you don't want to be a chef anymore?'

Eric had no ready answer, but he carried the plant down four flights of stairs as Kate mulled over her conversation with Charley. 'Do you think Charley will stop by the DA's office?' she asked in the lobby.

'No chance of that happening.'

'What about him making an anonymous phone call?'

'I would say 50-50. Keep your fingers crossed. Since you wouldn't let me shoot the guy, what's our next move?'

'I'm glad you didn't. Despite everything, I feel sorry for Charley. Let's hope he does the right thing. In the meantime, I need to get a hold of this person named Murphy at the prison since the warden never returned my call. Maybe he never got the message. Regardless, we must assume Liam's not in protective custody.'

They walked across the street to the shade of a large oak. Kate dialed the only number she had for Santa Rosa Correctional and used her most officious tone of voice. 'Good afternoon, it's urgent that I speak with Mr Murphy.'

'What's that? You mean *Doctor* Murphy?' asked a scratchy voice.

'Yes, that's what I said. This is Dr Gloria Tucker in Tallahassee. Please put me through immediately.'

'Hold one moment, Doctor, and I'll connect you.'

While Kate waited, Eric mouthed, 'Who is Gloria Tucker?'

Kate put her hand over the mouthpiece. 'She was my second-grade teacher. I needed a name.' While Eric grinned at her cleverness, Kate began to sweat.

In a few minutes, a man with an elderly rasp picked up the other end. 'Dr Tucker? This is Elias Murphy. Please refresh my memory as to how we know each other.'

'We don't, Dr Murphy, and I'm not a doctor, but please don't hang up. This is Liam Weller's sister, Kate. My brother gave a revised statement to the Escambia County DA's office which put his life in grave danger.'

'I'm not sure what I can do about that, Miss Weller. You should call the warden.'

'I did last night and left a message, but nobody called me back. I can't wait until tomorrow. Liam will be dead by then. Please, my brother said you were the only one I could trust in Santa Rosa Prison. Could you possibly transfer him to sick bay or something?'

Eric, who'd been craning his neck to hear, piped up. 'Place him in isolation due to a communicative disease.'

'How about that?' Kate asked, giving Eric the thumbs-up.

'I'll try, Miss Weller. But right now I must return to my patient.'

'Thank you, Dr Murphy. I know Eric did a lot of bad things in his life, but he never shot that guard. So he doesn't deserve to die at the hands of the man who did.' She heard only static on the other end. Liam's only chance had already hung up.

Kate threw her arms around Eric and hugged. 'That was a great idea. Let's hope that Dr Murphy takes the Hippocratic Oath seriously.'

FOURTEEN

Michael Preston, Price Investigations' forensic accountant, called them back before Kate and Eric arrived back in downtown Pensacola.

'Hi, Michael, did you dig up anything interesting about the three committee members?'

'You bet I did. Elizabeth Bronner, the treasurer, and Ann Hodges, the secretary, have no skeletons in the closet. They appear to be nice mothers, grandmothers, and generous philanthropists in their community.'

Kate all but rubbed her palms together with glee. 'But . . .' She dragged the word into several syllables and pressed the speaker button so Eric could hear.

'But Martha Collier, better known as Marti, has quite a colorful past. Her current husband met her in a bar and was instantly swept off his feet. After a whirlwind courtship, he married her in San Juan without checking into her past. Mr Collier was Marti's *third* husband. The first two are both doing time for financial crimes – everything from embezzlement to tax fraud.'

'They're in jail?' Kate squawked.

'The big house, federal playpen, sent-up-the-river – pick your favorite colloquialism.'

'What about Marti?'

'The new Mrs Collier has been convicted twice for impersonation and fraud for cashing checks that didn't belong to her. Apparently she once volunteered as a caregiver for the elderly. Both of the checks she stole were over ten grand each. But, thanks to an expensive lawyer, the charges were reduced to misdemeanors both times.'

'I can't believe she didn't go to jail!' Indignation left a bad taste in her mouth.

'Oh, did I forget to mention that Mr Collier is actually Judge Collier?'

Kate uttered a rude sound. 'As fascinating as this is, none of it has anything to do with Agnes Westin.'

'Don't be so impatient,' Michael chided. 'I'm just getting to that. Marti used to be *treasurer* of the garden club, until Agnes discovered the ledgers didn't match the club's bank balance. We're only talking a couple hundred dollars, but Agnes blew her stack. She called Judge Collier and demanded that he make restitution. The old guy probably thought Marti's life of crime was behind her. Her name came off their joint checking account and he cancelled Miss Sticky Finger's credit cards. Marti has only a debit card, which the bank monitors closely. One can only assume Mrs Collier is no longer a happy woman.'

Eric leaned closer to the phone. 'I can't even imagine how you came by this information.'

Michael laughed. 'And I'm not going to tell you.'

'My bet is that Marti holds Agnes responsible for her fall from grace,' Kate interjected.

'You got that right. Everyone in the club found out when Agnes stripped her of the treasurer's duties. Then Elizabeth Bronner, who was the VP, felt sorry for Marti and switched positions, but the damage had already been done. Everyone knows, plus hubby put Marti on a short leash.'

'I'm smelling motive.' Kate winked at Eric.

'I thought you might. I gotta run. Have any message for Beth?'

'Yeah, she should be nice to *you* until the wedding.'

'Only until? I shudder to think what will happen after.'

'Thanks, Michael. I owe you . . . plenty.'

'See you at the wedding, aka Natchez's Social Event of the Decade.'

When Kate hung up, Eric slapped her on the back. 'Sounds like you found another suspect,' he said. 'Marti Collier had both motive and opportunity. Where to now – back to police headquarters to talk to Detective Buckley?'

'No, let's ask him to meet us at the Westins'. What we need is a smoking gun, or Buckley might not want to change horses mid-race.'

'But Agnes was killed . . .' Eric thought for a moment. 'Oh, never mind. I had forgotten your fondness for metaphors.'

'It's from hanging around you too long. Pull into that parking lot and stop so you can listen to the call. This one might take a while.' Kate punched in the detective's number and waited.

'Ahh, Miss Weller,' Buckley said in his charming Jamaican accent. 'To what do I owe the pleasure? I assure you Mrs Gonzalez is in jail and that's where she'll remain until the trial. She's a flight risk.'

'Let's not throw the key away just yet. Do you still have the trash taken off the boat that day?'

'Yes, it was all logged into evidence.'

'Check the trash for a cork to a wine bottle. We're looking for the white wine cork in particular.'

'Why? The white had been finished and the bottle washed out, and the red wine contained no trace of poison.'

'Go along with me for the moment. Recently I found out Mark Harris didn't drink. Not at all. He neglected to mention that to you. Mrs Westin didn't want her boat neighbors to know she was a lush so she set out two wine glasses. Then Agnes drank both.'

'You're saying she consumed an entire bottle of white and then started in on the red? How was she able to snorkel around the marina? I certainly would have drowned.'

'Yep, me too, but alcoholics can build up a tolerance until their livers start to shut down. My theory is the poison was in the bottle of white wine. You should find a tiny hole in the cork from a syringe needle.'

Buckley remained silent while processing the information. 'The poison wasn't fast acting. It takes a while to be fully absorbed into the bloodstream and cause organ failure. But I don't think Luisa was savvy enough to inject poison through a wine cork.'

'I agree. That's why Luisa might not have been the killer.'

'You have my attention, Miss Weller, even though I don't like what I'm hearing. Even if someone put the poison into the white, what's the chance of finding trace evidence still on the cork?'

'Hope springs eternal. Could you have your lab techs search for the cork and send it to the lab?'

'Consider it done, but I'd love to hear about this new suspect.'

'I promise to divulge everything, but could you meet me at the Westin mansion? I also want to see if the household trash has been picked up.'

'Certainly by now. It's been over a week.'

'But with Mrs Westin dead and the housekeeper in jail, who knows which domestic tasks have been neglected?'

'You do realize that, unlike yourself, I have other cases.' Buckley sounded low on patience.

'Rest assured you won't be sorry you made the trip.' Kate had no idea how she could make such a bold pledge.

'I'll come, because I need to get out of the office. But you'd better not waste my time.'

Hanging up, Kate grinned at Eric. 'Full speed ahead to the Westin house with your fingers crossed. My case hinges on well-paid employees not doing their jobs if left unsupervised.'

Twenty minutes later, Eric pulled up the driveway and parked near the garage.

'You two back again?' Wiping his hands on a rag, the gardener appeared in the potting shed doorway.

Kate jumped out of the car. 'Yes, but don't worry. We're not here to grill you.'

'Then who? The only other person here is the cook.'

Ignoring his question, Kate asked one of her own. 'Where are the garbage cans kept?'

'*What?*'

'Tell us where the garbage cans are,' repeated Eric.

'On the far side of the garage, behind the rose trellis.' Chapman pointed in the general direction.

Kate and Eric sprinted around the garage. If the number of circling flies and noxious odors were good indicators, the trash hadn't been collected in quite some time. Eric reached for a lid, but Kate grabbed his wrist.

'Let's wait for Buckley. We don't want to taint the evidence. We're not law enforcement.'

Eric put his hands in his pockets. 'Good idea. You want me to stand guard?'

'No, you might pass out from the fumes. Let's go question the cook. What does that woman *do* all day?'

Inside the kitchen, the overpaid cook was emptying the pantry of canned and dry goods. 'Hi, remember me? Kate Weller. And you are?'

'Mrs Carter. I was the cook, but it looks like I'm in charge of packing boxes for the food bank now.'

'You did notice there's nobody here to cook for, right?' Kate laced her question with a tablespoon of sugar.

Mrs Carter dropped a can of split pea into the crate. 'What can I do for you, Miss Weller?'

'I was curious which day is trash pickup.'

The older woman blinked. 'It's every Monday.'

'But I noticed that every can is overflowing.'

'I am the cook, not a cleaning lady or a housekeeper or the gardener. I told that worthless Mr Chapman to drag out the cans, which he did. But they refused to pick up because the recyclables hadn't been removed. How dare that arrogant hauler refuse to pick up our trash?' Carter sounded as though she'd never suffered a greater injustice. 'I'm certainly not going to pick through that mess to remove glass, plastic, and aluminum. It can stay until kingdom-come.'

Eric held up a hand. 'Calm down, ma'am. We have people coming who will take care of it.'

Carter resumed packing boxes of rice, pasta, and paper products. 'It's about the time. The neighbor already complained once about the smell.'

'Is it all right if we wait for them in the study?' Kate didn't indicate who the *them* were.

'Wait wherever you like. People come and go around here like they're royalty. I hope Miss Lainey moves in soon. She'll put a stop to that nonsense.'

'What are we looking for in the study?' Eric asked, once out of the kitchen.

'Nothing, but I plan to set a trap for a greedy spider. If I were Judge Collier, I wouldn't drink any tea brewed by his charming wife.' Kate closed the study's door, punched in Lainey's number, and asked her to come to the house. Kate explained that she needed her to invite Marti Collier over this afternoon. If the invitation came from a private investigator or from Detective Buckley, Marti would become instantly suspicious.

However, Lainey refused to give up happy hour with her friends unless Kate spelled everything out, down to the last piece of evidence that hopefully would be in her mother's trash.

'You think that creepy Marti Collier killed my mother?' Lainey's indignation surpassed Mrs Carter's that someone so *classless* would dare to kill a Westin.

'Yes, I do, but I'll need help in proving it. Marti will smell something fishy if anyone other than you calls her. Tell her you have garden club materials that can only be entrusted to the vice president. Marti became the VP when she switched positions with Elizabeth Bronner. Actually, with your mom's passing, Marti just became the new president.' When Lainey began growling like a feral dog, Kate quickly added, 'Or you could imply Agnes left Marti a small inheritance, which you would like to take care of before probate.'

'My mother wouldn't leave a dime to that thieving gold-digger.'

'I understand, but a white lie about money will get her here for sure.'

'Fine, but you'd better be right, Kate. I'm giving up half-priced martinis all because of your hunch.' Lainey clicked off, leaving Kate dumbfounded.

The woman was worth millions, yet she hated to miss half-price cocktails? 'The rich definitely are different,' she muttered to Eric.

Her handsome boyfriend neither affirmed nor denied her assertion. Kate suspected Eric fit better into Lainey's category than hers. But she had no time to ponder the effect of wealth on people, because Julian Buckley strolled into the room looking calm and cool in a linen suit and white shirt.

'The churlish cook said I'd find you two here.' Buckley settled in a leather chair by the window. 'If I were Lainey Westin, I would fire that woman in a heartbeat. I don't care how good she cooks.'

'Thanks for coming so promptly, Detective,' Kate said.

'A team of forensic techs are combing through the trash, looking for a cork and the needle that might pierce through one. You'd better not be wasting taxpayer money.' Crossing his legs, Buckley shook his finger at Kate. 'Time for you to tell me what you discovered.'

'With pleasure.' Kate launched into an almost word-for-word recitation of Michael Preston's research.

'And you think Agnes calling Judge Collier and defrocking her in the garden club are motives for murder?' The question revealed more than a little skepticism.

'Absolutely, I do. These women believe status and social standing are everything. Agnes showed the other ladies that Marti didn't belong because she couldn't be trusted. That's a big deal for a wannabe.'

'Plus,' said Eric, 'Judge Collier was so furious with her that he took away her checkbook and credit cards except for a debit card. And he's keeping a close eye on that one. Marti had gone into this marriage with one expectation – plenty of cash to spend. According to our Price Investigations researcher, they had a pre-nup. So all Marti will get is what she can squirrel away from the judge.'

'And my mother wonders why I'm still single,' Buckley murmured. 'You'd better hope the techs find solid evidence in the trash. Everything else you've got is circumstantial.'

'We understand,' said Kate. 'That's why Lainey is calling Mrs Collier to request she swing by the house. She'll use the premise of turning over garden club materials to the new president.'

Buckley straightened in the chair. 'You set up a *sting*, Miss Weller?'

Kate couldn't tell if he was impressed or pondering charges of interference in a police investigation. 'I did. What do you think?'

'Hey, I still think the housekeeper did it, but I'm willing to play along. What do you see as my role in your plan?'

'I would like you to hide in there with a tape recorder.' She pointed at a closet with louvered doors. 'I wish I could hide with you, but Lainey will probably need me. So I'll pretend

I'm a paralegal from her law office settling her mother's estate. Lainey will try to get Marti to reveal something that only the murderer would know. I prepped Lainey somewhat, but mostly she will ad-lib this.'

They both glanced up with the sound of high heels in the hallway. Then Lainey Westin strode into the room.

'Detective Buckley, I didn't know you'd be part of my investigator's little scheme.'

'Just want to make sure the right person goes to jail.' Buckley rose to his feet. 'Sit here at the desk, Miss Westin. I'll be taping the conversation from inside the closet.' Opening the closet door, he got into position by perching on two boxes of copy paper.

Lainey focused on Kate. 'What do you want me to do?'

'First, trade shoes with me. I want to look more professional, plus Marti and I have met before.' Kate coiled her long hair into a bun, secured it with a butterfly clip, and grabbed a pair of huge tortoiseshell glasses from the desktop. Then she kicked her flats over to Lainey and slipped on the heiress's high heels.

'You'd better not stretch those out,' Lainey warned. 'They cost me four hundred dollars.' She put on Kate's sandals.

'Thanks.' Kate looked at the intricate straps securing the stiletto to her foot and shook her head. 'We want to keep Marti here as long as possible in hopes the techs find what I believe is in the trash. Just follow my lead in the conversation.'

Lainey snorted. 'Keep talking about the money Mom left her. That should hold Marti here for hours.'

Eric, who'd been watching for Marti's car, gave them a signal and disappeared into the next bedroom.

'Lainey, dig out anything you can find for the garden club. I'll be poring over papers in this filing cabinet.' Kate pulled out a stack of file folders, while Lainey sat down behind the desk.

In no time at all, Mrs Martha Collier breezed into the room in a cloud of perfume. 'Lainey, how are you dear? My deepest sympathy on your loss. Aren't we *ever* going to have the memorial service for your dear mother?' She sat in a chair opposite the desk without waiting to be invited.

'Thank you, Marti. I'm doing all right; still making

arrangements for Mom's service and tying up loose ends to process the estate. You know how complicated these things can be.' Lainey did an Oscar-winning job of hiding her contempt.

'If there's anything I can do to help, dear, just say the word.'

'Thank you so much,' drawled Lainey. 'My mother was so fond of you.'

'And that feeling was mutual.' Marti swiveled her chair toward the filing cabinet. 'Haven't you and I met before? You look familiar.'

Kate pulled her reading glasses farther down on her nose. 'It's possible, ma'am. I'm here frequently. I'm a paralegal from Mr Shaw's office. He sent me to do a preliminary financial inventory of Mrs Westin's assets. This will speed along the bequests, since there aren't many.'

'I'm sure you have your work cut out for you.' Marti smiled graciously.

'I do indeed. Since you were named as one of Mrs Westin's beneficiaries, I will need your complete name, address, social security number, and a contact phone number.'

'My pleasure!' Marti slowly recited the pertinent details while Kate took her time writing them down. Twice she asked the woman to repeat herself, as though she were hard of hearing.

'Great, got it,' said Kate. 'Now I just need the name of your bank and the routing number for your account.'

Marti's complexion paled. 'Why on earth would you need that? I would be happy to take the check to my bank.'

Kate pressed her notepad to her chest and smiled over her reading glasses. 'There is one *peculiarity* with the bequest. Mrs Westin set it up to be paid in monthly installments over a course of five years.'

The woman's eyes twinkled as the anticipated sum expanded in her imagination. 'Oh, that might make things . . . easier, but depositing a check at my bank would be no inconvenience whatsoever.'

'I appreciate that, Mrs Collier, but I'm forced to follow the exact instructions in Mrs Westin's will. I promise your personal information will be quite secure. You needn't worry about identity theft with the Shaw legal team.'

Lainey cleared her throat and picked up where Kate had left off. 'You know how . . . eccentric Mom could be at times. She was very old-fashioned and lived in constant fear of leaving the household cash-poor, even though she could get a cash advance from any one of her credit cards. I'm afraid that Mom's paranoia carried over into her estate. Were you aware that my father's divorce settlement has been doled out in installments?'

'No, I was not.' From Marti's expression, the plight of Robert Westin was of little concern to her. 'I'm sure Agnes set it up that way to make it easy for me. But I don't have an account in my own name, only a joint checking account with my husband, the judge.' She imbued the last word with special emphasis. 'And since *I'm* the named beneficiary, the funds should be deposited into an account that's all mine.'

'I understand perfectly, ma'am.' Kate made notes on her ledger. 'Why don't you open a new account tomorrow and furnish me with the details?'

Marti's expression resembled a weasel's. 'Or perhaps you could call your boss, Mr Shaw, and ask for his advice regarding a matter involving Judge Collier's wife.'

Kate's head reared back as though startled. 'Dear me, no. I'm the newest paralegal in the firm. I could *never* question a senior partner's judgement. You'll have to make that phone call yourself.'

'Let's move on to other matters.' Lainey thumped a stack of folders and a leather-bound journal on the desk. 'This is the garden club business that I've collected so far. Mom's agenda for the next meeting is in the top folder.'

Marti gazed at the materials as though confused. 'You want me to take all that?'

'Of course, as the VP you move up to the rank of president. You will chair the next meeting.'

'But I'd rather go back to being the treasurer.'

'You'll have to take that up with Mrs Bronner. For now, I prefer to separate garden club business from my mother's estate.' Lainey pushed the stack across the desk toward Marti.

'Anything to speed probate along.' Marti moved the stack of folders to her lap. 'Assuming I'm able to open a new bank account tomorrow, when can I expect my first check?'

'My mother's will was cut-and-dried, but we still have to wait for a probate judge to release the funds for distribution. Although as executrix, I could write your first installment out of her checking account.' Lainey tapped a pen on the desk. 'But there is the matter of my mother's murder.'

'What does that have to do with anything?' Marti almost levitated from her chair.

'Oh, a great deal,' chimed Kate. 'The senior law partner doesn't want funds distributed until the police determine who killed Mrs Westin. You know the law – a criminal can't financially benefit from his or her crime. What if Miss Westin inherits the bulk of the estate, but the police later charge her with murder? She could already be on a spending spree in the Maldives.'

'You impudent little—' Lainey's outrage sounded as real as it gets.

'I beg your pardon, Miss Westin. I wasn't implying anything, merely providing an example.'

Lainey threw her hands in the air. 'The cops already have Mom's housekeeper in custody. Why don't they just charge her and let the rest of us get on with our lives?'

Kate glanced at the doorway and dropped her voice to a whisper. 'I heard Mr Shaw talking to his friend in the District Attorney's office. Luisa Gonzalez confessed to buying the rat poison, but insisted she only killed rats with the stuff.'

'Like there really are rats in *this* neighborhood,' Lainey sneered.

'Unfortunately this house sits close to the bay,' Kate said sagely. 'There have been rats near the waterfront since the beginning of time.'

Lainey angled another frown in the paralegal's direction. 'Regardless, if Luisa confessed to buying and using the poison, I don't know why the facts aren't presented to the Grand Jury.'

'Oh, they will be, but Mr Shaw said the police can't find the container of poison. Luisa insisted she put it on the top shelf in the potting shed, because that's where she spotted a rat.'

'Did anyone even *look*?' asked Marti.

'Of course they did,' Lainey explained. 'I was here when

the police searched the shed, the garage, the kitchen, the cellar – all the logical places.'

'Did they bother to search the illogical places, like the housekeeper's room?' screeched Marti.

'I don't know.' Lainey arched an eyebrow. 'I'll check with Detective Buckley when I talk to him this evening. Right now, I want to make sure you have everything you need to prepare for the next garden club meeting.'

'Sweet mother of pearl!' Marti jumped to her feet. 'Your housekeeper is in jail, right? This house will soon be yours. So why don't the three of us search Luisa's room?'

The pseudo-paralegal shook her head. 'I don't know. Isn't that an invasion of privacy? Even housekeepers have rights.'

Marti leveled a glare at Kate that could peel wallpaper from the wall. Then she addressed Lainey. 'This is your mother we're talking about. I don't give a fig about that woman's rights. Let's see if that ingrate has something to hide.'

'You're absolutely right, Mrs Collier.' Lainey jumped up and followed Marti out the door and down the hallway.

'On behalf of the Shaw and Associates Law Firm, I'm coming too,' said Kate, tottering behind on her high heels. How Lainey managed to walk gracefully was beyond her.

In the austere bedroom of Luisa Gonzalez, Lainey rummaged through bureau drawers and dug beneath pajamas and sweaters.

Kate dropped to her knees and stuck her head under the bed. 'I see only dust bunnies,' she called, her head behind the dust ruffle.

'You two would make terrible investigators. The logical spot would be the closet.' Marti pushed the clothes over to one side. Then, arching up on tiptoes, she pulled boxes and bags of greeting cards down from the shelf, starting in the exact corner where the container had been found by one of Buckley's officers.

Kate scrambled to her feet. 'Find anything interesting, Mrs Collier?'

'Don't just stand there. Bring me a chair to stand on.'

Lainey moved a chair to the closet and helped Marti step up. Shoving clothes aside, Marti lifted a stack of shoeboxes from the shelf and handed them to Lainey. 'Let's look in these. You, paralegal, check those boxes on the floor,' Marti ordered.

'Yes, ma'am.' Kate dutifully opened each box and inspected the contents. 'Nothing in this box but letters from her sisters in Matamoros.'

'Then check the others,' Marti barked as she pulled off lids and emptied contents on the bedspread.

Lainey stepped back to watch. When Marti had dumped the last box of receipts and cancelled checks, Lainey murmured in a low voice. 'The box you're looking for isn't here.'

'What on earth are you talking about?'

'The shoebox where you hid the rat poison. The police took the container in as evidence.'

Marti's expression was a cross between confusion and rage. 'You said the police couldn't find the poison.'

Lainey smiled. 'I wanted to see your reaction. Sure enough, you went straight to the corner where you had framed the housekeeper.'

'Have you lost your mind? A closet is the logical spot where people hide things. My looking here doesn't prove I had anything to do with this. Why on earth would I kill Agnes? She was my best friend.'

'Cut the charade, Martha! You weren't Mom's friend. You resented her because she was a snob.'

Marti moved closer until she was in Lainey's face. 'If I killed all the *snobs* in the garden club, there would be no one left but me.'

'You didn't want to kill all, only my mother because she told the judge you were a thief. Apparently, this wasn't the first time your sticky fingers got you in trouble.'

Marti pushed Lainey so hard she lost her balance, landing in a heap on the area rug. 'You turned out exactly like her, didn't you? Despite the fact you couldn't stand to be in the same room with Agnes.'

'Ladies, ladies, let's please keep the discussion civilized.' Kate reached down and yanked Lainey to her feet. Over Marti's shoulder, Kate spotted Eric in the doorway along with a police forensic expert. Eric was grinning, while the tech held up a quart-size evidence bag.

'You're right, Lainey,' said Marti. 'I hated your mother. Taking away my treasurer duties was one thing, but Agnes had no business meddling in my personal life. Not after I kept her dirty little secret.'

'What secret was that?' Kate asked, grabbing her notepad.

'That she was a closet drinker. The woman used to sip white wine at lunch, but always had a pint of vodka in her purse for her frequent restroom trips.'

Lainey glared down her nose. 'You were eavesdropping on our conversation that day.'

Marti shrugged. 'You merely confirmed what I figured out. But I had kept quiet about it. I told no one in the club that Agnes Westin was nothing but a drunk.'

With swift precision from hours of yoga and Pilates, Lainey lifted her hand and smacked Marti Collier across the face. Before the two women could fully engage like cage combatants, Julian Buckley emerged from the doorway.

'All right, that's enough,' shouted the detective, pulling them apart.

'Who are you?' asked Marti, her hands balled into fists.

'Detective Buckley from Homicide.'

'Homicide? What are you doing here? You've got nothing on me.'

'I beg to differ, Mrs Collier. You had motive and opportunity. The garden club met the morning Mrs Westin died. The food had been prepared by Mrs Carter, but you had easy access to the picnic hamper. Plus, Luisa Gonzalez didn't know Mark Harris didn't drink wine. Unlike the other committee members, you did. You knew Mrs Westin would start with the bottle of white during lunch and open the red later. You found the rat poison in the garden shed and hid the bottle in Luisa's closet in order to frame her.'

'Good luck with that. As my dear husband would say, all your evidence is circumstantial.' With a flushed face, Marti tried to step past the detective, but two officers blocked the doorway.

'What about this, Mrs Collier?' The forensic tech dangled an evidence bag before her nose. 'We found a syringe wrapped in paper towels in the trash with a fine set of fingerprints on it.'

'I wonder who those prints will match?' asked Buckley.

'Martha Collier, you're under arrest for the murder of Agnes Westin.'

Lainey, Kate, and Eric watched from the sidelines while the detective read Marti her rights. Then, as the murderer called them every foul name in the book, the police hauled her to the squad car in handcuffs.

'I was really wrong about Mrs Gonzalez,' Lainey said sadly.

'We all were,' Kate agreed. 'Never pays to jump to conclusions.'

'I'll ask my *real* attorney to pick up Luisa upon her release. She can stay here until she makes other arrangements.'

'Would you give her the job back?' asked Eric.

'Of course, if she wants it. But she probably wants to get as far from me as possible.'

'I wouldn't be so sure. Anyway, it doesn't hurt to ask.'

Lainey extended her hand first to Kate and then to Eric. 'I certainly will. Thanks, Kate, Eric. You did exactly what I wanted and I'm grateful.'

Kate shook the woman's hand. 'You're welcome. Just remember, you're not your mother. You can be whoever you want.'

'I know, but my mom wasn't how Marti described. Agnes had many good qualities. *You* would've seen through her crusty exterior to her soft center immediately. I'm going to miss her. A person never knows how much until it's too late.'

'I'm sure Agnes was very proud of you.'

Lainey nodded. 'If Luisa agrees to stay, I'll do everything in my power to bring Miguel back to the US. It's what Mom wanted.'

Kate squeezed her hand. 'Let me know when the memorial service will be. Oh, I almost forgot. I need to give you back your shoes.'

'No, you keep them. They look great on you. And frankly, I love yours. I haven't worn anything this comfortable in years. How 'bout an even swap?'

'Fine, but you're getting the short end of the stick.'

'No, not by any stretch of the imagination.'

'Ready to grab some lunch, partner?' Kate asked. 'You did great in there, by the way.'

Eric opened her car door like a gentleman. 'You're the one who shone. You went out on a major limb, but it paid off.'

Kate waited for a break in traffic, then accelerated when a pickup flashed his lights. 'One thing about limbs – either they break and you fall on your face or you end up looking like a genius.'

'What made you think the syringe would still be in the trash?'

'I didn't know for sure, but since the cans hadn't been emptied, I thought there was a good chance. Marti only carried a small wristlet instead of a purse, so I didn't think she'd take the syringe home. Too great a chance of it being seen. Since Mrs Westin didn't die until later, Marti figured the trash would be in the landfill before anyone thought to check. However, if the syringe wasn't there, I'd just tipped off the killer we were on to her.'

'I think Buckley liked your sting operation, though he probably wouldn't admit it.'

'Only because it turned out well. Otherwise he could have charged me with interference in a police investigation. File that in your PI memory bank.' Kate winked at Eric. 'I'm starving. Should we hit a fast-food drive-thru on the way back?'

Eric pressed a hand to his gut and grimaced. 'No, I'll make us a nice salad from stuff in your fridge and grill some frozen red snapper. Let's go home . . . I mean, back to the hotel.'

Ridiculously Kate felt herself blush. 'Done. I'd never turn down your cooking.'

When they got back to the hotel, Eric set out the fish to thaw and went to his room for a shower. Kate washed up too, then decided to update the Westin case file. She'd barely typed fifty words when the phone next to her bed rang.

'Hello, who's this?' she asked.

'Angie at the front desk. One of our customers noticed a car alarm blaring in the parking lot. When I looked up the license-plate number, the car belongs to you, Miss Weller.'

Kate reflected for a moment. *Who in the world would want to steal her car?* 'Maybe someone backed into it. Thanks for letting me know. I'm on my way down.'

Kate considered calling Eric, but hated to cut short his shower for something stupid. Instead she tucked her handgun into her back waistband and pulled on a long cardigan. As long as she took every precaution, Eric wouldn't hang her by her thumbs. As she walked out the front door, sure enough the blaring noise was coming from her Toyota.

Shielding her eyes from the glare, she soon spotted what had triggered the alarm. Some careless driver had backed into her Toyota, leaving a long crease in the bumper. Luckily both taillights were still intact, so the dent only added to the assortment that Beth had already put there.

Kate unlocked the driver's door and slipped in behind the wheel. The only sure way to cancel the alarm was to turn the key in the ignition. When the engine sprang to life, the alarm ceased, but the cold press of steel against her neck indicated her troubles were far from over.

'Put your right hand on the wheel, Katie-girl. Isn't that what your worthless brother calls you?' The man laughed without humor. 'Now with your left hand, pull the gun from your waistband and hand it to me, butt-end first.' He pressed the barrel into the base of her skull. 'And don't try anything foolish. This Glock has a hair-trigger and no safety.'

Reluctantly, Kate did as she was told, then studied him in the rearview mirror. Around fifty-five, razor-short blond hair; clean-shaven, broad shouldered, neither thin nor well muscled. He looked like he might have been handsome at one time, but a habitual bad attitude had left him with a permanent sneer. When their gazes met, Kate glanced away quickly.

'See something you like, missy? We'll have time to get acquainted later. Right now, dig out your phone and pass that to me too.'

When she didn't immediately comply, Kate felt a sharp pain shoot up her neck as he jabbed her with the barrel. 'I don't believe we've met,' she said, handing him her phone. 'Since you know my name, mind telling me yours?'

He yanked the phone from her fingers. 'You can call me Ace.'

'How do you know my brother?' Kate shifted her position to relieve the pressure on her brain stem.

'We met briefly on the street one day. Let's just say I was the silent partner Liam didn't know about. Now, as much as I enjoy chatting with a pretty girl, we don't want your boyfriend to start missing you. Man, that guy is like gum on a shoe. I should've blown him up when I had the chance.' He leaned forward until she could smell cigarettes on his breath and smoke on his clothes. 'See what being *nice* got me?'

Kate forced a smile at the rearview mirror. 'I understand you've got a beef with my brother, so why don't we talk this over in the bar? Maybe we can reach a mutually satisfying compromise.'

Ace repositioned the gun to just below her left ear. 'You think you can sweet-talk me?' The sneer was gone, replaced by an expression of pure hatred. 'Back the car out slowly. Then turn right and head south on Main. Do anything to attract attention and I'll spatter your brain across the dashboard.'

Kate felt of frisson of fear that left her dizzy. 'Just relax, okay? I'll do whatever you say.' With muscles nearly paralyzed, she had to force her foot to depress the gas pedal.

Ace slouched down behind her headrest, but kept his gun in contact with her skin. As they left Pensacola's historical section, he ordered a series of left and right turns with no purpose other than to confuse her. Since it had been a long time since she lived in the area, his ploy worked well.

'Turn left into that alley.' Reaching across the seat, he pointed with his index finger. 'Slow down, so we don't get noticed.'

'Doesn't look like anyone lives here,' she said. Skirting around trash dumpsters, Kate narrowly missed a stray cat that darted across her path.

'Let's just say these aren't rent-paying customers,' Ace whispered in her ear. 'Right after the green recycle bin, pull into the garage on your left.'

Stopping in the open doorway, Kate realized it wasn't a garage at all, but the bottom floor of an abandoned warehouse, one that hadn't been used in decades. 'Look, Ace, I have a better idea than whatever you have in mind. My boyfriend is loaded. He'll pay plenty to get me back. Just let me call—'

Before she could finish her sentence, Ace slammed

something hard into the side of her head. As her vision clouded, Kate felt bile rise up her throat.

'Money ain't the problem. I've got loads of it too, but I've been too afraid to spend it. All that ends today. Drive in another twenty feet and turn the car off.' His tone didn't encourage negotiation.

Kate attempted to comply, but with the dashboard swimming before her eyes, she couldn't find the key to turn off the ignition.

'What's the matter with you?' Ace crushed her against the window as he reached around her. Then he jumped out of the backseat, yanked open her door, and dragged her out by her hair before she could regain her senses.

Ace laughed while she howled in pain. 'Scream all you want. Nobody will hear you, and if they do, they'll be too scared to do anything about it. Like I said, these ain't rent-paying tenants.' He dragged her across the dusty floor by her ponytail into an office, then slammed her into a straight-back chair.

When her vision cleared, she spotted a calendar on the wall for 1991. *Is that the last time anyone showed up for work here?* 'Where are we?' she asked, gingerly turning her head left and right. 'What is this place?'

Ace didn't answer immediately. Instead he took a length of rope from the desk drawer and tied her to the chair. Next he pulled out two pairs of handcuffs from the bottom drawer, fastened one to her wrist and the other to a floor-to-ceiling iron pipe behind her. Then he secured her right ankle to the leg of the desk. Finally he sat down and pulled a bottle of liquor from the drawer. 'That should hold you for a while, Katie-girl,' he said with a smile.

'Looks like you've been here before,' she murmured.

'I certainly have.' Ace poured a half-glass of amber liquid and took a sip. 'This used to be my dad's factory and warehouse, until he was put out of business by foreign competition. Who can compete with countries that pay people two dollars a day?' He took another sip and thumped the glass on the desktop.

'You hear that a lot from business owners these days.' Kate utilized her most empathetic tone.

'I told my dad that he and Mom shouldn't worry, because I have a foolproof answer to their retirement plans. And guess what happened, Katie-girl?' Ace swallowed down the remaining liquid in his glass.

Kate tried pulling against her restraints to no avail. 'I'm not completely sure, but I guess my brother is in the middle of it.'

Suddenly, everything fell into place in her mind – Ace's clean-cut appearance, professional grade handcuffs, and his reference to 'a lot of money' as opposed to 'chump-change' like Charley Crump insisted he got for the heist. If her right hand wasn't bound to the pole, Kate would've smacked her forehead.

'You're the second armored car driver,' she said. 'The one everyone thought ran away when the shooting started.'

'Bingo. Frankly, I would have thought a smart girl like you would've figured it out by now.' Ace refilled his glass from the bottle.

'It would've been easier if you had worn your red plaid shirt. Or if you'd thrown around a lot of money after the robbery.' Kate concentrated on trying to slip her hand from the cuff, also to no avail.

'Don't think I didn't want to, but the little woman – my wife – was against the idea. She insisted we keep it hidden until nobody could finger me to the police. Now she's dead so it don't make no difference.'

'You killed your wife?' she asked.

Ace's face twisted with rage. In one smooth motion he smacked Kate across the face. 'No, you stupid girl. Cancer took her last spring. So what reason do I have to hang around here?'

As her head bounced against the post, Kate gritted her teeth. 'What about your kids? You have two, don't you?'

'Ah, someone did their homework after all. My kids are grown. They have no time for me, so why should I wait any longer to start living?'

Kate had no logical answer for his question.

Ace lit a cigarette and inhaled deeply. 'I knew one day you'd get your memory back, so you and Liam are my last loose ends.'

'Did you kill Jimmy Russell?' she asked, stalling for more time.

He blew a blue stream of smoke at the cobwebby ceiling. 'Small-time hoods like him and Doug should've stuck to stealing GPS's and DVD players out of parked cars.'

'You killed Doug Young too? He wasn't even there.'

Ace's expression turned feral. 'Doug needed to be taught a lesson: you don't stand up your friends when they're counting on you.'

'You're forgetting about Charley Crump. The guy skipped town. But before he left, he gave a statement to the assistant DA. The truth was long overdue, but better late than never.'

Ace pulled a second tumbler from the drawer. 'You have underestimated me. I was across the street when you visited that lowlife Crump. But as soon as you and Romeo left, I offered my old pal a ride to the bus station. It took a little convincing, but Charley finally agreed.' Ace spun his gun on the desk. 'Good ole Charley didn't make any calls on the way to the pearly gates. If anyone does find his body, they'll discover he died of a heroin overdose, like so many of the lost generation.'

As Ace filled both glasses to the brim, Kate felt her stomach tighten. Charley Crump wasn't exactly a stand-up guy, but he didn't deserve to die like that. 'People will figure it out. I suggest you give yourself up.

'And I suggest you enjoy your last hour on earth.' He pushed one glass across the desk. 'As soon as I hear Liam has been taken care of, your time is up, pretty girl.' His smile never quite reached his eyes. 'What do you say we drink up and have some afternoon fun?'

'No, thanks. I prefer to die not knowing that particular pleasure.'

'Suit yourself, but cooperation might just buy you extra time.' He held the glass under her nose. 'How 'bout a drink for old times' sake?'

FIFTEEN

Eric took the fastest shower of his life, jumped into clean clothes and let his hair drip-dry. The sooner he got back to Kate's, the sooner he could relax with his new partner, the woman of his dreams. But halfway out the door, he remembered the fish and doubled back. This time when he bolted into the hallway, a man in a sport coat was knocking on Kate's door.

'Miss Weller? It's Detective Mendez from Escambia County Sheriff's Department.' He knocked again with more force. 'Are you in there?'

Eric closed the distance between them in a few strides. 'What's going on, Detective? Were you called to this hotel room?'

The middle-aged cop turned to face him. 'And who might you be?'

'Eric Manfredi, Kate's boyfriend and partner, sort of.'

'Which are you sort of – the boyfriend or the partner?'

'Both. Does this have anything to do with her brother, Liam?' Eric drew Kate's key from his pocket and unlocked the door.

'It might.' Mendez checked the bedroom and bathroom, while Eric opened the sliding door to the balcony. 'She's not here,' Mendez announced when Eric stepped back inside.

'And her car is missing,' Eric said, breathing through his nostrils like an angry bull. 'Of all the stubborn, obstinate women I could have gotten mixed up with! She took off without me, *again.*'

'Get mad later. Where do you think Miss Weller went?'

'First, show me some ID. Then tell me why you're here.'

After a moment's consideration, Mendez opened his wallet to reveal a badge. 'I know who's been stalking Miss Weller all these years. He was the mastermind of the crew, the one who bashed Liam on the head and left him behind to take the rap.'

'It was the other security guard, wasn't it? Kate said the police already checked the guy out and he was clean as a whistle.'

A flush crept up Mendez's neck into his face. 'Look, hotshot. I know how to do my job. He's who I liked for the ringleader from the start, but I couldn't find a shred of evidence. The guard went back to work two weeks later. He still lives in the same house, drives a ten-year-old pickup, and when his daughter got married, they held the reception in the backyard. Does that sound like someone who stole a million dollars?'

'*A million*? That's not what Liam thought they would split.'

'Yeah, well, Liam was odd-man-out. For years I kept tabs on Lester Owens to make sure his savings account hadn't skyrocketed. He's been broke for sixteen years. Then, after your partner came to see me, I checked out Owens again.'

'Finish telling me this in your car. I think I can find Kate.' Eric grabbed his computer and ran toward the elevator with Mendez at his heels. 'I stuck a GPS tracker under the bumper of her car. If the thing works like it should, we should be able to pull up her location from the company's website. Someone in her office helped me set this up.' Inside Mendez's sedan, he started tapping keys on the laptop.

'Wow, you're not a very trusting partner. Or does this have to do with the "boyfriend" part?'

'Pretty much both again. You'd understand if you knew Kate better.' Once on the website for Price Investigations, Eric typed in his twelve-digit registration number, hit enter, and sat back while the database searched for the signal. 'Okay, tell me what changed for Lester Owens?'

'Both his kids moved out, his wife died this past spring, and last week he quit his job without giving notice. So today when I went to chat with him, the front door was unlocked and it looked like he'd packed in a hurry. I've got an APB out on his pickup truck.'

'Where's he been stashing the loot all these years?' Eric didn't take his eyes off the screen.

'Who knows? Maybe it was buried in his yard. But I also found out that Owens inherited a warehouse when his dad died. Before I went to look at it, I wanted to check on Miss

Weller, to make sure her sort-of partner–boyfriend was still her bodyguard.' Mendez scowled at Eric.

Before Eric could retaliate, his laptop dinged, indicating the website had found Kate's vehicle. 'Head to 1452 Eleventh Street.'

Mendez muttered an expletive. 'That's the address of his father's defunct factory.' The detective radioed the dispatcher and repeated the address. 'All patrol cars must proceed cautiously and silently. Lester Owens has a hostage and should be presumed armed and dangerous.' To Eric he said, 'You wait here. I'll keep you informed.'

'No way, I'm coming along.'

'Stop wasting my time. This is police business.'

'If Owens moves Kate to a different location, I've got the best way to track her.'

'Fine,' Mendez snapped, 'but you'll stay in the car. I don't need a civilian getting in the way.' He peeled from the parking lot of the Vacation Inn and Suites.

'Agreed.'

It took ten agonizing minutes to reach the rundown neighborhood and another four to locate the correct building. When they stopped in front of the abandoned warehouse, the first responders were leaning against their vehicles. They straightened when Mendez and Eric jumped out and approached.

'What are you waiting for?' Mendez hissed. 'Owens has a woman in there he means to kill if he hasn't already.'

'I've assessed the building,' said one officer, stepping forward. 'There's a door in back and one on the side, plus these garage doors. Without knowledge of the building's layout, we were waiting for your command, Detective.'

Mendez, as well as Eric, gazed up at the four-story building: No windows on this side other than the garage doors which sat flush to ground. They had no idea what was happening inside. 'Block this exit with your vehicles and don't let anyone get past you.' Mendez pointed at two officers. 'You come in through the back, while you and I will take the side entrance as quietly as possible. Manfredi, stay with the vehicles. Don't go heroic on me,' Mendez said over his shoulder as everyone scrambled into place.

Or you'll do what – arrest me? The moment Mendez and the officers disappeared around the building, Eric headed to the opposite side, where a narrow alley separated the factory from the apartment building next door. Eric spotted an open window on the factory's fourth floor, along with a rusty fire escape still bolted to the exterior. At one time the metal steps could be used to go up to the roof or down to the ground in an emergency. Now the steps dangled twelve feet in the air. Eric picked his way through the trash, trying not to breathe. With few other options, he stacked two plastic milk crates atop an overturned garbage can, hoping they would hold his weight. He had no time to consider if the fire escape would crumble into orange dust or if he could fit through the window if he got that far.

But with Kate's life at stake, Eric sucked in a deep breath and climbed the precarious stack, grabbed the bottom step and with every bit of strength, pulled himself up. The stack swayed but didn't fall. The steps creaked and groaned, but supported his two hundred pounds.

'Hey!' A voice said from below. 'Where do you think you're going? You were ordered to stay by the cars.'

Eric looked down at a red-faced cop, one of the officers told to watch the front entrance. 'My partner's inside with a psychopath. I'm going in to find her. Either shoot me or follow me up.' Eric turned his back and squeezed through the window. When he glanced down, the officer was already pulling himself onto the fire escape.

It took a full minute for his eyes to adjust to the dim, dusty interior. And a minute more before Eric could breathe without coughing. By this time, the cop had crawled through the window.

'What's your name?' the cop asked in a hoarse whisper.

'Eric. What's yours?'

'Officer Frank Hegarty. I'm taking the lead. You got that?' Drawing his weapon, he motioned toward a set of stairs thirty feet away. 'Try not to make a sound.'

'Got it.' Eric pulled his gun from an ankle holster.

The cop's eyes rounded. 'You got a permit for that, PI?'

'Nope. Like I said, my partner is down there.'

'Then try not to shoot anyone. Let's go find her.'

It's not that Eric didn't trust Officer Hegarty, but he would do whatever necessary to save Kate and deal with the consequences later.

As silently as possible, the two big men crept down the first and second sets of stairs. Unlike the empty top level, floors three and two were strewn with abandoned machinery and equipment, probably too archaic to have resale value, along with shipping orders from better days at All-Best Tool and Die Company. No footprints in the dust indicated Lester Owens hadn't brought Kate to either of these levels.

As they crept down the last fifteen steps to the first floor, Officer Hegarty motioned for them to stop and listen. Eric wiped his sweaty palm on his jeans, trying not to make a sound. But as they reached the bottom stairwell with guns drawn, their arrival didn't come as a surprise to Owens.

'Welcome, join us,' Owens sneered. 'Look, Katie-girl, your boyfriend and Pensacola's finest have come to your rescue. Isn't that sweet?'

In an instant, Eric took in the surroundings. In a filthy office, Kate sat stiffly in a chair, lashed to an iron pipe. Her feet were bound, her blouse half-buttoned, and her face streaked with tears. Owens stood behind Kate with his left hand around her neck, spiking Eric's blood pressure into the danger zone.

'Lester Owens, step away from that woman.' Officer Hegarty leveled his service weapon at him.

'No, I don't think so.' Owens lifted his right hand, where a large handgun was pointed at Kate's ribs. 'Put down your weapons, or this pretty girl will suffer a gruesome end. She's been very uncooperative anyway.'

For half a minute, no one moved. Eric locked eyes with Kate, while the cop drew a bead on the killer's forehead.

'Lay your guns on the ground!' Owens yelled so loud, pigeons roosting in the empty warehouse took flight. 'Or I blow a hole in her head. I'm either leaving here today or some of you are dying with me.'

Eric took another look at Kate and lowered his gun to the floor. Hegarty hesitated a moment longer, then he too lowered his weapon. 'Fine, take the money and get out. That's what you want, isn't it?'

'*What I want?*' Owens screamed. 'What I want is my wife back and Liam Weller and his worthless sister dead.' Spittle flew from Owens's mouth. 'It was a perfect plan if those stupid hicks had just done what they were told. I have waited all this time and these two are still messing up my life.'

Suddenly, the jangle of a cell phone jarred everyone's attention, but brought a smile to Owens's face. 'Know what that sound means, missy?' He grabbed Kate by the chin. 'Your jailbird brother is dead. Nobody else has this number but my cousin, who just happens to be a guard at Santa Rosa. At least I'll know one Weller has been dealt with when I leave here. You, I'll take along for a bit of insurance.' Roughly he pulled Kate to her feet, unlocked the handcuff from the pole and attached it to her other wrist. 'If either of you makes a move, my gun goes off.'

Eric and the cop exchanged glances. With Owens's gun stuck in her ribs, neither had time to reach their weapon. As Eric helplessly watched, Owens released the handcuffs at her ankles, then yanked on the ropes until they came loose.

Kate winced in pain but didn't cry out. 'Could you at least tell me where we're going, Mr Owens?' she asked. 'So my mom and dad know where to find my body. I deserve a decent burial, same as your late wife.'

Owens dragged Kate by her cuffs toward the main part of the warehouse. 'You ain't got no parents. They were killed in a car accident. You're the last Weller left in these parts.' He laughed manically.

'I do too have parents – Dolores and Ken. I fostered with them until I left for . . .' Kate stopped short, her mouth pulling into a grimace. 'I think I'm going to be sick.' Suddenly she doubled over and began to retch.

Just as suddenly, Officer Hegarty bent for his weapon and shot Lester Owens squarely in the forehead. The man staggered a bit and then crumpled, dead long before he hit the floor.

Freed from her captor, Kate ran to Eric, her fake nausea gone. 'Look at you – my partner, the hero!' She turned her face up to his.

Eric wrapped his arms around her. 'Officer Hegarty shot the guy. All I did was crawl through an open window.'

Hegarty dug the key from Owens's pocket and released Kate's wrists. 'Look, Manfredi, part-time partner, part-time boyfriend, put your gun away before Mendez sees it. You've never seen that guy mad before.'

Just as Eric slipped his gun into the ankle holster, Mendez with two other cops reached their part of the warehouse. Mendez looked at Owens in a pool of blood on the floor, then looked at his officer and finally looked at them. 'What do we have here?' he murmured.

'He left me with no choice, Detective,' Officer Hegarty explained.

'Put it all in your report. Are you all right, Miss Weller?' Mendez asked Kate. 'Nobody told me Owens's father owned only half the building. It wasn't easy getting through from the other half.'

'I'm fine, Lieutenant Mendez, thanks to your officer and Mr Manfredi.'

'I'd get a new partner if I were you. This one doesn't know how to follow orders.' Mendez scowled at Eric.

'True, but every now and then he comes in handy.' Kate smiled at him.

'Look at what Owens stuck in Miss Weller's trunk.' The other cop who'd been watching the garage doors held up a duffle bag. 'Looks like we found the million dollars.'

'Wow, who gets to keep that?' Kate asked.

'You can always put in a finders-keepers claim and fight the insurance company for it. But for now, I need to get both of your statements.'

'No, we need to get ahold of someone at Santa Rosa Correctional,' Kate said, remembering what Owens had said with frightening clarity. 'Owens left my phone out in my car.' She and Eric sprinted toward the open garage doors.

'Don't go anywhere, you two,' Mendez called.

'Thanks, Eric,' she said when they reached her Toyota. 'Pay no attention to him. As partners go, I think you're pretty awesome.'

*   *   *

As soon as Kate found her phone in the back seat, she dialed the number for Santa Rosa and asked for Elias Murphy in the infirmary. She held her breath until someone picked up the other end.

'Infirmary,' barked an elderly voice.

'Doctor Murphy? This is Kate Weller. Did you get my message? Were you able to move my brother someplace safe? I didn't know who else to call.'

'Yes, Miss Weller, Liam is here now, recovering from a sudden bout of the Zika virus. Would you like to speak to him?'

Kate opened her mouth to answer, but not a sound came out as tears ran down her cheeks. Helplessly, she handed the phone to Eric.

'Doctor Murphy, this is her partner. At the moment Kate is very emotional. Could you put her brother on?'

'Hello. Is this Eric?' asked a deep voice. 'Tell my sister to stop crying. I feel fine. As viruses go, this one ain't bad.'

Since she had heard every word Liam said, she grabbed the phone from Eric. 'Excuse me for worrying about you, Liam Weller.'

'Settle down, Katie. I'm not a pregnant woman, so I should survive the Zika virus without permanent consequences.' Liam sounded like her brother used to – dismissive of any attempt to care about him.

'Fine, I'm not worried. So I shouldn't bother to visit tomorrow?' Kate made sure she sounded just as obstinate as him.

'I would love it if you visited. But they won't let you into the infirmary with something so contagious.'

'When we hang up, talk to Dr Murphy. I think you're about to make a *miraculous recovery.*'

Liam paused while he considered. 'I'm starting to understand why I don't feel sick. So if you do come tomorrow, bring Eric with you. I want to meet the man who can put up with such a crybaby.'

Kate handed the phone back to Eric as her eyes filled with tears again. Tomorrow would be soon enough for snappy comebacks. Today she planned to just let the tears fall. Liam was alive and well. And maybe, someday, she would get her brother back.

'Hey, Liam? This is Eric again. We'll both see you tomorrow. In the meantime, better do everything the good doctor says.' Eric hung up and handed her back the phone.

For a while they sat in her Toyota, running the air conditioning and waiting for Detective Mendez to take their statements. When he finished with them, Eric drove back to the hotel, while Kate tried to process everything that had just happened. For the first time, she tried to picture her future without Lester Owens or anyone else threatening her. She could come and go without looking over her shoulder or checking her rearview mirror.

I no longer need a bodyguard.

That realization hit her hard. 'I suppose you'll be heading back to Charleston soon,' she said when Eric pulled into the Vacation Inn and Suites.

'Well, as you pointed out earlier, it is my home while your home is here. It's too bad, really, but maybe we can stay Facebook friends.' Eric turned off the ignition and handed her the keys.

'But I don't want to stay here. Pensacola no longer feels like home.'

'Where would you like to go, Kate?' Eric looked downright perplexed.

'I'm hoping that suite above your restaurant is still available.' She turned toward him.

'I could possibly ask my parents if they've rented it or not, but what about your brother? Liam doesn't get out of jail just because the ringleader set him up.'

'I can drive from Charleston to Milton every time Liam is up for parole. Maybe Detective Mendez and the DA will speak on his behalf. And when Liam's released, he'll probably be ready for a fresh start too.'

'What would you do in Charleston? You can barely cook ramen noodles.'

'Maybe I'll open a satellite office for Nate Price. With Lester Owens dead, I don't want to be a roving PI anymore. Then, in my spare time, I can teach you what I know about investigations. Or weren't you serious about leaving the family business someday?'

Eric arched an eyebrow. 'Oh, I was dead serious. Do you think Beth can teach me to shoot like her?'

'Beth has a God-given gift, but I know she'll do her best. What do you say, Eric? Will you call Alfonzo about the rental?'

At long last, he smiled. 'I will, if you're serious about letting me be your partner. There are lots of variables here – Nate's willingness to open another office, Beth's willingness to take on another trainee, plus my parents' willingness to rent you the apartment. If you recall, a lot of *bad things* happened when you lived upstairs.'

'I understand, and I promise to train you no matter what happens with Nate or the suite. If necessary, I'll pitch a tent behind the restaurant until the tenant moves out.' Kate offered her hand to clinch the deal.

'In that case I'll put in a good word with my parents. After all, you do need a real home now that you adopted Charley Crump's pink geranium. But I do have one more contingency.'

'Name it.'

'You'll say nothing about me eventually leaving Bella Trattoria. I'll tell my parents when I'm ready to go work for Nate or whomever.'

'Agree.' Kate's outstretched hand remained in mid-air.

'Then you have yourself a partner.' Eric shook with bone-crushing intensity.

Kate didn't mind. Broken bones healed. But she wasn't taking any more chances with a friendship . . . or any other kind of relationship any time soon.